THE TIPTON'S OF TYBBINGTON

Before and Beyond, Part One

The Tipton Crest "Causam Decidit"
"The Sword in This Hand Caused the Decision That Ended the War"

REBA RHYNE

The Tipton's of Tybbington
Before and Beyond, Part One

Copyright © 2020 Reba Rhyne

ISBN: 978-1-952369-49-00

When the author started this epic tale, she knew the story could be lengthy, but certainly not as extensive as it turned out to be. If placed in only one book, the font or print would have been very small, and the book would have been weighty and cumbersome — maybe over three pounds — too heavy to hold for any length of time.

She had no choice but to think of two books for her story. This narrative is not complete or finished unless you read Book Two. And, starting the second book without reading the first, means less understanding of the setting, characters, and actions described therein, because some references, needless-to-say, are back to Book One.

So, she highly advises YOU, the reader, to buy Book One and Book Two as a set.

All Scripture quotations are taken from the KING JAMES VERSION (KJV): KING JAMES VERSION, public domain.

Published by EA Books Publishing a division of Living Parables of Central Florida, Inc. a 501c3
EABooksPublishing.com

Acknowledgements

Thanks To:

Ken Raney for the excellent cover work. This Crest is the official one of the Tipton Family Association of America. All members are descendants of Jonathan Tipton of Anne Arundel Co., Maryland.

Ben Belandres for the first two maps. He sure outdid me on the last ones, but I got the message across.

Maria Kercher for her editing skills.

Dawn Staymates, my formatter, for putting up with me, and EA publishing for another great job.

Foreword

Have you ever been to a show or seen one on television where they said, "This will require audience participation?" Well, *The Tiptons of Tybbington* **requires reader participation**, beyond that of reading. So, if you aren't willing to put the effort into doing the research, which is provided within its pages, then this book may be the most boring book you will ever read.

This is a book of history. It starts in 500 A.D. or thereabouts, and ends around 1700 A.D.

First, let me explain about the word *"thereabouts."* Since a lot of the book is written before names, dates, and actions were adequately recorded, this writer used her imagination and made up *rational facts* to go along with the time period and story.

Mark Twain once told the English poet, Rudyard Kipling, "Get your facts first, and then you can distort them as much as you please." Mr. Twain would not be happy with me, because I tried not to distort the facts. But as I gleaned information from one chronicler to another, I did find *the facts may differ.*

So where does the reader participate?

The book covers around 1200 years of history, in places where most of my readers haven't been, and within situations they haven't participated. You'll start at Germania in the 500 A.D.'s or *thereabouts.* **I have added maps** so you can maintain a reasonable idea of where the characters are in the world—at least, the point where they are in the present time period being covered. In most cases, I've been there and can describe the area. You can go to the internet and find other information between chapters for further facts if your interest is piqued and if you desire.

I've also **added a chart** of the important rulers and Kings of England and coupled them to my characters, those in the same time period. So, instead of being confused, you can put your finger on each, as they are in chronological order. How many Kings were named Edward or Henry in 1200 years? Several, I can tell you.

At the start of each chapter, I've **given a brief summary of the events between time periods**. This shows up in a different font. I know this will be boring to some, but read it. The commentary leading up to the next section, in most cases, is very interesting.

The settings in this book are true, and the Tiptons lived through these times, but in order to people the story, it was necessary to put fictional persons through the history, alongside some real ones.

Some of the Tipton people are real, but their interaction in the historical activities are fiction—but possible? Since most of the Tipton descendants that I know have been honorable, God-fearing, support-your-government kind of people, this is the way they are portrayed in the book. My Tipton family is full of fact and fiction, legend and lore, each addressed in these pages.

This is a fun story of several generations, reminding me of where I came from, how I got here, and the sacrifices my ancestors may have made to dream of a different life.

Dedication

At times, I've found the dedication for a book a bit tough. But not this time. This very intelligent man is a keeper of his word.

Starting a project of this magnitude (which I hadn't planned to do) is a daunting task. I needed someone in England to keep me on track—read the manuscript, point me to websites, and make suggestions ... someone who would stay with me from start to finish. He promised to do just that, and he did.

We have e-mailed back and forth for many months as we worked on the manuscript for *The Tipton's of Tybbington*. Slowly, we have gotten to know each other much better.

Jeff Worsey has lived in Tipton all of his life, and is proud of his country and his town. As an avid reader, he became Chair of the Friends Group of the Library in Tipton, England. That's how I met him.

The Tipton Family Association of America planned a trip to England to visit the town where *it is believed* our family originally settled. Several signed up to go. When time came to finalize our arrangements, I couldn't find anyone planning on making the trip. I e-mailed this stranger. He hadn't heard from anyone ... but me. I told him if no one else came, he and I would have all the fun. He had planned several activities, but couldn't complete the arrangements until he knew the final number. In the end, he had seven coming, all at staggered times, making his job even harder.

Without his help and traveling alone, I would have struggled with logistics, especially getting back and forth to my lodging and the library. At home, I drive a car and have little experience in riding the train, bus, or calling a taxi, especially in an unfamiliar location. He gave excellent instructions.

It turned out that most places were in walking distance. My Travelodge was next to the Dudley Zoo, in the shadow of the ancient castle on Castle Hill, next to the Dudley Archives, and in a short walking distance of the Black Country Living Museum.

At the library, Jeff had arranged for our group to be honored with an English Tea, hosted by Edwina and other ladies of the Friends of the Library. The ladies 'did us proud.' Keith, from the Tipton Civic Society, and David, whose family once operated businesses in Tipton talked to us about the history of Tipton. There was also commentary and slides on the canals and narrow boats from a lady who lived it with her parents. Graham, who teaches an art group at the library, presented signed prints to the Tipton Family Association of America. Robert Hazel, the library manager, made sure our stay while there was comfortable—meeting any other need.

The following day, we attended the Canal Festival and went on a narrow boat trip along the canals. Sadly, Jeff did not arrange the weather. It drizzled almost non-stop. He did make sure we met some of the locals, and their cheery welcome soon drove the dark clouds away. This included two women who were patrolling the area as Bobbies. We stopped to take pictures.

In particular on day three, I enjoyed the Black Country Living Museum with his daughter, Caroline, as my tour guide. The BCLM took me back to the glory days of coal, blast furnaces, and steel. Within its boundaries, I visited period homes, observed a school session, and talked with people who told and showed me some of the history of the area. It's a must for anyone staying in Tipton or Dudley. Finally, to cap off a wonderful day, we had an early dinner in one of the museum's restaurants.

Jeff Worsey, you were there to help with great directions and support. So, as you folks in Tippin say, "I ull tek me cap off to yow."

In *The Tipton's of Tybbington*, I wrote the story, but you gave it more English places, language, and flair than I could have. Your fingerprints and suggestions are everywhere in these two books. It is fitting that this book is dedicated to you.

So, I say a simple, "Thank you, so much."

Introduction

Have you ever wondered how far back you could go in your family history? Since my mom was the genealogist of the family and researched many sides of my ancestors, I was interested in just this. I'm not a genealogist, but I am a lover and an avid reader of this world's history—from the ancient Israelites in the Holy Bible, Egyptians, Romans, and English, right up to how the United States of America came to be.

This two-part book is written as a history and should be read as such. It is the fictionalized story of the Tipton Family, who left Germania in 500 to 550 A.D, or *thereabouts*. This was the time period when many of the tribal peoples left the coastal regions of northern Europe for more favorable areas in Brittania. After many years and a sojourn in the West Indies, my Tipton ancestors arrived in the Chesapeake Bay of the New World in the late 1600's, *or thereabouts*.

This manuscript encompasses around 1,200 years of European and New World History, and includes some of the historical happenings during this time. I concentrate on the areas the Tiptons inhabited— Germania (now northern Germany), Brittania (England), Barbados, Jamaica, and the New World (North America). I've traveled through most of the areas in the book.

Many of the characters are real, such as the first recorded Tipton who went by the name Tybba. In 500

A.D., people generally went by only one name. The community he founded on the River Tame in Brittania was called Tybbington, meaning Tybba's farm or village. This name changed several times over the centuries before it became Tipton, England.

The interactions of the characters in the book are totally fiction, but based and set against actual movements and activities in the different areas. You will discover what is happening around the Tiptons and their possible response to the situation.

Almost two years were dedicated to this manuscript. Lots of hours to write down descriptions of areas, events, and people who lived during these centuries.

In 2018, on my third trip to England, I visited Tipton, and walked in the area where *it is believed* my ancestors had walked before. I looked up at Dudda Hill (Dudley), saw the ruins of the castle, stood outside and felt the drizzling rain, and watched the sun come up and go down. Many of these activities would feel the same to Tybba, should he come today.

But, I'm sure Tybba would be totally bewildered if he could return and walk down shop-lined, busy Owen Street, through modern Tipton Green and past the statue of the Tipton Slasher. He would see the canals which have replaced the River Tame, cross multiple paved roads, and look confused at a traffic-controlling roundabout, filled with horseless carriages and flashing red or green lights.

What would he see, if he climbed Dudda Hill (Castle Hill) and looked over his old home? What had transpired during the years to make Tipton the town it is today? These two questions will be answered at the end of Part II. Instead, we start at the beginning.

So, let the adventure begin ...

Contents

Rulers of England

Tybba's Family

500 A.D. or Thereabouts		Cassius, Tybba, Gemma to Brittania And Tybbington
Small Tribes and Chieftains	500-626	
Æthelric's son CombinesBernicia and Deira BecomesKing of Northumbria	593-604	Below Hadrian's Wall
Penda, King of Region as Mercia. Tamworth Favorite Home	626-655	Roman Christianity Spreads
Æthelbald Calls Self King of *The Brittanians*, Mercian King	716-757	Murdered by Bodyguards
Offa, *King of English*, Most Powerful of Mercian Kings Tamworth Home	757-796	Alwin, Eggen, and Dever
King Alfred the Great Father of Æhelflaed and King Edward the Elder	871-899	Fortified Cites, Created Army, Started Navy. The Danes established Danelaw, Taking Large Parts of Mercia and Wessex
Lady Æthelflaed of the Mercians, Battle of Tettenhall War Against Danelaw or Vikings	911-918	Briallen, Elis, Meta, Elric

King Edward the Elder, Battle of Tettenhall, Brother of Lady Æthelflaed, Took Mercia And East Anglia Back	899-924	
Æthelstan Illegitimate Son of King Edward the Elder, Raised By Æthelflaed, Conquered Northumbria	924-939	Defeated Army of Scots, Danes, Celts, and Vikings. Anglo-Saxon Kingdoms Forming England
William of Normandy, Defeated Harold Godwinson. King Came From France. Died in France	1066-1087	Started Feudal System
Henry II, First Plantagenet King	1154-1189	Thomas Becket Murder
Richard I, The Lionheart	1189-1199	Third Crusade
John I, Brother of Richard a Terrible King	1199-1216	Magna Carta or Bill of Rights for the Common People
Edward I or Edward Longshanks Battle with Prince Llywelyn the Last	1272-1307	Anthony Tipton, Slays Prince Llywelyn, Knighted at Rhuddlan Castle by King Edward
Edward II was a Weak and Incompetent King. The Plot Against Edward by His Nobles And Son, Edward III	1307-1327	Henry, Margery, Roger of Tipton Ralph of Stafford
Edward III, Fifty Year Reign Victory at Crecy and Start of The Pestilence	1327-77	Adventures of Roger of Tipton, Sir Ralph de Stafford. Ralph's Marriage to Margaret de Audley

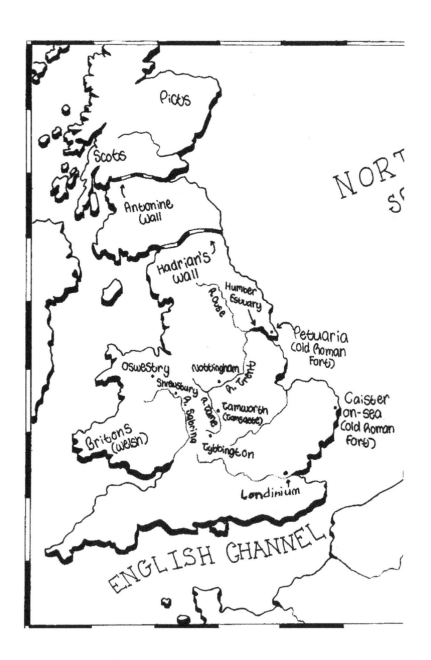

Picts

Scots

Antonine
Wall

Hadrian's
Wall

R. Ouse

Humber
Estuary

Petuaria
(old Roman
Fort)

Oswestry

Nottingham

Shrewsbury

R. Trent

R. Tame
(Tamsaete)

Tamworth
(Tamsaete)

R. Sabrina

Caister
on-sea
(old Roman
Fort)

Britons
(Welsh)

Tybbington

Londinium

NORT
S

ENGLISH CHANNEL

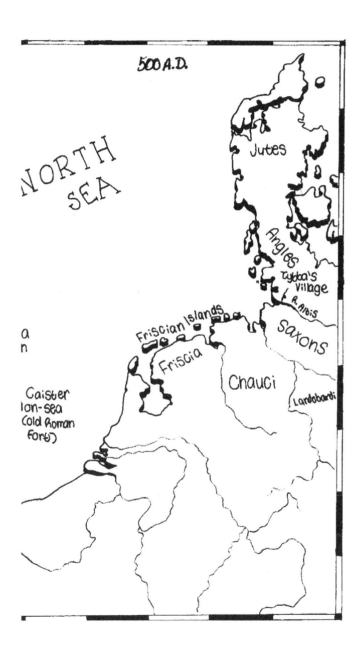

500 A.D.

NORTH SEA

Jutes

Angles

Tydda's Village

R. Albis

Friscian Islands

Friscia

Saxons

Chauci

Landobardi

Caister
Ion-sea
(Old Roman
Fort)

a
n

Setting the Stage

Being attacked from all sides and needing their legions elsewhere, the Roman Empire finally withdrew all their forces from their province of Brittania in 410 A.D. This information spread rapidly up and down the seacoasts of Europe.

~

On the coastal lands of southern Denmark and northern Germany (known as Frisia), many small European tribes were poised to cross the North Sea to the newly vacated lands of Roman Brittania, the land which would later be called England. At first, this migration was light, but it grew in quantity and intensity, until much of the southern isle and the Brittanian Midlands was overrun with Angles, Saxons, and Jutes.

There was more than one reason these Germanic people were willing to leave their native soil and move across the North Sea to a new home. The Frisian coast was low, protected from the sea in most cases by a chain of low-lying islands, some no more than sandbars. Raging storms often caused the sea to rise dramatically, breeching the islands and flooding the mainland, ravaging their crops and drowning their cattle, horses, and sheep.

Even their homes were no match for wind-driven, twenty-foot coastal waves, which raced inland and then back to sea. This invasion of water spoiled the hard work of the tribes living close on the coast. Made of wattle and daub and placed on a terpen (a raised, manmade mound), these rude dwellings were easily destroyed, and often looked like they floated in the water during floods. These barbarians couldn't go inland because they would be fighting the Chauci and Landobardi, who were ferocious fighters and blocked the pathway to a more habitable area to the east.

To worsen the situation, the Chauci and Landobardi were being pushed west, against the coastal tribes by people to the east, putting more pressure on them to abandon their homeland, and strike out for a new home. No wonder the Angles, Saxons, and Jutes were looking for a more suitable place to grow their crops and raise their livestock.

The climate of the land of Brittania, especially the Midlands, should be more moderate than in Frisia, where the chilly cold winds from the north and off the northern sea, with no natural barriers, often cut to the bone. Surely, in the midst of this new country, storms would not ravage the hard work of building homes and growing crops.

The story these tribes had heard from sailors coming off the trading vessels, plying up and down the coast, was that the heart of Brittania had better soil and plenty of acreage to spare once the forests were cleared. While they hoped to settle in peace, these *noble savages* were willing to fight for a better opportunity—for change, for family, for future.

With the Roman departure, the northern Scots and Picts, natives living on the northern edges of Brittania, were moving south, across the high, stone wall, built under the orders of the Roman Emperor Hadrian, which ran east and west. Once there, the northern tribes sought to expand their influence into the coveted southern lands. Other Britonic (Welsh) tribes, who lived across the River Sabrina (Severn) to the west of the Midlands, were raiding east across a ridge of low-lying mountains.

The Roman's tight rule had left the native peoples of Brittania unprepared for fighting. Incessant in-country fighting disrupted the family units, upset the growing season, and caused herds of abandoned animals to roam wild in the land. The native people were weak and unable to deal with the vast influx of invaders, people not native to Brittania who trespassed on all sides. If the coastal tribes of Europe wanted to move, this was the perfect time. Their arrival caused more tribal upheavals within Brittania, resulting in conflicts continuing for hundreds of years. The trespassers would claim small kingships and lordships in different parts of the country.

These disturbances continued until Middle and South Brittania were brought under control by someone who was respected by all—Æthelbald of Mercia in the 8th century. He established control of all territory south of the Humber Estuary, including the southernmost lands, Wessex and Kent. But not the west coast, which remained with the Britons (Welsh) or the land above the Humber Estuary—Northumbria and Cumbria. These last separated to the north by the Roman's Hadrian's Wall and soon to be called Scots Land. A united England or Brittania would come hundreds of years later.

～

Realizing the need for transportation of these barbaric tribes from the European Coast to the Brittanian mainland, sea captains and their boats were for hire, and whole families embarked across the North Sea to England. This included one from a tributary of the River Albis in Saxon territory. This is the story of Chieftain

Tybba, and his descendants, and how after hundreds of years and many adventures, they came finally to the New World to establish the Tiptons in America.

THE TIPTON'S OF TYBBINGTON

Before and Beyond, Part One

Tipton.

The Tipton Crest "Causam Decidit"
"The Sword in This Hand Caused the Decision That Ended the War"

REBA RHYNE

❧ Chapter One ❧

550 A.D. or Thereabouts, Chieftain Tybba and Wulf

The <u>BRITTANIAN</u> Midlands/Tybbington/Dudda Hill

The crowing of a rooster woke Tybba from his dream—one he was having frequently for the last year. He was with Gemma. They were young, and she was beautiful. He stood on the bank of the River Albis with his arms around her. Her warm breath touched his cheek. She was his, and he was hers. Once pledged to each other, their union had survived for many years and twelve children—four of them born before they crossed the North Sea to Brittania. Now, she was resting with some of their offspring in the burial ground outside the settlement known as Tybbington. He missed her.

When Tybba opened his eyes, it was still dark. The glow from the raised fire pit was dim, but still emitted the warmth needed to ward off the night chill of the Brittanian Midlands. He could hear low breathing from others in the stone hut. His eldest son, Averel, softly snored on the other side of the room.

Tybba's shoulder ached. He grinned in the darkness. So much for the muscles his late wife had found attractive. He moved his fifty-year-old body into another position, touching Wulf, his grandson.

Wulf was a chip-off-the-old-block, following his grandfather around and soaking up everything his elder said, imitating his every move. He'd stayed the night so he could accompany Tybba on a trek to Dudda Hill. There were many grandsons who could have made the trip, but Tybba had chosen him. Wulf had stars in his eyes and reminded the grandfather of himself at the age of twelve on the northern seacoast of Europe, where he'd poked his nose into anything slightly interesting.

A faint light filtering through the cracks in the doorway told of the sunrise. Yesterday, it had drizzled much of the day, and he was sure clouds still floated in the sky. Tybba arose and quietly pulled back the leather opening of the door. Looking east and over the wooden palisade surrounding the enclosed village, the sky was ablaze with orange and red. Scattered yellow-tinged clouds of light and dark gray dotted the sky.

He stepped outside and looked to the south above the hills, where the sky was clear. The old chieftain stretched his arms to the sky, easing his aching body. This was going to be a perfect day for their climb.

∼

With the first light of dawn, the village was stirring. Shadowy figures moved to start cooking fires and soon the smell of smoke and cooking food drifted among the wattle and daub houses. In the central pathway of Tybbington, Tybba stood with his back to the entrance gate, eating his morning meal of bread and fried pork. His home was the first one inside the compound. He looked past the housing and commons area to the sheep cote, where the animals were herded into their compound for the night.

Averel had told him yesterday, the night holding area needed to be expanded. Their herd was increasing rapidly. The sheep, goats, and ponies along with several black horses, were descended from those they had brought across the sea. Pigs and cattle were products of the wild ones roaming the forests. The oxen they'd bartered from a roving merchant, who came through the area—these to help with plowing the hard clay soil. Rabbit's and chickens were in separate areas within the compound. They were too small to be let out into the surrounding area, where they would become food for wolves and foxes, roaming the woods and making these predators a greater nuisance to the larger livestock.

The crops, the village planted on the lower green to harvest, would not be safe from the smaller animals and fowls.

"Tybba, I have your pack and waterskin ready for today's climb." Hildi, his son's wife, appeared from the hut and held out two leather bags with straps to be hung over his shoulder. "There's food inside for you and Wulf."

Tybba took the packs. "Good. Where is Wulf?"

"He said he forgot something and went home. He should be back soon. Ah, here comes the bearn now," she said, waving her hand toward the running Wulf.

Wulf came hurrying down the village path. "I forgot my walking stick, Tybba," said the young lad, holding the wooden piece up in the air, swinging it, and narrowly missing a woman carrying a bucket of water from the nearby spring.

"Watch it, Wulf," the woman admonished, giving him a hard stare.

"Sorry," Wulf ducked his head and kept walking, this time using the stick as it was intended.

"Your grandfather needs to get his," Tybba said as Wulf drew near. The old man headed toward the stone hut.

"I'll get it." Wulf started to run ahead of his grandfather.

Tybba caught him with his hand. "No. I need to fetch it, Wulf." Tybba was pleased at his grandson's enthusiasm, even if he was a bit clumsy.

Inside the hut, Tybba retrieved his walking stick from a corner and placed something wrapped in leather into the larger bag with the food. He hefted the packs to his shoulder, touching the silver amulet—a hammer—to the god, Thor, which was tied on a leather cord around his neck. The tribes of Germania worshiped many gods and goddesses with secret rites in sacred groves of trees.

Although Cassius Aurelius had talked to his friend, when he was asked, about his faith in Jesus Christ, Tybba had not changed. He'd brought many suspicions to Brittania with him, and now he asked the god's blessing and, with determination in his step, walked out the door ready for the climb up Dudda Hill.

"Be careful, you two. Remember a wolf was spotted down the river two days ago. It could be anywhere now," warned Hildi.

"Ah, Tybba can kill an old wolf with his bare hands. Can't you, Tybba?"

Tybba laughed and patted the knife on his belt. "Come on, Wulf. The sun's getting up and we have some ground to cover and a stop or two to make on the way."

Two hundred feet later, Tybba halted and pulled some leaves off an alder tree, which was growing beside Dudda Brook. He found a rock, sat down, and pulled off his leather shoes. Carefully he placed a layer of leaves inside both shoes, put them back on, and tied strings to ensure they wouldn't come off.

"Tybba, what are you doing?" Wulf's eyes had gotten bigger as he watched what was happening.

"Wulf, everyone knows that a few alder leaves in your shoes keep your feet cool and your feet won't swell if you're taking a long journey. I don't need my feet to swell."

"Ah, Tybba, I heard father tell older brother there was no truth to that old tale."

Tybba got up and leaned toward Wulf. "Just in case there is, I've got it covered," he grinned. "Let's go."

A few steps later, as they followed the brook, Tybba took out his knife and cut two twigs from a willow tree. With two swipes of his hand, he removed the leaves and handed one to his grandson. "Here chew on this and rub your teeth," he added, continuing his walk at a fast pace.

"How did you know about that, Tybba?" The lad put the large end of the twig in his mouth, chewed the bark off, and spit it out. He started nibbling at the exposed core inside.

"My friend, a ship's captain said the Egyptians used the willow to clean their teeth and for medicine to cure aches and pains. He got this information from his seafaring grandfather."

"What's Egyptians?" asked Wulf, his brow furrowed.

Tybba was already breathing hard. "Can't walk and talk. Right now ... walking is more important ... than talking."

～

The trip up Dudda Hill was never easy. To ensure he reached the exact spot he wanted, he crossed the grazing meadow and headed for a tunnel or path cut through the trees and thickets of thorny, hawthorn bushes which led to the start of the ascent up the hillside. The climb was steep and rocky, and at times he grasped the hand of Wulf, pulling him up and around rocks in the path, that is, when the youngster wasn't off exploring some interesting rock or plant.

"Wulf, if you don't quit lagging behind, one of the white ladies will get you," admonished Tybba, repeating something he'd heard as a child, when he'd wandered away from his mother or father. White ladies lived underground and snatched travelers at night or any who were alone.

"Now, Tybba, father said those were left behind when you came to Brittania. There are no white ladies in Tybbington."

Grinning, Tybba grumbled under his breath, "Confounded son. What does he know?"

During the climb, there were many times he counted twenty steps and paused to breathe, especially the closer to the top he came. Finally, he was on the highest part of his world, but he was only interested in one side.

The old tribal Chieftain Tybba sat down on a rock, resting from the steep climb up the hill and above the village named after him—Tybbington. It was from Dudda Hill he first viewed the land he and his family would claim as their own. Since then, when threatened by other tribes, his perch afforded a vantage point to observe the area should intruders intending to raid his village be spotted.

Yesterday, wanting to make the climb, he decided to do it, even if he never came back down. That was a possibility, because he'd been having pains in his chest area, and he had an idea why. This trip served two purposes. First, he wanted to look at his beloved Tybbington one last time. Second, he needed to start teaching Wulf the history of his family. His intention was to have a member of the family carry on this tradition. He pulled off the two packs, handing Wulf the waterskin so he could drink first—the water carried from another spring at the base of Dudda Hill which ran to Lea Brook and finally into the larger river below.

He loved the view from this high place, especially the silver thread of the River Tame—what he could see of it, because his eyes were dimming. The river snaked through tall sturdy oak, slender alder, and filmy, drooping willow trees. Many times, it disappeared altogether. Several small brooks came close or through his tiny village, the source of which the residents obtained their drinking water, and in the end making the river he lived beside.

Crossing his hands on the top of his walking stick, he could see from his perch the settlement below him. Outside this area, plots for gardens or farming were framed by hedge rows or stone fences, designating each family's area of responsibility. Some fields were dotted with the white forms of sheep, grazing on the meadow grass. Forty years had cleared the forest of two hundred, back-breaking acres — this included the smaller clearing his family had first used on the River Tame bank. Plainly seen from the hill was the large, fortified stronghold with homes on pathways, a central common's area, and places for their livestock to spend the night.

The gate stood open, meaning struggles in the immediate area were non-existent. For several years, conflict had ceased, as most of the ancient tribes of Briton had gone west beyond the mountains ... although there were always rumblings of happenings around the area. War could break out on any given day. If it did, he would be required to send men to join and fight with the friendly tribes around him. Those included the Saxon Snotta's compound, whose large tribe inhabited the River Trent just before you rowed south on the River Tame — three days hard march to the northeast, if you didn't have to go around itinerate swamps on the way.

Outside the compound, where the gardens dotted the meadow with each family tending their own allotted spot, several beautiful black horses grazed in a field by themselves. The horses were descendants of the two brought from the banks of the River Albis forty years ago.

Ah, those were the days, thought Tybba.

Beyond the garden spots and grazing grounds, the communal areas started, where anyone could hunt or cut wood for a fire. Slowly, the folks were clearing other areas for the village to farm with their pursuit of warmth in the winter.

Over the years, other families were admitted into the Tybba family farm. Some because of skills they had which were beneficial to the tribe, and others because of a recognized union between a man and woman. Even a few Britons, captured when trying to raid Tybbington had taken an oath to serve him and joined the group. Tybba hadn't restricted anyone coming in peace who could add to the talents of those already there. He estimated over two hundred families lived down in the valley. Almost every week, the cry of a newborn baby was heard, and he was blessed to hold the little one in his arms.

The smoke from many cooking fires mingled together and hung over the wood houses. His son's wife would be cooking wild greens with parsnips and shallots in an iron pot over an open fire outside their hut. He'd gathered the greens from the forest yesterday in-between the drizzling rain. On an outside spit, she would tend a dressed red squirrel caught in one of his many traps in the forest. The small squirrel would be joined with a plucked chicken on the same spit. Tybba felt his mouth water at the thought of fresh meat cooked and smoked over an outside fire.

An insistent nudge from Wulf, who had been entertaining himself, made Tybba tear his attention away from the scene before him. "What is it, bearn?"

"You promised to tell me a story, Tybba." Wulf's twelve-year-old eyes were questioning.

"Yes, and I will." He patted his grandson's head and pulled him upon his aching knee. Pointing his finger at the young boy, he said, "Wulf, you must listen carefully, so you can tell this account to *your* grandson."

"Oh, Tybba. Mama says I can't remember anything," laughed Wulf.

"We'll have this talk again and again. You'll remember."

"Did your grandfather do the same thing to you?"

"No, not quite the same thing. So, we're going to start on how *your* grandfather came to Tybbington from the continent of Europe. I hope I can remember all the details. Here goes. I once knew a Roman sea captain by the name of Cassius Aurelius. Listen carefully."

❧ Chapter 2 ❧

Forty Years Earlier – *Or Thereabouts*

Germania, Chieftain Tybba, and Cassius Aurelius

Roman Captain Cassius Aurelius grasped the bar connected to his two outside steering oars. Sailing north, he turned the boat starboard or right, into the calmer waters of the River Albis Estuary on the coast of northern Frisia and into Saxon territory. Passing two islands, he continued until he was close to the mouth of a shallower river which came from the north.

His crew chief, Maximus, called for the single sail to be pulled to the yard arm on the mast and tied off. Immediately, sixteen oarsmen methodically dipped their oak oars against the ships progress and slowed the boat to a crawl. Cassius steered to port or left and five hundred feet later, his boat floated above the green water of a small harbour. The crew threw lines to the wharfmen and the ship was tied up to the dock. With gangplanks installed, he watched as the men abandoned ship and disappeared along with the men working the dock ropes. They scattered throughout the village. After many visits, each sailor had a definite place to go. So, did he.

News of his coming always traveled fast throughout the compact family village. Being a month early, there was no sign of young, Chieftain Tybba and his family. He knew they would be close-by and probably on the way. No other craft the size of his came into the cove, although several smaller fishing boats plied its water. These local fishermen ventured into the estuary and on short day trips up and down the coast, looking for food and trading partners, swapping their handmade items, produce, and gossip, keeping up with what was going on in the world.

Docked at the wharf, his boat was a reason for celebration. Tomorrow, he would set out some of his cargo for barter with the community, but that wasn't the main reason for his visit. He and Tybba had other plans.

~

For three generations the Aurelius family had visited this Germanic Saxon tribe, becoming friends and then establishing trade with them. The first time for the Aurelius family was while the Romans were leaving Brittania. Trade was interrupted, because the shore forts were being shuttered, wasting a sea captain's time in stopping to sell his goods. Most boat captains weren't interested in transporting possessions, soldiers, and slaves back to Rome. These trips would take several months without payment, since Rome was financially insolvent. Cassius's grandfather had no intention of returning to decadent Rome with a boatload of rowdy, drunken soldiers. He ran a tight ship. And, from the scuttlebutt he'd heard, his native country wouldn't be around long.

Taking a breather and looking for other trading partners, Cassius's grandfather had rowed his ship up the River Albis and into this river, finding a welcome in the Saxon village. An accomplished Roman merchant, he could afford to take a break. He and his wife had stayed for several months, establishing close relationships with the villagers. Romilius, his third son was born while he was here—the only one of his children to survive.

With the Roman exit finished, he resumed his former trading route. The elder Aurelius visited all of his favorite places and started a new trade of bartering with the natives. From Brittania, he loaded their excellent wool, tin to make bronze, and animal hides for leather tanning. At favorite harbours on the Brittanian and European coast, he unloaded his bartered cargo to trusted merchants for gold or silver coins and took on new items to trade. He stayed a few days to rest, and headed to sea again. His crew was loyal. They enjoyed the short voyages and the time ashore with family.

That generation passed and with a new boat which had a sail, Cassius' father, Romilius, took over the captain's post. He increased the trading route, sailing as far as the warmer climes of Hispania, through the Pillars of Hercules, and to the island city of Palmaria on Mallorca. This port city, under Roman rule was the stopover for ships from the eastern Mediterranean to the western provinces beyond. During his many trips there, he had a villa built high on the hillside, overlooking the sea, where when his sailing days were over, he could feel the balmy breezes and smell the salty sea air. This would be the perfect place for his family to visit and rest.

Adding different types of cargo, he reversed course and sailed west to Brittania and the coasts of the continent to barter and trade.

On one trip into the village in Germania, Romilius found a new wharf had been built to make his landings easier, and he found his wife. In front of the village, they'd pledged themselves to each other, and she'd boarded the boat to sail with him. This was many years ago. They were both gone, as was the old, Saxon Chief, Tybba's father, who Cassius first knew as a little boy.

Chief Tybba was Cassius' age and until Tybba settled down with a wife, they'd sailed much of the Brittanian seas. And once, Cassius took his friend to Palmaria to show him his villa, which his family would inherit from his father. They contemplated going on to Rome, but gossip said the city wasn't safe, with wars continuing, unrest disabling the markets, and rulers changing quickly.

On the way back to Germania with a hold full of bartered goods, they'd survived each other, bad storms, and outrun a boatload of pirates. Tybba loved the ocean and knew the shipping business as much as he did. If there was such a thing as brotherly love, without being close blood kin, these two men had it.

In Londinium, during the three-month winter hiatus when most boats were idle, Cassius had longed to get back on the water. Germania and Tybba's village were his first destination.

Before he pulled his heavy, wool cloak tightly around him and moved out from under the aft deck canopy, the captain paused and touched the ichthys, or fish symbol, of his belief in the Lord Jesus Christ, which he wore on a delicate chain around his neck. He said his thanks for a safe journey. The symbol of Christ was old—ancient his grandfather had said, and passed down from generation to generation, farther back than his old ancestor could remember.

Stepping down from the deck's raised surface, he immediately felt the sun's rays on his brown, curly hair. Squinting his dark eyes against the bright sun's reflection on the water, he headed toward the gangplank, which connected the boat to the wharf. Six smaller boats of various sizes were tied up to the dock or pulled up on the shore. These belonged to people living in the village, who used them to fish in the river and along the Germanic or North Sea coast.

Stepping onto the dock, he headed toward land, grinning at his unsteady steps. Losing his sea legs would take a day or two.

"Cassius." A young boy waved and called from the closest hut. He was dressed in layers of wool clothing, trimmed in fur with leather trousers and fur-lined, lace-up, leather boots.

"Sutt, you made it through the winter. How are your parents?"

"They're in good health. We're going with you on your journey."

"Good," said Cassius and kept walking, hoping to discourage the blue-eyed, blond-haired youngster from following him. Sutt hadn't stopped talking since he learned his first words as a toddler. "Is Chief Tybba close by?"

"Yes," Sutt responded, taking a few steps in his direction and then stopping. "He's with the sheep. One of the ewes is having a lamb."

Cassius looked around the settlement as he walked quickly toward the sheepcote. Coastal Germanic villages looked the same. This one started several feet back from the water's edge—a hedge against the incoming tide. There were no mountains and almost no hills in this land. Since it was mostly flat—only trees broke the landscape view. Houses were built on man-made mounds. These mounded terpen made a half-hearted attempt to keep the raging sea from flooding and destroying homes. When an unusual neap tide surrounded the terpen, it left the homes looking like they floated in sea water. The angry sea was the biggest reason to leave this land. Moving anywhere, even inland to higher ground, did not change the villager's situation and backed them up against their cousins the Chauci and other militant tribes.

Tybba's family settlement was made up of semi-permanent, thatched-roofed, wattle and daub houses. This type of home consisted of about equal parts of mud, straw, sand, clay, and manure, mixed together and smeared, inside and out, on woven, thin wooden canes, or straight sticks gathered from the banks of the river or forest's edge. The daubed mud dried in the sun and became brick hard. Several homes made up a compound determined by blood ties and surrounded by a single picket fence, which became part of a larger designated village area.

Cassius stood in the midst of the village, looking from one well-known hut to another. Piles of bog peat rested against the sides of the homes waiting to supply warmth in the living area. Smoke from inside fires curled upward through a hole in the roof and mingled with the clear blue sky. The smell was one of pungent, burning peat. Since the season was late winter, the people inside their homes were enjoying the heat of the flames as the food cooked. He could hear the faint murmur of their voices. He heard other noises—the occasional bleating of a sheep or mooing of a cow in the pastureland beyond the small community. There was one path running through the village. He took it, starting up a slight rise, and heading toward the only hill in the area. He passed to the side of gardens where the villagers grew vegetables — each one with their own defined plot.

"Cassius, you're early."

Grinning broadly, the sea captain turned around and answered in the Saxon tongue as Tybba came from a pen of sheep nearby. "Tybba, 'ow bist yow?"

"I'm fine and ready to set sail, my friend. Come with me, and I'll show you my cargo." Tybba embraced his childhood friend, then he turned to walk the short distance to his home. This single stone house with thatched roof was surrounded by several wattle and daub homes, all part of his immediate family. Smoke curled lazily from the roof. "How was your trip?"

"Smooth as silk. The Lord made sure the sea was kind to us. Are we still on schedule?"

"Yes. I've seen no reason to change. Of course, since you are here, maybe we'll go earlier." Tybba stated. "If the gods are with us, next year at this time we'll be wintering in our new lands and eating our first harvest."

The intention was to arrive in the Midlands before seed planting time, so the tribe could plow, plant crops, and harvest them in their new homeland.

What they would encounter after arriving in Brittania was unknown. They would be travelling up a river and through lands settled by other fierce Saxon and Angle tribes, going deeper inland to find a protected place in the middle of the country. Tybba had a rough Roman map which his friend had given him and a place picked out. He and Cassius had had many discussions on the particulars of the trip. The plan was to come in peace, but conquer, if necessary. Gossip said the lands were sparsely populated, compared to Tybba's homeland.

Cassius had even traveled up the estuary where the tribe would first see their new country, as far as the River Trent. Once the small ship couldn't be sailed or rowed, the people from Tybba's village would leave the boat. They would be on their own, and Cassius would return to the sea.

~

The lane to Tybba's house wasn't long and led across a small, wooden bridge with water as clear as a crystal flowing underneath.

"Wait." Cassius hopped down the bank and got down on one knee. He cupped his hands and drank in the water with big gulps. "It's been too long since I had a sip of good water, and this water is the best in the world."

"We're sure to take some full barrels with us on your boat." Tybba babbled on as Cassius joined him on the path. Finally, he said, "I have a new little one since you last left."

"What! Is that the cargo you were talking about?" Cassius teased.

Tybba doubled over with laughter, his face redder than usual. "No." He managed to say.

"Another one. Boy or girl?"

"Only four, Cassius," Tybba replied, pretending indignation. "A little girl. We've named her Randi, after her grandmother and to remind us of the land she was born in."

"How's the wife and other children?" Tybba was living with the most beautiful woman in the village— long, blonde tresses, blue eyes, and graceful figure. Cassius regretted not being more aggressive in his relationship with her, but he was glad she belonged to his friend.

Tybba stopped in the middle of the path. He turned toward Cassius. "Sailing with you was the greatest experience of my life, but I'd have given it up for Gemma and the little ones. Having a family is my best achievement in my short years on this earth." He turned, pulled on his long blond beard, and started walking again. "When are you going to find a good wife?"

"Someday, my friend. I'm in no hurry." This was a true statement. He wanted to be as happy as Tybba, and there was no one in sight to make him this way. A woman was hard to find when you only stayed four or five days in a place, and he shied away from the women who hovered around the smelly wharf in Londinium where he over-wintered.

The thick fur hanging at the entrance to Tybba's house flew open. "Cassius, it is you. You're early!" Gemma exclaimed, her face showing her pleasure at his coming. He walked toward her, giving her a hug.

"Evidently, I am," he teased, as he and Tybba stepped inside the fur covered door. "I hear we've got more cargo?"

Gemma's brow furrowed—then she smiled. "Oh! The little one." She didn't blush as Tybba had done but waved her hand toward a wooden box covered by a warm fur coverlet. "Yes, she'll be a big load. Come on in. We have rabbit stew with peas, cabbage, and carrots. Tybba went hunting this morning." She moved aside, making way for the men to warm by the fire.

"Cassius, we'll check out the big stuff after we eat." The two men sat cross-legged on thick fur mats next to the fire in the dim interior, while Gemma dished the food into bowls.

"Where are the youngsters?" Cassius knew they were nearby, because he heard them snickering and moving about. He was poking fun at them.

"Don't turn around, but there are several beady eyes looking at you from their fur beds next to the wall," Gemma said.

Tybba laughed. "Come on boys. I know you want to greet the captain."

The youngsters threw themselves on Cassius, almost knocking the soup bowl from his hands. The youngest, a little more than a toddler, lost his balance and fell onto the sea captain's knee.

Quickly setting the bowl down, Cassius grabbed an armful of boys and rubbed each blond head with his fist. Then Gemma sent them back to their furry nooks.

"Three boys, Tybba. Having a little girl will be different." Cassius picked up his bowl and took a sip of the rabbit broth. "What did you say you named her?"

"We've named her Randi after her grandmother— my father's wife."

The rest of the meal consisted of the men eating and making plans for loading the boat. Afterwards, the two headed to the back of the cottage. Under a thatched lean-to, they looked at the stash of supplies for the trip to Brittania.

🦋 **Chapter 3** 🦋

500 A.D. or *Thereabouts*

The Trip to Brittania

Cassius couldn't help but smile as he looked down at the hodge-podge on his deck. This included twenty-nine passengers of various ages besides his crew and a menagerie of animals—the start of new herds in England. Tybba had selected the best ram, two ewes, three good goats, and two of the beautiful black horses the Saxons were known to raise. To say the ship was crowded was an understatement. There was just enough room for his rowers to sit on their benches at the gunnels, and a pathway through the maze on his deck—all supplies secured tightly to his boat.

Tybba could have left the animals and taken from the inhabitants who lived along his path to the Midlands, but he wanted to make friends not enemies. The chief had women and children to be concerned about. Fighting might come, but it was not on his agenda. He was a farmer first, and a fierce warrior second.

Two of the boats that had been tied up to the dock were now lashed onto the deck of Cassius's small ship. The larger one was packed with supplies—hides sewn together to make tents when pulled over poles and tied off, wooden stools for sitting, armour and wooden boxes containing cooking supplies. The smaller boat was empty and would be used to row ashore to cook for the night. Two small carts were directly in front of his perch underneath a canvas covering. They could be pulled by horse, goats, or two men.

Cassius watched as Tybba supervised the last of the provisions going into the hold of the boat. He hadn't read much of the Bible, but from what he knew, his boat was a miniature Noah's Ark.

He wondered how much of his cargo would make the trip inland to the place marked on Tybba's map. He wished he could go with his friend, but his responsibilities as a ship's captain would not let him.

The tribe's chief bounded upon the raised deck where he stood. "I've checked and double-checked. I think we're ready to sail." Tybba was all smiles and excited about this adventure to find a new home.

"I understand. Are you sure you don't want to stay here where you know what to expect on a day-to-day basis.?"

"No. Our group has had many discussions. We are agreed. This is what we want. A new land awaits us." Tybba turned to the expectant faces below him. "Are you ready," he called.

"We are ready," came the chorus of responses. "We will follow you, Chief Tybba."

"One word of caution, everyone," Cassius said, addressing the upturned faces below. "Take control of your small children. After we reach the open sea, our travel will not be smooth, but rolling and unsteady. After they get accustomed to the moving ship, sailing will be easier for them, and they can run and play."

Cassius gave the order for the ship to move out from the dock. Maximus walked down his lines of oarsmen, who were in place along the gunnels of the boat with their oars in the water. The lines attaching the boat to the dock were thrown aboard and stowed in their boxes. A quick dip of the oars and the boat moved slowly and gently away from the wharf. Out in the river mainstream, the bow was pointed forward— downstream.

"I will be back," Cassius called to the new chieftain of the village.

"We will expect you, Cassius Aurelius," the chieftain called back. He continued, "May the gods go with you, Tybba."

"Take good care of my village," Tybba responded and waved.

The sound of oars dipping in the water was the only sound for some seconds as the ship pushed into the river. The people aboard were filled with wonder as they felt its movement for the first time. Some went close to the boat's gunnels and waved to those on shore. Some cried. The children seemed in awe as the boat moved beneath their feet. Several went running to their mothers, hanging on tightly to offered hands.

Those left standing on shore waved and called to family and friends. Many walked down the sandy shore as the boat picked up speed, until they couldn't distinguish the passengers, which they would never see again. Then the boat went starboard into the estuary and headed for open sea.

At the mouth of the estuary was the deep, aqua-blue of the North Sea. Some of the oarsmen unfurled the sail and tied it off. It caught the wind and the oars went motionless. Keeping the shore in sight, the boat moved forward and south on its first roll. Tybba's journey to his new home had started.

For the passengers, the moment was poignant with unexpected thoughts. There was something Tybba needed to do. He walked to the stern and looked at the mouth of the river up which he and his ancestors had lived for hundreds of years. His eyes were wet with tears. He wanted to wave goodbye, but didn't. No respectable chieftain would do that! Whatever happened to him in the future, he'd never regret his decision to go to this new country. He turned his back on the past, walked to Cassius, and looked ahead to the life before him.

Today, Cassius would send his boat south along the coast of Frisia, until he encountered a long chain of islands. He would follow those until the islands became unbroken land. At that point, he'd cut straight across the North Sea and sail for a large English headland below the Humber Estuary and north of the English Channel. His destination or point of interest was an abandoned Roman stone fort on a low hill where marshlands filled the lowlands down to the sea. Once he came to this jut of land, he would turn north, past an inland sea of marsh and mudflats called The Wash, and sail until the mouth of the Humber Estuary came into view.

When he'd first took over the captain's duties, he'd often consulted maps and used instructions his father, Romilius, had written down on scrolls. He needed them to navigate his established shipping lanes. Cassius had packed the rolls away. He knew the area he traveled well.

To cover the route they had chosen, he and Tybba estimated three to four days of sailing. The plan was to anchor close to land each night. All depended on mother nature. Ahead lay the channel currents, winds, and whitecapped waves.

～

With the first swell of the Northern Sea, three of the oldest women headed for benches on the deck. They made a small group midship, where the surface movement of the water was felt less. Others stood by the rail, watching the waves crashing on shore, the rolling sea, and the scenery slipping quietly by. Sea birds flew overhead, calling their sad goodbyes to the people on the boat. The ship hugged the coastline, trying to keep seasickness to a minimum.

The children getting their sea legs started a game of hide-and-seek, squealing and running on the deck—sometimes bumping into the stacked boxes when an unexpected wave caused the boat to pitch and roll. The older ones chaperoned their games, laughing at their antics and making sure they were safely navigating the deck.

～

"Cassius."

Hearing his name called, the captain turned from the helm and looked down to the deck. "Sutt, how are you doing? Are you enjoying your first trip at sea?"

"Oh yes. I was wondering if I could come up and help you steer."

Cassius chuckled. "Sure, come on up."

The young lad bounced up three steps and joined the captain at the steering bar. "Do you know how the steering bar works, Sutt?" he said, pointing to the cables and pulleys which worked the steering rudders.

"No."

"Cassius, I'm going down and see how the family's faring. See if you can teach young Sutt how to sail the boat." Tybba grinned, punched his distant kin on the shoulder, and walked down the stairs that the lad had just come up. He headed for Gemma, who sat on a chest away from the rail, and assumed a seat beside her.

"I don't feel so good," she told Tybba. She held Randi and looked like she was going to be sick.

"Seasickness will be a problem with some of our travelers. I was hoping you wouldn't be one of them. Keeping the shore in view helps some people, but you need to stand up." He helped her to her feet and guided her to the rail so she had a clear view.

"Could I sit on one of the rower's seats?"

"I don't see why you can't, but you need to face the shore as much as possible."

She sat down and followed his instructions. "The baby seems to be faring well. She's such a good baby."

Tybba peeked under the edge of the blanket. Randi was fast asleep. "Maybe we should have called her Frith, since she is so peaceful," he suggested, grinning. "How are the rest of the children doing?"

"Off playing. Averel took charge of them. They're exploring the rest of the ship." Gemma rubbed her forehead with her hand.

"You don't feel any better, do you?"

"No! Here, take Randi." Gemma jumped up and leaned over the rail. After being sick, she sat down hard on the rower's seat. "I feel better now," she said, grinning weakly.

"I'll get you a cup of water." Tybba handed the baby to her mother and headed for the water barrels. With a full cup, he went back to Gemma.

"I do feel better," she said, spitting some of the water out but drinking the rest in gulps.

"Feeling better probably won't last long. Let me see if I can find someone to help with Randi. If the wind holds up, we may make better time today. If we do, I'll suggest to Cassius we stop earlier to cook our food and then you and the others who are having difficulty can stay on shore, maybe even sleep on shore tonight."

"Tybba, I could hug your neck."

"Hey, don't let me stop you," he grinned, checking out the sail which was taut with the wind's strength.

"I'm afraid to get up."

He leaned over and gave Gemma a quick peck on the cheek. "I'll search for a woman who's not feeling the effects of the waves and send her to you. Look for a place to stretch out and rest on the deck—or below where there are bunks for the sailors."

Tybba hunted among the women and found a young girl who could help Gemma. He looked for Averel and made sure his boys were safe, then he returned to the stern where Cassius stood watching Sutt.

"Look, Tybba. I'm 'holding the boat steady.'" Sutt was beaming, standing as straight as an arrow.

"Sure enough, you are. I'm proud of you."

"Is Gemma adjusting to a seafaring life?" asked Cassius, who had observed her struggle.

"No. The motion of the boat is not helping the motion in her stomach. I sent one of the women to help with the baby. If we make good progress today, I promised her we'd stop early for cooking the evening meal. Any chance of that?"

Cassius looked up at the sail. "A good possibility if the wind holds fair." Cassius motioned to Maximus, who was standing by. "Will you take over the steering rudder? I think Sutt has had a good lesson today. Maybe he can help tomorrow. What about it, Sutt? Would you like that?"

"You mean it?"

"Sure, but don't come early. I don't want you here at first light. Now, go and find Averel. He's probably missing you."

"Cassius, if you need another hand with the boat, I'm available," said Sutt.

"I'll think about it," the Captain returned as Sutt bounded to the deck.

Cassius and Tybba watched the young boy thread his way through the cargo and stop to tell a friend of his adventure. Tybba spoke first. "All we'll hear about is his seamanship from now on."

Cassius laughed, "At least this story will be different." He changed the subject back to Tybba's wife. "I knew some of my passengers would probably have seasickness, but I wasn't thinking about Gemma. She's such a strong woman."

"Do you think she'll get over it? I know I did." Tybba was remembering his time on the sea with Cassius.

29

"Let's hope so. Be glad our trip will not be long and when we get to the Humber Estuary, the rest of the trip will be *calm and peaceful*, at least on the water."

Tybba looked quickly at his friend, realizing he'd put emphasis on the calm and peaceful part. Was he teasing? Or, did he know more than he let on? "I hope you're right."

~

In the late afternoon, they anchored between an offshore island and the mainland. Shielded by the island, the sea settled down and the boat rested in calmer waters.

"Tybba," called Cassius, "first we'll take the supplies for cooking and the night stay to the island. The people can elect to go or stay on the ship. If they go, each family will need to supply us with their tents. Then we'll row to the mainland and look for meat for the evening meal. The deer should be out grazing soon." He knew it would take a large animal to feed his passengers—maybe two.

The chieftain was checking on his wife, who had survived the day. "I'll make sure that the supplies are ready to go. Will you see that the boat is hoisted over the side?" Tybba turned back to Gemma.

"I feel better already," she said. "You go on and help Cassius, but I want to be in the first boat to shore."

~

After making several trips to row supplies and people to the island, the men started a fire with flint and steel and dry materials brought from the ship packed for that purpose. Leaving the women with the responsibility of keeping the flames going, they headed for the mainland, looking for meat to roast and eat for the evening meal. The only sound breaking the peace of the island's solitude was the delightful sound of children playing and sea birds winging over the tidal flats near the shore, calling to the seals frolicking in the shallow water.

Gemma, along with the other women, was glad to be ashore. She tested her legs by walking around on the hard, sandy beach. Randi, encased in fur, slept in the wooden bed Tybba had made for her, shaded by a lone bush on the windswept island shore and tended by the young girl.

"Averel," called Gemma, walking toward her son, "you and Sutt get all the driftwood you can gather. We need a large pile for cooking and to build a fire for tonight." This wouldn't be hard because there were piles along the shore. "Try to get dry wood," she instructed. "And watch your brothers."

As they'd sailed south, the boat had passed several islands large enough to accommodate a tribal village. Cassius had pointed out one. He traded with the folks living there. When asked what on earth these people had to trade, he'd replied—seal skins. The island where they'd dropped anchor wasn't very big—not much more than a sandbank with a few surviving shrub bushes. But it was adequate for today's needs. Tidal flats held hundreds of barking seals as they rummaged through the shallow water, looking for food or fun. Hundreds of sea birds flew overhead in sweeping formations in search of scraps left by the seals.

Joined by Sutt's mother, Gemma set out to explore the area. The women trudged for the highest point, walking through a bank of grasses, short bushes and loose sand.

From their perch, they could see over the boat anchored in the waterway between the mainland and the island they stood upon. Marshes were scattered along the coast. An opening in the grassy wetland allowed a glimpse into the interior—more water and marsh.

"Do you think they'll find food in that tangle of water and weeds?" asked Gemma.

"I don't know," replied Sutt's mother, shaking her head. She had turned toward the open sea. "Look Gemma. A boat."

"I wonder if it's headed toward the English Channel crossing?" This crossing was the shortest distance between the continent of Europe and Brittania.

"Is that how we're going?"

"I hope not," replied Gemma. "That would add two or more days on the water. I heard Cassius and Tybba talking. There is another way, but it's riskier. The sooner we can get to the Humber Estuary, the better I'll like it. We'd better head back and make sure the fire's still burning. Randi may be getting hungry also."

～

The men did find meat. Tybba told Gemma on return, "A small herd of deer was swimming through the water looking for solid ground. We were able to get two, so we'll have plenty to eat tonight and tomorrow."

"Should you check on the animals on board ship?" asked Gemma.

"Yes. I'm going to row to the ship and take care of them."

Averel came running. "May I go with you, father?"

"Yes. We'll get done faster."

Averel grabbed his father's hand, and the two headed for the beached boat, pushing it into the water. Tybba lifted Averel aboard and jumped in. Soon the oars dipped in the water.

The women boiled whole parsnips, carrots and shallots to make a tasty stew with some of the meat and a little saltwater. Other large parts of deer meat were roasted into the night over the glowing fire. This would be tomorrow's feast. Later, in her snug, fur bed by the fire and under the stars, Gemma told Tybba, "I feel much better. What should I expect tomorrow on the boat?"

"After we leave the islands behind, we'll be out in the open sea for about two days. The waves and swell will be worse. Once we see the seacoast of Brittania, we'll find an abandoned Roman fort called Caister-on-Sea. We'll stay there overnight. This is one place we can unload the animals from the ship to graze. The next day we'll head north. After that, there'll be one more day of sailing until we get to the Humber Estuary and start on our trip inland to our new home."

"So, I'll have to survive for three more days?"

"Yes. I wish I had better news," Tybba turned to put his arms around her. Over her shoulder he could see Randi's sleeping box. They'd made a shield out of sticks and fur to hold the warmth in her area. He pulled in a sigh and let it out in a rush. Was he doing the best thing for his little girl? What would her life be like in this new country—Brittania? He tightened his grip on Gemma and went to sleep.

❧ Chapter 4 ❧

The Humber Estuary and Beyond

Late afternoon on the fourth day of sea travel, Gemma stood by the gunnel, looking at the calmer waters as they moved into the Humber Estuary. After the last few days, seeing even the ripples they were sailing through was enough to bring tears of relief to her eyes.

The second and third day of crossing the North Sea had been a nightmare. The wind stopped and drizzling rain started when they were within sight of the Brittanian coast. The ship had sat in the water tossing up and down, up and down for hours. Just thinking about it made her stomach churn. Almost everyone on board was sick, except for the rowers. They sat on their benches, dipping their oars into the water against the current, pushing them south from their destination. Even Tybba stretched out on the deck of the boat at midship, determined the wave action would not get the best of him.

The rain stopped and the sea calmed down somewhat in the morning of the third day, allowing them to tie up to the dock at the fort, hoping to set foot on dry land. No one got off the ship due to the wave motion against the ship and wharf. The cold and incessant rain returned before nightfall. No one ate the evening meal, and there was no dry wood to even attempt a fire on the shore.

Before dark, the wind started blowing, bringing with it cold and icy droplets. That's when everyone went below deck and experienced ship life in a new crowded way.

Hoping to put the storm behind him, Cassius decided to keep going north since there were no obstructions in the sea. Even with the harsh wind and rain, he could make out the dark coast outline. Sometime during the early morning after the rain subsided, he'd turned the helm over to Maximus and gone in search of sleep. Remembering what Tybba had said earlier, he wished for a warm woman to ward off the chill he felt. Below deck, he pulled several layers of fur over him in his small cabin. "This will have to suffice," he said to the empty room.

Day four was little better. The rain and wind returned and everyone struggled with the cold and cramped quarters below deck. Cassius stood at the steering bar, spelled by Maximus and Tybba. At noon, the sun appeared through the clouds and so did the Humber Estuary — land out of the mists.

∼

The last days with the churning sea, cold and hungry, were the worst ones Gemma had spent in her life. She was grateful her seafaring days were over. She hoped the days ahead on the river would be an improvement.

"Gemma."

She jumped when he spoke to her, loosening two tears which ran down her face. "Tybba, you scared me."

"I'm sorry." He put his arm around her and rubbed her shoulder. "Are you better?" Gemma quickly disposed of the wet spots on her face. "I think I'll live. How did you sail for days on end? I couldn't do it."

"You get used to it."

"Not me. I don't care if I never see another sail or sailing boat, but you don't have to tell Cassius I said that," Gemma stated with conviction, breathing in a full lung of sea air. "And please, don't tell me you have changed your mind, and we are going back to our old home."

"No, my wife, we are staying here, and speaking of Cassius, he says there's a tribe ahead on a river tributary. We can go ashore, greet them, and dry out. They were friends of the Romans and live in one of the forts the legions left vacant. They have plenty of room, and he thinks we'll be able to stay overnight and cook our evening meal over their fires—warm food, dry clothes? What do you think? We'll get there late afternoon."

"Sweet words to my ears, Tybba. I'm all for stopping."

"I promise you the rest of the trip on the water will be calm. None of us will have trouble eating or sleeping." As soon as he made the promise, he wondered if he could keep it. *I guess I'll find out shortly,* he thought.

~

The Saxon group from the River Albis stood staring at the stone fort walls of the Roman Fort of Petuaria. Most had never seen a building so imposing. With the boat docked at the wharf and the gangplank extended the people were ready to go ashore, but Cassius and Tybba went first to greet the leader of the tribe which now inhabited the fort. The harbour gate was on the west wall, facing the river. A cobble stone pathway led to this entrance.

Cassius explained to Tybba as they walked to the gate, "This was an active Roman fort when my grandfather traded here. He would stop and take on goods, grain, and corn for transport to other forts and trading partners in the area, but it has deteriorated over the years and become inactive. Most ships pass by it. Not me. I still stop because the leader is my friend."

"The outside walls look fine," observed Tybba, standing inside the opening and looking at a set of steps leading up to an observation point on the gate's summit. He'd seen Roman forts before on his jaunts with Cassius on the sea. This one was small compared to some he'd observed.

"Yes, they do. Stone survives the ages, but inside where wood was used, there's much decay and original buildings have been replaced with round huts and thatched roofs much like you lived in on the coast of Germania."

"Who's that waving at us?" Tybba was looking at a plump man advancing toward them. He was covered with a long cloak, touching his boot-shod feet. It swayed awkwardly at each step.

"His name is Valerius. He's the local merchant with whom I trade and the head of the village people. Just as you are Saxon. He is from the Parisii tribe."

Tybba nodded in understanding. He stopped to look around at the buildings inside the fort compound.

"How did the village head get a Roman name?" he asked as he caught up with Cassius.

"Intermarriage with the Roman soldiers or slaves. There was much influence over the Parisii people who weren't chastised or subdued like other tribes in the area—sort of a mutual cooperative interaction. So, the native tribe kept the name, not wishing to change it." Cassius stopped walking and waited for the village chief to close the distance between them.

Valerius was dressed in layers of wool clothing complete with trousers and leather boots which laced up and enclosed the foot. The weather was cold even though the sun shone brightly in the late winter sky, and this man was dressed for it.

"Salve, Captain Cassius. This is an unexpected pleasure. You are early this year," Valerius said, extending his hand and arm toward his friend in the Roman greeting of welcome. "And who is this?"

"Salve, Valerius. I *am* early." At first, Cassius thought it better not to tell the Parisii leader that Tybba was heading inland to establish a home in England. Some Saxons weren't welcome on the Humber Estuary, due to raiding of their settlements after the Romans left for Rome. Instead, he said, "Your visitor is Chieftain Tybba of the Saxon tribe. He's my good friend and a trading partner across the North Sea. He and I would like to obtain permission to overnight here in your village. I can vouch for him."

"A Saxon, huh. I hope you are not after my lands like those Angles who live across the river." The chief looked Tybba up-and-down. Did he guess the reason this Saxon was in England? Then he smiled. "Salve, Chief Tybba. A friend of the Captain is a friend of

Valerius." He extended his hand and arm to Tybba and turned back to Cassius. "Is there enough room in the building where you usually overnight?"

"Yes. Do you mind if I show Tybba and his family around your village?"

"Please do and then come to my home for refreshment. I will be expecting you."

"Tybba, we'll walk back to tell the others. And Valerius, when we finish with the unloading and tour, my friend and I will come to your home."

"Very good, Captain. I need the news you always bring."

~

Gemma, along with the others, had no idea what a Roman fort should look like. She stood at the boat's gunnels staring at the massive stone fort walls. Other than the gated fortress, the area had the same river marshes and low terrain as where she'd come from. She could be back home where major floods took the lives of humans and animals alike. She saw Tybba and Cassius turn and head back toward the boat.

"Gemma, bring the load of supplies for eating and staying the night. Tell the others," called Tybba, waving from the gate. "Get the boys to help you."

Anticipating going ashore, she had a pile ready to go. "Averel, you and the others get the animals off and gather all you can carry for what we need tonight. Make other trips, if necessary," she instructed and picked up a large iron pot which contained wooden bowls and stirring spoons. "Be careful. The boat is moving a little against the wharf."

Each family hurriedly gathered what they needed, making a ragtag procession off the boat and up the cobblestone walkway. They were followed by the crew. The group endured stares from the villagers as they paraded by, and stepping faster, they caught up with Cassius and Tybba. Tybba took the iron pot from Gemma.

"Are these people friendly?" she whispered to Cassius.

He laughed, "Yes, they're not used to being invaded by so many strange people at once. They'll warm up to you." A few feet later, he stopped at a door and said, "This is our home for the night—one of the old Roman barracks. Find a spot and make yourself at home."

"We need wood," said Gemma, after opening the door and looking into the dim interior. The men and women started filing into the building to establish their room for the night.

"I'll send the crew for it," said Cassius, looking at Gemma, "and make sure the animals on the boat have been tended too." Without entering, he called Maximus and gave him instructions. "Come on, Tybba. I want to show you the rest of the fort."

"Do you mind if I go with you?" asked Gemma.

"No. Join us," said Tybba.

"Let me talk to Sutt's mother. We'll make plans for the evening meal." Gemma disappeared into the building and was shocked to find individual rooms, separated by wood walls. A long central hearth with a rusted iron grate was available for cooking. "Hum. The layout of the building is interesting," she said to herself.

"Yes, it is, Gemma. We'll have to keep this in mind when we build our new homes," Sutt's mother responded.

The hearth was surrounded with small rooms. The whole building had a central corridor with doors on each end where light could filter into the dark interior. "I like this arrangement." Gemma made plans with the other women on the meal preparation and made sure Randi was with her caretaker. Then she walked outside and joined the two men.

"Sutt's mother is in charge until I get back." She linked her arm into Tybba's, drawing a deep breath and letting it out in a quick rush. She turned to Cassius. "I'd like to climb up to the gate and look over the land around the fort, if we have time."

"We can do that. But first, I want you to see the old market place, Tybba."

Cassius turned and strolled down a wide street, talking as he went. "The Romans were very conscious of order. We're walking down the center street in the old Roman village. The tribe now utilizes the market place. Note the streets crisscross the main path." Cassius waved his hand indicating a crossing route. "There are many family workshops here. The home has a lean-to or front room where the goods made or grown are traded or sold to other villagers or visitors. See, here is the smithy's shop under the lean-to on the front of his house."

The smithy was not there, but they looked at his forge, tools, and some iron encased wheels he had leaning on his house wall.

They passed a pottery shop and a bakery. Tybba bought bread for their evening meal and tomorrow's voyage.

"We'll pick it up as we come back though," Cassius told the woman, who smiled at Gemma.

Gemma headed for a home with small tables displaying cloth made of woven wool. She ran her hand over a strange looking material with zigzags on its rough surface—totally different from the wool cloth her family made which was simple and serviceable.

"That's herringbone weave, Gemma. Doesn't it look like a fish bone?"

Gemma nodded. "Yes, it does." She walked to another table and ran her hand over a beautiful smooth material.

"Silk made from a thread spun by a worm." Cassius kept pointing out other types of cloth such as linen and cotton. He often carried them for trade on his boat, but never displayed the materials in Tybba's old village, because they'd not be of serviceable use to the women on the River Albis.

"What's this," she asked of a tiny piece of shiny gold material prominently displayed by the store's owner.

"All she could afford," Cassius laughed. "Silk with spun gold interweaved in it. Very expensive and definitely not usable for a working woman's clothing."

Gemma shook her head, amazed at what she was seeing. "I didn't know so many kinds of material existed," she said, looking reprovingly at Cassius.

"Gemma, I didn't show them to you, because you had no need of them in Germania. You made excellent clothing from your sheep's wool, which fit your lifestyle." Cassius was on the defensive.

During this conversation, Tybba had stood in the background. He spoke up. "If we're going to see the view from the top of the gate, we'd better go."

The trio continued by other enclosed rooms holding goods made by the families to be sold. Gemma wondered what treasures would be in the darkened rooms. "The sun *is* going down," she observed.

"Yes, we need to hurry to the northern gate." Cassius made a sharp left turn down a narrower street and picked up his pace, scattering chickens everywhere. The three climbed the steps inside the gate to the upper wall.

To Gemma the view was fascinating. Before her were rolling hills as far as she could see. Tybba had described them. But this was the first time she'd seen them.

"Those are the forested hills of the north," explained Cassius. "There are other higher mountains in the world and in Brittania."

Gemma stood looking over the rolling hills bathed in the sunset glow of the west. The mists of the marshes were already filling up the valleys where they stretched down to the river's edge. She'd never seen anything so high or beautiful. Plots used for gardens lay outside the fort and beyond that, sheep, cattle, and horses grazed in fields. There were fenced areas and areas with cages of rabbits next to the fort.

It was the sight of earthly hills which made her stand in awe. "What's that?" she asked, pointing to a separate part of earth near the fort. From where she stood, she saw stones set on end, and they seemed to have inscriptions on them.

"That's the cemetery where the Romans buried their dead."

"Oh," was her reply.

"Cassius, we'd better hurry or it'll be dark before we get to Valerius's home."

"Yes, let's go."

The group hurried down the stair and back the way they'd come, stopping to pick up the loaves of bread Tybba had bought.

"Valerius may ask us to stay for the evening meal." Cassius told Gemma as she headed back to finish fixing the food for the night.

"We won't wait on the both of you." With that, Gemma pulled her cloak close to her body. The penetrating night chill was settling on town and human alike.

"Are you ready, Tybba?"

"Lead on, Captain," the chieftain answered.

⁓

Valerius placed cups of hot spiced wine before his visitors. "We grow our own grapes and make our own drink here in Petuaria."

As he talked, Tybba had a chance to look around. The house where he sat had faded colored wall plaster and mosaics arranged in circles on the floor. Worn padded couches and chairs, including the one he sat on—leftovers from the Roman exit of England, were arranged around the raised fire pit which warmed the area.

After pleasantries, Valerius asked Cassius, "Have you heard the latest from Bernicia?"

"The last time we talked Ida was King. What else has happened?"

"It seems King Ida has his hands full because of his lust for power. He's trying to keep hold of his pitiful kingdom, and his attempts to take our territory here above the Humber Estuary are causing more trouble. He's really stretched his military thin." Valerius's face showed his disgust with King Ida.

"Do you think he'll breach Hadrian's Wall?"

"I doubt it. And if he heads south, he'll be at our backdoor. My villagers may have to join with others and fight him to keep him out of Deira." Valerius shook his head. "I hope that doesn't happen."

"For your sake, my friend. I hope it doesn't either. Is there news of the Midlands? How is it faring? Is there war?" asked Cassius.

"Is that where you're heading, Chieftain Tybba?" asked Valerius, turning his gaze on the chieftain and shrewdly guessing the reason for the question.

"Yes. I have to admit I am." The chief was honest.

"I thought as much," Valerius smiled and stroked his chin. "Hum-m, the Midlands? A few years back, another Saxon went through here with his family and stopped—Snotta, that was his name. I believe he established a village on the River Trent, just before the first shallow place where most Britons ford. What are you planning, Cassius?"

"I'm to take my friend as far upriver as my boat will go. From there, Tybba will continue with smaller boats on up the River Trent and into its tributary the River Tame. His intention is to go almost to the River Tame's source."

"You will have an easy trip at first, but then the tribes, shallow rivers, and marshes will complicate your progress. I really can't say. With floods, those streams change courses and the depths never stay the same. I've heard of trips where you have to walk by the water and pull your boats beside you."

"You sound like you've been there," responded Cassius.

"No, but my village gets many visitors with news of the area. When the Romans were here, we had regular courier service. Not now, the news is spottier. I'm afraid Brittania has gone downhill since the legions went back to Rome. Abandoned forts and homes tell the story. And, speaking of stories," he motioned to a bookshelf with some volumes, "Latin and written language has all but disappeared. I didn't like being subject to Rome, but there were some advantages, including an uneasy peace."

"Valerius, we must go and check on the accommodations for tonight. It's been a pleasure seeing you again. I'll stop on my way back from the River Trent, and we can talk some more." Cassius and Tybba got up to leave.

"Come by and see me before you sail. I'll give Tybba some things to take with him — to remember his visit. Valete, Cassius and Tybba."

"Vale, Valerius."

Outside in the dark, Tybba said, "Seeing him has been profitable, Cassius."

"Yes, I'm glad we stopped. You should look for this Snotta on the River Trent. He may be able to help you. At the very least, with information on the area you'll be traveling through." Cassius yawned. "I'm tired."

"The last two days and nights were a horror for our passengers and you."

"Yes. You and I could have weathered the storm without a problem, but with our travelers —." Cassius threw his hands wide. He didn't know Tybba had stretched out on the wooden deck to keep from being seasick. "Here's our home for the night. I'll see you in the morning, my friend."

As Cassius hurried inside, Tybba said, "Have a good sleep." Instead of going indoors, he stood looking at the stars — the same ones he saw over his former homeland. He jumped sideways as something moved in the darkness. A rabbit had escaped from its cage. Recognizing a man's presence, it hopped quickly out of sight.

Tybba pulled in a breath and released it in a rush. Cassius. Always in the back of his mind was their last goodbye. Parting with his friend was going to be difficult, and tomorrow might be the last time he would see his lifelong friend. All would depend on how far his ship could go up the rivers they would encounter. Time to get some sleep. Tomorrow would be another eventful and maybe stressful day.

Tybba found Gemma and snuggled into their fur bed.

~

When the two had started talking about the chief moving to Brittania, Cassius had come across the North Sea and traveled some of the route he knew the trip would involve. Part of that trip had included a part of the River Trent.

He'd seen people walking along the river bank. Some jumped into boats pulled up to the bank, rowing toward his ship. He had ignored them, so he had no idea of their intentions. At the mouth of the River Trent, Cassius took Tybba aside to talk to him about the day's sail. "You might want to break out your bows, arrows, swords and shields for the rest of the trip. There may be attempts by the Angles to board the ship or at least make contact—better to be prepared. Warn everyone to keep their eyes focused on the shore for any movement. The children might be better below deck."

Tybba nodded. "I'll see that your suggestions are carried out. Trying to board the ship won't be an easy task."

"True, but it can be done."

Tybba left to warn the other men. The armour was stowed in the second boat where it could easily be reached. Spears, axes, swords and wooden shields, were placed within arm's reach for hand-to-hand combat.

Pulling his sword out of its scabbard, Tybba tested its sharpness with his thumb. Made of steel, he'd honed it before he left home. "Ouch!" Yes, the blade was sharp. He swung his hand as a small cut oozed a few drops of blood.

"Ah, Tybba didn't your mother teach you the edge of a sword or knife is sharp," the other men teased.

Tybba grinned ruefully and let their comments pass as he put the sword on his belt. These men were his best friends. Their ties of blood formed the bonds within the greater community and forced fierce loyalty to each other. There was no need for an oath. Those unspoken words were understood. These men knew the strongest survived. The weak didn't. They would fight, if necessary, to defend each other.

He headed for Gemma and the women to give them instructions on the children. On the way, he noticed the men who rowed the boat had weapons beside their benches. Cassius had provided protection for crew and passengers. The rest was up to the skill of all on board.

~

Sailing the River Trent was a slow business, especially the farther they went upriver. Sand banks appeared in the most unusual places. And whole trees floated in the water—partly submerged and ready to take out the rudders. Finally, they put the empty boat overboard so they could take soundings to see how deep the water was ahead of the ship. If the natives on shore decided to cause difficulty, those in the small boat would be the most vulnerable. Tybba sent men forward to the bow as lookouts to oversee their progress. He instructed them to keep a close check for movement on shore.

~

"I wonder how far it is to the mouth of the River Tame?" asked Maximus standing next to Tybba who was steering the boat. Cassius had gone forward to look upriver and access the situation from the bow. The river banks were slowly closing in. How far could they travel before turning the boat around in the river would be impossible?

"Have you ever sailed backward?" asked Tybba.

Maximus laughed. "We do this at harbour sometimes, but only for short stretches — with oars and not with the sail unfurled. It might be interesting to find out."

"How much farther before the mast is pulled to the yardarm?"

"Cassius will make that decision."

As long as the sail could be used, the men didn't have to row. One thing in their favor, should this become necessary, was the sluggishness of the river. The current wasn't strong — yet. But, the shallower the river and with progress up the River Trent, the flow should soon be felt.

"I don't know if we can make progress rowing against a strong current," Maximus observed. "We can try."

Tybba's heart thumped a little harder in his chest. They had gone almost one day of slow travel on the River Trent — about as far as the boat could float, and the sun was heavy in the west. He drew in a deep breath, letting the air out slowly. Life was fixing to change.

Cassius came back to the stern, the strain of the last days of sailing showing plainly on his face. Frowning, he told his second in command, "Maximus, pull the mast to the yardarm and drop the anchor, I'm afraid to go further," he ordered. His mate left to follow his instructions. Turning to Tybba he said, "I don't want to run aground. In the morning, we'll check the tidal bore. If it reaches here, we may be able to ride the wave and go upriver more hours, but I don't want to risk damaging the boat tonight."

"I agree with you."

"Overnight on the ship, and we'll check in the morning?"

"Alright. I'll go tell the ones in the boat to come on board, and get the others ready to go ashore to cook the evening meal." Soon his little band would be on their own, and he would say goodbye to Cassius forever. He dreaded the goodbye.

"Gemma, is everything ashore to fix our evening meal?" Tybba stood on the bank, sorting out the supplies and putting them in place.

"Yes, everything's here, including the pig to roast," she responded and pointed to two men coming from the forest with a small dressed pig slung on a pole.

Using a board between two flat rocks, Tybba pulled out his knife, squatted, and cut the pig into smaller portions, pushing them onto an iron bar. The smaller cuts would cook quicker and they could get back on the boat by sundown. Tybba didn't want to be on shore after dark.

Gemma positioned the pieces on the iron bar over a hot fire which had burned down to coals. Soon the pig was sizzling, with the fat falling in drops into the fire, making a spewing sound—and smelling better than honey on toasted bread. A smaller fire with a grate over it, allowed water to heat in an iron pot. Gemma cut up cabbage and shallots, throwing them into the water. She added a little bit of honey and salt and let it boil. After the smaller chunks of meat were done, she'd cut tinier pieces and put some of them in her boil, making cabbage stew.

It didn't take long before everyone on the boat was standing on shore with their noses stuck in the mouth-watering aroma of roast pig, cabbage, and shallots.

No one heard a noise until someone let out a gasp, alerting the crowd that unknown men stood in their presence.

In the rush to get supplies off the boat, no one had thought to bring shields and swords—hunting blades they had on their belts. Tybba and Cassius turned to face the intruders, pulling their knives from their belts in one smooth operation.

The twelve new men went on the defensive—spears raised and shields at the ready.

"Who are you?" the leader of the group managed to ask as his eyes darted from one man to the other. His men were outnumbered by the boat group, but they were heavily armed while those from the boat were not.

Tybba jerked his head backward. "You speak our language!" he said in astonishment.

"Are you Saxon?" The leader said.

"Yes. We are seeking a new home on the River Tame."

The leader nodded his head, lowered his spear, and acted in a peaceful manner. He stepped forward. The others remained in a position to fight. "I am Cynebald, a son of Snotta, who rules this area. Who are you?" he asked again.

"My name is Tybba. We are from the River Albis, on the coast of Frisia."

"I know the River Albis. My family is from far up river. We welcome you." Cynebald smiled and motioned to the others to lower their spears. "My father will want to meet you."

"We are cooking our evening meal. We ask you to join us." Tybba motioned to a flat area where the men could sit, and he could join them along with Cassius and others.

"It was the smell of your food that brought us to your camp. We are honored and hungry," he smiled, stepping toward the area pointed out. "We'll be glad to help you eat *our pig*. We've been trailing it and it's been dodging us since noon."

Tybba couldn't help but laugh. "At least, you won't have to dress it or cook it."

Cynebald nodded and sat down in the grassy area with his men.

As the others talked about the home they'd come from, Tybba and Cassius plied the leader with questions of the River Trent and River Tame. During the conversation, Tybba went back on board the ship to get his Roman map.

After Cassius oriented Cynebald to the map, he pointed to it and followed the River Trent with his finger. "Here, where you sit, you are at a shallow place in the river. Just beyond, the river deepens until you pass our village. There the water is shallow again. Your large boat will not go further, but your smaller ones will be fine."

"That's good to know," Cassius said, nodding at Cynebald and Tybba.

"How far to the River Tame after that?" asked Tybba.

"Two to three days by smaller boats. When you get to the River Tame, you'll run into marshy areas where you may have to get out and carry your supplies around the swamps. Or the river may be high enough so you can row right through. The river's course changes with each flood. Some places you can save several miles by going across land, but you'll need to know where those places are."

"How about rival tribes? Are there conflicts going on which Tybba should worry about?"

"We keep the area fairly calm. Most of the tribes are small, but the place you pointed out on the map is at the far reaches of our territory. All we do is show up once a year. This lets everyone know Snotta is still a force to be reckoned with. So, I don't know." Cynebald held up his hand and shook his head. "Except for the Tomsaete."

"Who are they?"

"A fierce Angle tribe who are very protective of their territory. We'll figure out something to keep them from knowing you're in the territory, and the place where you're going is far enough away that it shouldn't cause them to worry about your presence."

Tybba leaned forward, "Could we impose on you and your men to travel with us and help?"

"Snotta will have to make that decision. You'll be there tomorrow, and you can ask."

Gemma motioned to Tybba. "The food's cooked."

Exhausted after the stressful day of keeping watch on the river's depth, the men remained seated and let the women bring wooden bowls of steaming stew to them. Tipping the containers of potage, the men sipped the hot soup. They cut chunks of cooked meat off large hunks, placed in several places around the sitting group and served off wooden boards used for dicing vegetables. Each man took his knife and cut his fill. The women and children ate by themselves while sitting by the fire.

When Cassius pulled anchor the next morning, he had new passengers. Accepting an offer to take them home by water, the twelve men were on board, enjoying the ride.

❦ Chapter 5 ❦

Snotta's Village, The River Tame, and Home

Snotta's village was easy to spot by water. It sat on the highest hill around and was clearly visible from downriver.

"We'll take you to Snotta's hut." Cynebald said as Cassius and Tybba stood at the rail, watching the crew anchor the ship. They were ready to board a boat to the shore.

Minutes later, the men walked a dirt path up the hill to the village.

"Something's wrong," Cynebald observed, looking at the vacant huts facing the footpath.

"Why?" asked Tybba.

Cynebald continued, "Even though we were on your boat, someone should recognize us and come to greet us. With your ship sailing into the River Trent below the village, we should have several excited people to welcome us. Not often do we have a ship the size of yours."

At the top of the hill, the reason was obvious. A cart, bearing a shrouded body in white cloth, was being pulled by a horse.

"Snotta's mother has been very sick. We will follow the cart to the burial ground and participate in the ceremony. This may be her."

As the group passed, Tybba noted some of the people carried grave goods to be placed beside the deceased. These could be personal belongings of the departed or special offerings of good friends. One was especially beautiful—a red, glossy bowl with a lid and dancing figures on the sides.

"Yes, it is Snotta's mother. I recognize some of her special cooking pots and wooden spoons, including the bowl you are pointing out."

"There must be a story behind it. I've never seen a piece of pottery so beautiful." Tybba craned his neck as the piece went from sight.

"Yes, the story goes that the Samian pottery piece was given to her father by a Roman cohort for his help in defending against a Gaullist invasion in the north of the Roman Empire on the European continent. He was hired by the Romans as a mercenary, as a fighter paid for his inclusion in the army. He saved the cohort's life."

"She's your grandmother?" asked Cassius.

"Yes."

The group joined in the procession at the end. The walk went down a winding path in an attempt to disorient the dead person's spirit so it wouldn't go back and inhabit the old dirt hut, the deceased's former home.

The cemetery was outside the village in a clearing between the hill and the forest. The group walking behind the cart stopped, while the horse and cart went on, traveling around the graveyard three times before the burial started. Tybba watched as the body was put in the grave. The ceremony was familiar because his tribe had used it for centuries.

Slowly, several of the mourners approached the grave and, bending over put pots, jewelry, and even food in the grave beside the body. All this to help the spirit go to the new world. A tall man, who seemed to be directing the crowd, added coins of gold.

"That's Snotta," whispered Cynebald, as the tall man, with an air of authority, scooped up a handful of dirt and threw it onto the white shroud.

"Come," said Cynebald. "We will go to my house until things settle down. I don't want to disturb him at the moment."

Tybba still hadn't calmed down from the whirlwind of the last day. Snotta had received them graciously and, listening to Cynebald's wish to explore the River Tame to its source, had given his blessing.

"Please escort our friends to their new home and scout out the territory between here and there." The chieftain turned to Tybba. "We never know when someone will decide to increase their territory, especially the Britons or Tomsaete, by attacking us. As Saxons, we need to stand firm, if and when this happens. Can I count on you for help?"

"You can count on us," responded Tybba. "Are other Saxons in the area?"

"Cynebald, do we have neighbors?" Snotta turned to his military chief. "He's the one with the answer to that question. I send him all over the territory to keep an eye on our neighbors. That's how he found you."

Snotta's son nodded. "We have Angles and Saxons in the area—small tribes who've settled in the Midlands. I'll point them out to you as we travel the River Tame. None are very close to our village."

A few minutes later, Tybba had walked down the hill to Cassius' boat.

With several extra boats from the village, the supplies had been off-loaded from the ship. The largest boat which had been stashed on the ship contained the most supplies. It was emptied of cargo and floated in the water. The animals on the ship were led down a heavy gangplank to the floating boat. Safely on board, they were rowed to shore, offloaded and left to graze overnight. Now, they were tethered to iron loops on the same boat with grain placed aboard for them to eat. Several men would board to row.

There was plenty of room to stretch out in the boats, for which Gemma was thankful.

The gathering had ballooned to over fifty people. The whole armada looked like an invasion, which it probably was in many ways.

In late afternoon, Cassius had called him to his quarters below deck. "Tybba, it seems the time has come to part, my friend."

What could Tybba say but, "We've been friends many years, and I'll never forget you. I wish the best for you in the future, I—" that was as many words as he could get out, past the lump in his throat which was as big as his fist.

He'd stepped forward and grasped Cassius by the shoulders.

Cassius did the same, "You will be a great Chieftain here in your adopted country. May God go with you." He stepped back and smiled, dropping his arms to his side. "Every time I enter the Humber Estuary, I'll think of you. If you are back there at any time, leave Valerius a message for me. I'd like to know how you are faring."

"I will, my friend. Vale, until we meet again." Tybba took a step toward the door.

"Wait, Tybba." Cassius went to a small table with two books lying on it. The books had tooled leather covers of a ship with a sail and expanding metal clasps. "I have two of these. This one is yours. Each one gives our history before we met and after—our travels and your village in Germania. Add to it and keep it safe. I'll do the same."

Tybba opened the leather clasp. The writing was in Latin. He recognized his name. "I'll take good care of it, my friend. I'll get Gemma to make a leather pouch to keep it safe."

"Vale, Tybba."

Chieftain Snotta stood on shore to see them off.

The last he'd seen of his friend was him standing on the stern of his boat with the sail unfurled, heading down the River Trent. Tybba and Gemma had waved and Cassius had waved back.

On the morning of the third day, after two days of hard rowing, Tybba and Cynebald stood in their boats, looking at the wide mouth of the River Tame.

"I can't believe we're finally on the river where we'll establish a home," Gemma said with excitement in her voice. She was looking at the water flowing into the River Trent.

There was hardly a ripple on the surface. Underneath, the current flowed strong and relentlessly — the sea far behind them was its destination.

Tybba's voice was hushed as he spoke, "Almost home," he nodded. The sun was up and warm on his back, knocking off the late winter's chill.

Grinning, Cynebald added, "Are you ready? We're floating backward."

"Yes." Tybba dipped his oar into the water, signaling to the others it was time to continue their journey. They pushed ahead, and soon the river's mouth was behind them. Since the elevation of the Middle lands wasn't much above sea level and the river sluggish, it did not flow in a straight line but made many dramatic twists and turns, following the slightest depression in the countryside.

After several hours of traveling the river's bends, Tybba called to his leader, "If I were a bird, I'd be home tomorrow. I do believe I saw that tall oak tree much earlier. We just made a circle around it." He pointed to one on some higher ground they were floating by.

Cynebald laughed, "Yes, your front meets your back in some places on the river, but, be happy, there are no areas where you deal with rapids. Going upstream is an easy row. The biggest problem is getting lost in the large marsh mazes or grounding the boats in the shallows."

As they traveled up the River Tame, where the scene was much the same as in their old home, a haze hung over the river, while rushes grew down to the river's edge. A flock of orange-breasted birds flapped their blue wings, diving down and gliding just above the open water, dipping for a minnow or water insect. A rarer sighting was a wading bird with brown plumage. The waterfowl stalked minnows or an unsuspecting lizard in the shallow marshland.

They startled a wolf, drinking on an open bank. The furry beast took a second look and slunk into the thick forest growing behind it. Willow trees drooped over the water and alders, roots exposed, hung tenuously to the river bank. That is, where it had a bank. Their denuded limbs stood out against the blue of the sky.

When the river narrowed, Cynebald went ahead in the first boat. He was followed by Tybba. The others came behind them in no certain order. For a while, there was chatter up and down the line of boats. The men and women of both groups were getting more acquainted with each other. With fatigue, the chatter stopped and there was only the sound of oars dropping into the water.

～

In the late afternoon, Gemma said, "I smell smoke." She sat wriggling her nose and turning her head in different directions.

The smell of smoke could only be attributed to two things—the forest was on fire or people were in the area.

Tybba tested the air. "Yes, I do too." He called out to Cynebald, "Gemma and I smell smoke."

"I know," he replied. "We are close to a village of Angles. This is the Tomsaete. The village is bigger than the others around. When Snotta said not to get them riled up, he meant it. They like to fight, and my father doesn't want to fight them another time. So, we will pull into the opposite river bank, eat our evening meal without building a fire, and wait till dark—try to go by their village quietly without disturbing them."

"Waiting till dark means wasting several hours of good traveling time," observed Tybba.

"Trust me," Cynebald returned. "You do not want to tangle with them. We would be evenly matched, but they never give up. They'll follow you, and you will confront them more than once. If he were here, Snotta could tell you about them. I wasn't born when they were fighting. It's better if they don't know you are around." He pointed, "Up ahead is a bank where we can get out of the boats. We'll stop there."

The bank was on the right side of the river, away from the village. Everyone alighted, happy to step ashore. "How far is it to the Angle tribe's settlement?" Tybba asked.

"Far enough away. We won't be disturbed unless there's a scouting party heading home from this side of the river. We haven't seen any boats tied up to the bank, so I'm thinking they're all snug in their warm huts *with a hot fire burning.*"

"You're making me cold!" Tybba said, shivering and knowing his guide was teasing him.

"Sorry." Cynebald laughed. "Remember, no cooking fires. The wind may shift. They have good noses like Gemma."

The two men stood watching the others unload the things necessary for a short stay on the river bank.

Finally, Cynebald asked, "Do you want to unload the horses and other livestock?"

"Yes, there's not much to eat here in this spot, but what there is will save us grain." Tybba went to give instructions to the men taking care of the animals.

This gave Tybba a chance to consider Cynebald. He was a fair and very affable leader and obviously liked by his men. He laughed easily and, so far the chieftain had not seen him angry. Tybba was glad to call him a friend — a bond which was growing.

It was cold on the river bank with no fire. Mothers rummaged in leather bags for more clothing — for the children and themselves. They ate cold meat with bread bought from the women in Snotta's village. Better than nothing, Gemma thought. She held baby Randi beneath her fur coat, letting her nurse. Randi was as warm as the bread she sometimes toasted over their cooking fire, while Gemma shivered, and her stomach growled.

At the first hint of darkness, Cynebald gathered the group together on the river bank. "Here's what's ahead," he started. "As soon as you see the fires of the Tomsaete village, *don't talk!* Don't talk until we *can't* see the glow," he emphasized, holding up his finger and shaking it. "Remember to whisper only. Sound carries a long way. Try to keep small children quiet. Women with small babies might nurse them. Other sounds coming from our boats will blend with their own normal sounds — such as our horses neighing or chickens clucking."

Seeing Sutt standing next to his mother, Tybba leaned toward him and asked, "What did Cynebald just say."

"He said to be quiet." Sutt put his fist to his mouth.

"Can you do that?"

"Can I sail a ship?"

Tybba grinned and nodded at the young lad, as Cynebald continued. "Once we get past the Tomsaete village we are not out of danger. There are two huge marshes beyond. One we must navigate in the dark, but since there are no clouds in the sky, we can continue in the moonlight. Stay close together. Don't lose sight of the boat in front of you. We will travel as far as we can before dawn. Please don't get lost. After the first marsh, we will traverse the second and rest for a few hours on higher ground. Ask the gods for a heavy river mist and we'll chance a fire. That is our plan."

Tybba stood in front of his family group. "Sutt, what did Cynebald say?" he said loudly enough for all to hear.

Sutt grinned, "No more talking until we pass the Tomsaete village."

Tybba held up his hand. "Does everyone understand?"

Several of the men and women nodded their heads.

The trip past the Tomsaete village proceeded without misfortune. *Good planning by Cynebald*, Tybba thought. The next morning, they rested before travelling on, but progress was slow. Stopping early, they pulled to the bank, made camp for the night, and ate a decent meal of roasted deer shot with a bow and arrow. Everyone sat around picking the last morsel off the animal's bones.

The next morning, the movement forward was even slower. The River Tame was shallow and the large boat with the animals had run aground. Tybba stood watching Cynebald and his crew struggle with moving the boat off its rocky perch in the middle of the river. Being thirty feet long, the boat was too large and heavy to continue up the shallow river bed. He needed to make a decision

"Cynebald," Tybba called. "Unload some of the animals."

Crates of chickens and rabbits — gifts from Valerius at Petuaria were off-loaded onto the river bank. Enough of the other animals and supplies were lifted off to float the boat. The heaviest cargo left was the two black horses.

Tybba knew he needed the boat to get his supplies or horses to his new home. The one thought he couldn't shake was *should they set out and strike across land*. He was leaning toward this plan. What were his options? Could he trade his large boat for one of Cynebald's? He'd seen them looking at it. He went to talk to Cynebald, who was still working to get the boat close enough to land and remove the horses.

"If we went west across the land from here would we cross the River Tame again?"

"No. A journey southwest would let you cross the river. What are you thinking?"

Tybba looked at Cynebald. "We can't take the large boat any farther, especially with the animals inside. I'm wondering if we should unload the carts and hook the horses to them and start overland with the other animals and some of the men and women. We could meet later on the riverbank."

"That might work." Cynebald said, absorbed in his immediate problem. The keel of the boat was stuck again. He handed Tybba the horse's rope. "Here, let's see if we can get the horses to land." The gangplank from the boat just barely touched the bank. His men stood knee-deep in the river. They steadied the boat as the horse's weight shifted and displaced the water.

As it was forced onto the suspended board, the horse, white-eyed and scared, reared upon its hind legs, throwing its front legs high in the air. The unstable board collapsed into the shallow water, but the horse took three steps to shore, ready to be rid of the whole affair and Tybba too. Still clutching the rope, the chieftain fell, while the black horse recognized freedom ahead. The animal ended up dragging the offending man across the spongy ground and through a bunch of new-growing, baby nettles. Tybba let go the rope. Sutt ran after the animal.

"Ouch! Ouch!" Though he was clothed almost from head to foot, the nettles quickly stung and brought angry red welts on Tybba's hands and exposed arms. Pulling out and rubbing at multiple burning stings, he jumped up and danced around the area.

Everyone, including Cynebald, stood around laughing at the embarrassed, hurting man, who kept slinging his arms, obviously in agony.

When Cynebald could talk, he said, "Won't hurt long, my friend. Gather some dock leaves and squeeze them onto the red welts. They will ease the stinging." Cynebald pointed toward a clump on the ground.

"Yes," exclaimed Tybba. "After I pull out hundreds of stems." He kept yanking at the nettles, while looking at the dock leaves.

With one horse off the boat, it floated higher in the water.

Tybba rubbed his arms with the juice of the dock leaves and watched as the men pulled the boat close to shore, steadying the gangplank on the dirt bank.

"We'll put a bag over the head of the last horse." There was no problem getting this one off. And Sutt came leading the other by its rope, which had gotten tangled in a hawthorn bush, stopping the horse in a headlong rush to freedom.

Cynebald came over to Tybba after the last animal was unloaded. "What did you want to talk about?"

"Our plan needs to change, since we can't take the big boat any farther. So, I was going to suggest using the carts and horses, starting overland with supplies, some of the men and women, and meeting the boats up-river. The large boat should float if it isn't loaded with provisions."

"That would work, but I've a better plan. Two of my men have been discussing a proposition—their two small, flat-bottomed boats for your large boat. You could use the two smaller ones where you're going, and they can easily manage the big one back home on the River Trent. We'll hide it in the rushes and pick it up as we go back down the River Tame. My men can take the horses, pulling the carts with enough of the supplies, so all your people can continue to travel on the river. I'll go with you as your guide."

"You're a good friend, Cynebald, and your plan is excellent. I keep shoving problems on you. I wish our trip wasn't such a burden to you and your men."

"I consider our trip a challenge, and I like challenges. Let's go implement our plan."

∽

Tybba and Cynebald watched the carts being hooked to the horses. They were filled with goods and animals, as many as could be put aboard. Two men rode the horses pulling the carts and two climbed inside, joining the animals. Each man was fully armed, although if confronted by several warriors, they wouldn't stand a chance.

"You'll get to the river before we will. Don't start a fire, because there's another tribe close to the area. Wait in complete silence. We'll be along as soon as we can row up the curvy river."

"Will they run into trouble?" Tybba asked, as the group disappeared inland.

"Not likely. We've traveled through this area many times and never seen a soul, but they need to be prepared. We're getting closer to small villages in the area, who may not take kindly to our presence. The largest tribe is a settlement called Beormingham on another tributary of this river. Come on, let's find a place to stash the boat."

Back on the river, the group rowed upstream, with six people in each boat and pulling the large boat behind them. When Cynebald had said curvy river, he'd meant curvy.

Tybba thought they'd never get through the section. There were low lying hills on both sides of the river, and no rushes until the mouth of a stream on the left appeared. There they left the boat, pushed into the tall matted stalks.

"That's a good place," said Tybba, nodding his head.

"No one will find it in the maze of reeds," agreed Cynebald.

They passed the mouth of the River Rea and the River Tame became shallower still, even sluggish in some places. Rowing upstream was easy because of the lack of current. A day-and-a-half passed before they met the men on horseback with the carts.

"Heave to," shouted one from the bank, waving his arms. "Are we glad to see you."

After several minutes of greetings, the men told of unhitching the horses and riding them up the river to another sharp curve south. "The river is low from here, but I think a good spot for your settlement is maybe two or three Roman miles in that direction." The man pointed west. "You'll cross the River Tame, and there's a grassy meadow with a small brook running into it. A great place to graze your animals and set up your tents until you can build houses." He suggested Tybba and Cynebald ride across to look at it before going further. "Oh, and something else, there's a high hill. You could climb it and look the area over."

Tybba was filled with excitement. *Could it be that they were close to home?* He motioned to Cynebald, who had guessed his next sentence, because he was leading the horses toward him. The two men mounted up. "We'll be back soon," Tybba told Gemma as they rode out.

∾

The men were right. The place was ideal, but there was one thing Tybba wanted to do. Leaving the horses at the bottom of the high hill, the one that Cynebald's men had mentioned, they climbed to the top.

"Have you been here before?" asked Tybba.

"I've been all around it, but not on top."

"Is that smoke to the northeast?" Tybba pointed in the direction of a hill which appeared to have smoke coming from the top.

"Yes. There's a hilltop enclosure and a few farmers living there—not very big at all. The people call it Wodensbyri." Cynebald twisted around. "See the smoke from the southeast?"

Tybba turned around and shielded his eyes with his hand. In the lower valley, there was a thick forest with tall trees. The smoke was barely visible.

"That's Beorma's people. He's an Angle. His tribe and village aren't any bigger than Wodensbyri. I met some of his men when my group went south of this hill last year. He won't give you any trouble, although he likes to lord it over everyone."

Tybba nodded his head and moved toward Cynebald. "You've traveled this area extensively. You know the people and the lay of the land. Do you think this is a good location?" He waved his hand over the area below the hill toward the River Tame.

"Yes. You have water for your animals and to grow crops. Plenty of wood. It's not likely this area will have a great flood, because you are almost to its source, and you can easily use the river for travel. You might even come and see me some day," Cynebald grinned and clapped Tybba on the back.

"Then I think I am home." Tybba pulled in a lung full of air and let it out in a rush. His eyes ran over the earth below him. He couldn't control himself, but stretched out his arms as if to embrace the land.

"We should probably stay where we are tonight and start moving everything tomorrow. By nightfall tomorrow, you will be sleeping here at your new home."

"When are you leaving, Cynebald?" Tybba hated to ask the question. He needed his friend's help to start the camp and get him acclimated to this land.

"If you don't want to get rid of us, we'll stay a few more days to help you get set up. We might even go to Wodensbyri to meet and greet the villagers. With your men and ours and in full armour, we'll make an awesome group, maybe give them an impression of a larger tribe. Wouldn't hurt to try. Then you will be less likely to run into trouble with them."

The two men hurried down the mountain and back to the main group. Tybba couldn't wait to tell Gemma they were home.

～

"Tybba, Tybba," Wulf pulled at his shirt sleeve. "I'm hungry."

"What?" exclaimed the grandfather, struggling back to reality. He pushed Wulf off his throbbing knee and stood. The old joint made popping sounds as Tybba walked around to relieve its aching. His stomach growled, saying he was hungry also. Opening the food sack, he pulled out bread and meat, handing chunks to his grandson and taking some for himself. With a sigh of relief and sadness, he sat back down and took a bite. "What did you think of the story, bearn?"

"Exciting! Have you ever been back down the River Tame to see all the places you traveled through? Can we do that?"

"Tybba's too old to go back. We, you and I, need to go forward. There's so much more to do, and for me, not much time to finish it."

"Tybba's not old," declared Wulf, getting up from the rock he'd sat on and hugging his grandfather.

"Wulf, there's something else to this story. Do you remember Cassius giving me a book to keep safe with our history and the times we had on the sea?" Tybba cleaned his hands and pulled the leather-wrapped item out of the bottom of the food sack. "Here it is." He handed it to Wulf.

Wulf wiped his hands on his trousers and unwrapped the book, running his hand over the etching of the ship's motif. "I've never seen anything like this." He opened it up. "What's this?"

"It's Latin writing. Cassius could write down thoughts and read books like this. He taught me some of the words."

"Read? Why don't we do that?" Wulf raised the book and traced some of the writing with his finger.

"Good question. Maybe one day writing will happen again. But for now, you must keep the book safe and pass it on to your grandchildren like I have to you. And, you must remember the story I've told you. It's important."

A folded piece of parchment fell out of the book onto the rock. Tybba picked it up. "This is the map

Tybba used to get to Tybbington. Keep it with the book. Do you understand?

"Yes, Tybba. I understand."

After resting for a little while, the two started down toward the village. Tybba's knee was unsteady on the steep, rocky hillside. Wulf stood to his side and held the old man's hand to keep him from falling down in the worst places. When they were at the bottom, Tybba gave his grandson a hug.

"Bearn, I couldn't have made this trek without you."

"Ah, Tybba can lick hills, too," said Wulf, smiling at him. They walked on through the forest and to the edge of the fields, where they rested.

Wulf said, "Who's that coming from the village?"

Tybba could see a form and, as it got closer, he recognized Cynebald, Chieftain Snotta's son. "Do you remember the man who brought Tybba to this place and went up Dudda Hill in my story?"

"Yes. His name was Cynebald, wasn't it?"

"I think that's him," said Tybba, nodding and pleased that Wulf had remembered.

The man was Cynebald, Tybba's former young friend. He was gray-headed and walked with a limp, the same as Tybba. The two old men laughed at their infirmities and returned to the feasting area of the village where rude tables and chairs were for resting. Tybba noticed a strange bundle on a chair as they sat down to talk.

"It's good to see you again, Tybba," said Cynebald. "I bring you greetings from my tribe and news of my father, Snotta. During the cold winter months, he became ill and did not recover. He joined his fathers, and I am now chieftain of his village. I came to tell you this, and as you can see, I have problems with old age myself. As chieftain, I will not return to the River Tame, but my oldest son, Theobald, will come in my place."

Tybba returned, "This news makes me sad. Life is changing, and it is so short. I too am feeling the effects of my old age. I fear I won't be around long, and I have more than one reason to think so."

Both men sat for some minutes, thinking their own thoughts and contemplating a spot on the ground, where ants busied themselves with cleaning out the entrance to the mound which was their home. One of the men had disturbed it upon sitting down.

"I have something for you, Tybba." Cynebald got up to retrieve the strange bundle Tybba had noticed before sitting down. "It's from Cassius, your Roman friend. He left the package at the old Roman fort of Petuaria on the Humber, and a ship captain brought it to me by water." Cynebald hefted the bundle as if weighing what was inside and handed the parcel to Tybba. "It's fairly heavy," he concluded.

"Yes, it is. Should I open it?"

"If you don't, I will," said Cynebald with his old familiar laugh from their former journey down the River Tame. "Do you remember when you fell into the nettles on our journey here?"

Tybba looked at him. "Why do you bring my infamous fall up each time you come?" But he was not upset with his friend, and they both heartily laughed at the memory.

When Tybba opened the package, he found a beautiful bolt of expensive blue silk and the fish medallion in a small leather pouch—the one which Cassius had worn on their many journeys.

Tucked into the edge of the silk was a note. Both men bent over the words, and between them they deciphered it. The message said, "*The last I heard from the Parisii by Snotta's family, you were well. I have decided to retire to my father's old home at Palmaria and enjoy the warm breezes of the Mediterranean. My eldest son, Marcus, will take over the ship and the trade route I have established. Enclosed is a bolt of silk like the one Gemma admired at the Roman fort on the Humber. I've always felt sad that I didn't make it available to her and the other women in Germania. Also enclosed is the ichthys I always wore. The fish symbol of two intersecting arcs started not long after Christ died in Jerusalem. The Roman persecution made it necessary for his worshippers to establish a way to recognize other believers.*

My grandfather often told me this story. When a Christian met a stranger on the road, the Christian sometimes took his staff and traced one arc as if drawing in the dirt. If the stranger drew the other arc, both believers knew they were in good, safe company. Remember our talks? Someday, I feel your tribe will worship my God. Pass this symbol on from eldest son to eldest son until that time. Go with God, my brother."

Tybba patted his chest with his hand. The hammer of Thor was gone. He hadn't noticed its disappearance. The ichthys was on a leather cord. He could wear it. Instead, he placed the silver fish back into its pouch.

Cynebald stayed for several days of feasting. The parting between the two men was longer than usual, and then the new chieftain of the Snotta tribe went home.

~

Tybba called Wulf and placed the fish medallion into the larger leather pouch. To make sure it would not be lost, he punched two holes in the large bag and one in the small pouch and tied them together with a leather thong.

Every chance Tybba received, he kept telling his story to Wulf and pressed upon his grandson the importance of remembering the story he'd recounted on top of Dudda Hill.

And Wulf did as he was told, relating Tybba's story, keeping the leather pouch and its contents safe, and passing it on to his grandchildren, while adding the oral history of his lifetime.

❧ Chapter 6 ❧

Late 700 A.D *or Thereabouts*

King Offa, Alwin, Eggen, and Dever

ENGLAND

With the invasion of the Angles, Saxons, and Jutes in the 6th century, the whole of the English Isle became unsettled. During the next two hundred or so years, distinctive areas produced dominant rulers—kings and kingdoms emerged. The seesaw of a multitude of rulers in the many realms of England continued with numerous deadly battles fought on the land. These clashes split-up kingdoms and established other or larger kingdoms. To the north of the Humber Estuary but below Hadrian's Wall, Bernicia and Deira combined to become Northumbria with Æthelric as its first King.

Fergus Mor crossed from Ireland to found the Kingdom of Dalriada in Scotland. Penda became the first King of the Middle English, who attempted to combine the middle and southeastern part, calling his Kingdom Mercia. The Britons or Welsh continued to be the thorn-in-the-flesh of all these kingdoms—at times friend, at times foe.

Alliances and broken agreements between these factions made strange bedfellows. Revenge, feuding, rivalry, or just plain warmongering for food or plunder underlined the many battles fought between the mixture of tribes in the country.

At the same time, Roman Christianity was spreading across the realm. The rulers were turning from paganism to the Church with monasteries being established in the countryside villages and large towns. Aidan, Augustins, and Paulinus traveled different parts of the land, preaching the Holy Bible and Jesus Christ and converting the Kings and people.

Penda allowed the missionaries and monks to preach, but he himself did not convert, although many of his kinsmen did believe.

The veil of history covers the Kingship of Penda, with many theories as to his reign and time period. But he was a King and the ruler of Mercia during the 7th century. His residence changed with his travels, but his favorite and semi-permanent homes were at Repton, Tamworth, and Lichfield. His attempt to unite England into one country failed, but one of his descendants succeeded— Æthelbald in the early 8th century.

In the years between Penda's reign until Æthelbald became King, Mercia slowly waned under Kings whose ability to govern diminished. But Æthelbald restored the Kingdom to the prominence of his ancestor and subdued the southern kingdoms of Wessex and Kent, making Mercia larger than before. He became King of all the area below Hadrian's wall and essentially King of England—all except the Britons (Welsh).

Although Æthelbald united the Kingdoms of Mercia, it was King Offa who brought the realm great fame. Offa favored Tamworth as his capital. This is where he went to be crowned—*Rex Anglorum*, or King of the English. Tamworth was the original home of the militant

Tomsaete—the same village Chieftain Tybba had avoided in the dead of night.

Through all the Kings, kingdoms, battles, and intrigue, the village of Tybba or Tybbington had prospered, being prominent in the valley on the upper reaches of the River Tame and known to Penda's Mercia Kingdom and swearing allegiance to King Offa.

Being the King's vassal obligated the village chieftain, Alwin, to support the royal ruler in return for keeping his beloved land. Its position between the protection of a range of small hills, including Sedgley and Dudda to the south, marshland to the north below Wodensbyri Hill, and the River Tame to the East had kept it from hosting major battles fought near and far, although they did support the wars with men, cattle, and other food.

The fertile land supplied nourishment for crops, animals, and men alike. Tybba had chosen wisely.

Eggen stood watching his father, who was shearing the last sheep. The exposed animal sat on its haunches, between Alwin's knees, with its hind legs extended to the front and Alwin bent over it—an awkward position for the animal and a back-breaking one for the man. With the expertise of one who'd done this thousands of times during his life, Alwin used his spring-steel scissors, and calmly chopped away at the wiry wool on the immobilized beast's stomach, ignoring a new blister on his middle finger. The older man was hot and tired.

"How is it we pick the fieriest week in June to cut the wool from our flock?" asked the twenty-year-old Eggen, scratching at the fibers mixed in with hair on his arms—red streaks running up his arms from the force of his fingernails. He'd rubbed so hard his arm was irritated and burning from the salt in his sweat.

He stood in the wool shearing lean-to dressed in a sleeveless tunic with rivulets of perspiration running down his face. His job was to bring each animal into the shed, help his father get it positioned to cut, and bundle the shorn wool into bags for transport to their buyers at Tamworth.

From there, the wool would be transported down the River Tame to the River Trent and sold to merchants on the Humber Estuary, to be shipped to Londinium or France or other thread spinning and cloth making facilities in England or Europe. The Tybbingtons were known for the highest grade of wool in Mercia. Every year, they always sheared their sheep at the same time.

His brother, Dever, who swapped jobs with him on a day-to-day basis, stood outside and shepherded the shorn sheep back to the field to join the rest of the flock. After two weeks of back-breaking work, the season of trimming the wool was over.

"Just be glad this is the last one, Eggen," exclaimed his father, his arm and leg muscles bulging with the effort. After the initial help to position the selected animal, Alwin continued his work without help. His son understood he was an expert, and as such, another person was unwanted and in the way. For several minutes, the father kept moving the animal into the best shearing position using his feet, knees, and free hand to hold it and give him ease of clipping, and the least hurt to the sheep.

Alwin released the shorn sheep, which fell awkwardly onto its side, flailing its legs to stand on four feet.

Eggen quickly helped the exhausted animal to an upright position and walked it toward Dever and the herders. He gave it a pat on the rump and a small push toward the pasture. The herders guided it in the direction of the field and to the rest of the flock.

Eggen, cupping his hand, called across the field, "Last one, brother."

Dever pushed his shepherd's staff into the air in triumph, acknowledging his words.

Alwin put his spring scissors on a wooden peg protruding from the wall, rubbed off the clumps of wool on his sweaty arms, and gave a sidewise glance at his son.

Eggen was looking back at his father.

Suddenly, the two men broke into a run and dashed straight for the brook, running through the pasture, taking their belts, tunics, and sandals off on the way, but leaving on their loose-fitting, sweaty loin cloths which went between their legs and covered front and rear.

A hundred years ago, at the edge of the field, the people of the village had used rocks to dam the running stream. In summer, those of the village bathed and cavorted in the water. The pool soon became a social place for visiting and taming the heat of the day.

After the last sheep was shorn, Eggen and Alwin had performed this ritual, as long as the young man could remember, and with cries of shock as their mostly naked bodies hit the cool water, they did belly flops and plunged beneath the surface. Coming up, they spewed water from their mouths and laughed with relief.

"I'm glad that's over for this year," Alwin said, sending a handful of water in his son's direction as a punctuation mark for his words.

"I'm hungry," returned Eggen, ducking the rush of droplets.

"Son, you're always hungry. If I didn't have to feed you and your brothers, I wouldn't have to work so hard."

"Ah, father, you wouldn't know what to do if you didn't have so many good-looking boys."

"Looks like we're going to be joined by your older brother," Alwin motioned at the young man striding toward them at a fast gait. He continued, "I'm thankful Chad and Godwin have established homes of their own, but what about you and your brother? It seems the two of you should take some of the women up on their obvious attention."

"Are you trying to rid yourself of me?" Eggen continued, "Ah, I would Father, but none of them interest me. We grew up together and they're more like sisters than a partner."

"What are you two taking about?" Dever asked as he threw his tunic and shepherd staff on the ground. He didn't wait for an answer, but stepped out of his sandals and jumped into the pool of water to join his father and brother.

When he surfaced, Eggen said, "Women, that's what we're talking about."

Dever raised his eyebrows and said, "Oh, that subject again. I thought for sure you were talking about our mother's lamb stew — the one she's going to fix for tonight's feasting," a wide grin on his face, showed white teeth in the midst of his dripping, wet blond beard.

"See," said Alwin, shoving a handful of water toward the second son. "That's exactly what I'm talking about. You're just like that flock out in the field," he waved his arm at the newly shorn sheep, grazing on green grass in the pasture. He continued shaking his head, "All you two think about is your stomach. I guess that means we'll have to kill and dress a lamb for the feast tonight." Alwin was teasing. All of his sons worked hard. He had no reason to complain.

"That's what we were thinking, isn't it, brother?" Dever replied, rubbing his chin. "Lamb chops, lamb stew, whole roasted lamb—"

Alwin threw up his hands. "Then, I assign that task to the both of you. You select and dress the lamb, since you'll eat a good portion of it." Grinning, Alwin got out, pulled on his single garment, and belted it. Slipping on his shoes, he headed back toward the shearing shed, calling over his shoulder, "I need to put the last wool in with the rest, pack the bag, and start loading the carts. You have your chores to perform. Get to it."

Eggen and Dever shared a laugh. "How many times have we heard the same speech," Dever said. "Do you think we'll be like him when we have sons of our own?"

"We have to find a woman who can stand us first."

The two men hauled themselves out of the water and pulled on their tunics.

Sheep were easily spooked in the field, causing them to be stressed. Running one down in the open pasture was not an option. For this reason, a few were selected and kept in a pen close to the village. Fattened-up, they became food for the inhabitants. The two men headed for the sheepcote.

"Look, Eggen. The traveling tinker is in the market place with his waggon. He must smell the end of sheepshearing and know exactly a feast is in the offing."

Dever pointed at a chubby, bald-headed man. His five squealing children ran around an area normally left vacant for visitor's carts and located next to the feasting area. A charcoal fire burned hotly in the raised spit, which would soon hold the roasting lamb and melt the man's solder. He would use the liquid metal to mend a pot he was carrying around in his hand.

The young men dodged the area and walked on toward the sheepcote. "Are you going with us to Tamworth?" Dever had hesitated to go, thinking someone needed to stay behind and watch over the village and his mother.

"Yes, I decided to go. Chad will be here for the feast. He's bringing his brood and staying to help our mother while we are gone." The first-born son had taken a woman from Wodensbyri, or as Alwin always stated with a grin on his face, 'the next high hill to the northeast.' Dever continued, "How many herders are going?"

"Everyone. We were the last to get our shearing finished. They've been waiting on us. Alwin always gets the highest prices for our wool. None of them would think of going without him."

Alwin and Eggen's plans were to take horses and carts loaded with wool to Tamworth. They also planned to present King Offa with two more of their prized black horses. The Tybbingtons had been raising them for hundreds of years. Alwin said they were brought over on the ship with the first of their family to come to England. The horses were distinctive, sturdy, and in demand—solid black with feathers hanging over their hooves.

"I've been planning on going for several days," Dever repeated.

"If you do, you'd better not drink too much tonight. We'll need all our abilities to drive the carts and tend the stock going with us tomorrow—no headaches."

"Ah, little brother, don't worry, I shall drink only small ale. It's just above water, and you know our table ale requires gallons before you feel its effects. Don't worry."

The two brothers continued down to the sheepcote, and soon their mom was roasting a newly skinned and dressed sheep over another fire, which they had built using charcoal next to the tinkers, on the communities raised spit under a shade tree. When meat was cooked here, everyone knew they were invited at sunset and asked to bring food and drink. Oak trestle tables with benches stood in rows waiting for the celebrants. This wasn't the only feasting place in the village, but it was the principal one, for the village chieftain presided over the meal. His name— Alwin of Tybbington.

Alwin's wife, Aisley, stood fanning herself with a reed fan, trying to cool off. "Twill be good eatin' when it's done," she observed to the boys as she called them. She loved her sons, and these would be the last to leave the nest. She hoped to keep them both near.

The tinker came over to visit with Eggen, Dever, and Aisley. "Smells mighty good," he noted, still holding the pot he intended to fix in one hand and a short, hollow cane stick in the other. Eggen noticed the stick had scorch marks on one end.

The lamb was starting to get hot as Aisley turned the spit for even roasting on all sides.

"My son could turn the spit for you, lady. He's an old hand at it," offered the tinker.

"I'll take you up on your offer." Aisley had other jobs to manage for the makings of the feast. "You and your family are welcome to join us. Sheepshearing is over this year, and we are celebrating tonight."

"Thank you, lady. We would be honored."

The tinker called to a young, barefoot boy, who took over the work of turning the spit and, Aisley, after making sure he was doing the job to suit her, headed in the direction of her stone cottage to finish her preparations for the night's meal. As the village expanded, other stone cottages with thatched roofs were built. Some had separate rooms inside dedicated to sleeping and cooking in the winter.

"Would you lads like to help mend this pot? It has a narrow crack in the side."

"Sure, we'll help." Dever replied.

They watched as the tinker put a patch on the outside of the vessel, using thick clay mud and shaping it with his fingers to match the arc of the metal object. Then he sprinkled tiny chunks of metal in a small iron bowl with a long handle and set it on top of the charcoal fire. "We need to reduce the metal to liquid by using the hollow cane." He demonstrated the technique and allowed Eggen to handle the blowing torch as he called it, making the charcoal glow almost white, sending the heat onto the pot and over the soft metal lumps.

If Eggen thought the heat of the day was over, he was wrong. He practiced blowing through the hollow cane, sending sparks and flames everywhere, his face feeling the heat of the hot fire. A thought ran through his mind. This mending process had better not take long, or I'll be roasting like the lamb.

"Not so hard," cautioned the tinker. "Blow more softly until the metal turns to liquid."

Dever put on leather gloves and held the pot, as the tinker facilitated the melting metal by punching at it with a flat piece of iron. The solder melted, and with a thick leather glove the tinker carefully gripped the long handle of the bowl and guided the hot liquid metal to the pot, smoothing it as best he could along the arc of the mud and over the crack. "That should be enough," he told Eggen, while Dever kept holding most of the pot out of the heat. "We'll let it cool and then I'll take off the mud mold and file it until it has no rough spots."

They stood and watched as the glossy surface of the metal turned to a dull gray as it cooled. "You can set it down now," the tinker told Dever. Both men stood back from the fire to cool off.

"Will this be used over the cooking fire in the future?" asked Eggen.

"No, only for holding water or other liquids or solids. It's not useable for the hottest of fires."

The two brothers stood, watching the tinker remove the mold and smooth the metal's rough edges. He set the piece on the edge of the hearth to cool.

"When are you going to take your wool to Tamworth?"

"We leave tomorrow," Eggen said as Dever pulled the gloves off his hand and gave them to the paunchy man.

"Tamworth will be crowded. Everyone in the Mercia Kingdom will be there after shearing their sheep in June. They'll stay awhile to hear all the gossip and intrigue surrounding the King's activities. By the way, have you two heard about King Offa's latest idea?"

"No, what's going on?" Dever asked.

The King had seized power in a civil war which followed the death of his distant cousin, King Æthelbald. Offa was ruthless in his dealings with his subjects and other kingdoms around Mercia. When he couldn't overcome or establish an uneasy peace with the other realms, he married his daughters to their rulers as a cushion against all-out war. He had established a mint and was coining his own silver penny at Canterbury, and he'd sent emissaries to other countries, including Europe, to establish a rapport with their leaders. Offa intended to join the world community and exclude any who wouldn't come along—this meant the Britons or Welsh, his biggest thorn-in-the-flesh.

"The King is building a dyke."

"A what?" asked Dever, raising his eyebrows and looking in amazement at his brother. Had he heard right?

"He's tired of fighting the Britons, and he has a scheme to cut them off by building a defensive wall on their side of his Kingdom. I'm sure you'll hear all about it in Tamworth. He's been hiring and conscripting men to work on it. In fact, there's work happening on the ditch right now, and for some time, I think. And, the slaves or former captives of your wars, who were working on building bridges and roads in Mercia, have been directed to this project. Everyone in Tamworth says he's crazy, but you know when he sets his mind on something, it happens."

"He's crazy like a red fox," responded Dever.

"Never underestimate King Offa," agreed Eggen.

"Boys, I need you." *The boys* turned at the sound of their father's voice. He motioned for them to come and help him finish loading the last cart.

Tamworth, the old village of the Tomsaete, a fortified enclosure at the intersection of the River Tame and River Anker in the English Midlands, was a busy settlement as the group from Tybbington soon found out. From the road south of the town, the royal palace could be seen on the highest hill. Its rock walls, with the proud Mercian banner of blue with a diagonal yellow cross, stood out against the puffy, white clouds seen floating in the sky.

As the group approached the village, the built-up road through the marshes became a muddy mire of ruts, causing each supplier of wool to pass one at a time through the slimy bog. With all humans grunting and helping the process of pushing and pulling the wooden conveyances along, the sellers breathed a sigh of relief as they approached the stone and wooden bridge across the River Anker. At this point, they were on the palace grounds, where progress forward was at times down to foot traffic. Everyone had wool to sell — bundled on carts and carried on their backs. Boats floated in tight formation on the River Tame to take the bought and bundled wool down the river to the sea.

"Everyone in Mercia has had a good growing year," observed Alwin as they crossed the bridge. "The buyers won't be paying as much this year."

From the bridge and looking east, the end of a defensive burh or dyke Offa had built around his royal residence and surrounding grounds, stopped at the marsh on the River Anker. It extended north and turned west to the River Tame. Formed by digging a ditch ten or fifteen feet deep and piling the dirt and rocks upon the ditch's side toward the village, the finished dyke was twenty-five feet high and made anyone attacking the King's people more vulnerable to arrows and spears.

The whole sight was impressive, especially with the rock palace sitting splendidly atop and the burgeoning village surrounding the area. Nothing could rival the view from the river, and the city throbbed with movement and excitement.

Alwin spoke first. "Let's head to the buyers on the wharf. Get rid of our wool so we can leave our carts where we will stay. I'd like to deliver the King's horses today."

Dever exclaimed, "King Offa's royal residence is buzzing with activity."

"Yes, and the pickpockets will be out. Watch your valuables!" Alwin cautioned.

Alwin kept his entourage moving toward the merchant's quarter of the wharf and stopped in front of the home of his buyer. The man sat on a chair under the lean-to in front of the two-story stone building, fanning himself and doling out coins to one of his wool suppliers.

Alwin got in line as the representative of his group. The others waited in the street, knowing the chieftain's ability to bargain for the highest price the merchant would pay.

Suddenly, a yell, "Stop thief," grabbed everyone's attention. A young urchin ran down the street in the direction of the Tybbingtons. Dever stuck out his foot, sending the young boy flying onto the flagstones making up the pathway. His hat continued on without him, landing at Eggen's feet. He picked the cap up and dusted it off.

A fat, greasy-haired man waddled down the street and grabbed the fallen youth by the collar, standing him upon his feet. Checking the pockets in the thief's ragged clothing, he pulled out a bulging bag. "Here's my sack of coins!" He gave the boy a push, sending him to meet the pavement again, and plodded off without another word.

Eggen strode over and picked up the long-haired boy, offering the cap to him. In amazement, he realized the boy was actually a young girl.

She was unkept, sobbing, and mumbling something. Tears streaked her cheeks as she picked at a bloody scrape on her elbow. "We was starvin', we was starvin', we was starvin'." she said again and again, blubbering as she wiped her nose on the ragged sleeve of her tunic.

Eggen and Dever looked at each other. "Who's starving?" asked Eggen.

Two wet blue eyes turned upon the young man. "Me an' me family. I asked fer a coin, only one." She held up one finger—hope in her eyes. Maybe this blond-headed, blue-eyed, bearded man would help.

Eggen and Dever exchanged glances. The other herders milled around. "Who wants to help this young girl?" Eggen asked, waving his hand in the air. He took a silver penny out of his pocket and put it in the dirty hand the girl offered. Soon several pennies flashed in the sunlight.

More tears flowed. "Thank 'e kindly, sir."

"Go home," said Eggen.

Before he could stop her, she grabbed him, and reaching up gave him a grubby hug. Then she ran into the crowded market and disappeared.

While all this was going on, Alwin was bargaining with the buyer. He brought back to his group another bulging bag of coins. "Let's find the place we always leave our carts and horses, and I'll dole out the money. I know some of you want to start home immediately, and some want to stay a couple of nights."

King Offa stood stiffly at the only window in the corridor, looking down on his courtyard. He was dressed in a red tunic with blue alternating panels, sandals, and a short, matching blue cloak with fur trimming. The cloak was fastened with a metal brooch which sparkled with embedded precious gems. Rivaling his contemporary, Charlemagne of the Holy Roman Empire, was his aim. The two had exchanged emissaries and gifts.

On Offa's emissary's return home, he had brought back glowing reports of the emperor's court and several gifts. One of them Offa proudly displayed on his side. It was a bejeweled, Hunnish sword, complete with belt from the treasure captured at Charlemagne's great battles with the nomadic horse warriors of Avar.

The King sweated profusely, even though a slight breeze blew through the opening into the stuffy, semi-dark hall. Below, the black horses the Tybbingtons had brought stood nibbling on the grassy square in the care of the King's stableman. A good way to get an audience with a King was to give him something he considered important.

"Beautiful," he exclaimed, sucking in his breath and swiping with a white kerchief at his brow. "They'll look perfectly handsome with my entourage riding them."

This was as much of a thank you as Alwin got. The King already had two of this breed of horse, brought by the Tybbingtons last year at wool harvest. Being the vain man that he was, he realized four would command more attention and make a greater appearance of royalty when traveling.

Fit for a King, Offa thought. Wiping his face again, the King turned from the window, crossed a narrow hall, and stepped through a large door.

The Tybbington village people had a reputation of being hard workers with skills in many areas. He did have respect for Alwin as a loyal subject, but he had need of Alwin's boys, and no one turned him down.

The King hadn't dismissed them, so Alwin, Eggen, and Dever followed, stepping over a dark spot on the stone floor and continuing into the reception chamber.

A man, the Steward, came out of the shadows in the farthest reaches of the room. He stood close to the ruler.

The room was walled with marble and furnished with gold-gilded furniture brought from Londinium or the continent. Tall golden stands, holding five candles each, lighted the throne which sat on a raised dais, with a red carpet in front of it. His castle was known as the most opulent in England, and built in a Romanesque fashion with huge columns in front.

When the King reached the throne, he did not sit down, but paced back-and-forth. "Alwin, I suppose you've heard that I'm building a dyke between Mercia and the Welsh. I'm tired of the problems my Kingdom has with the Britons—raids into Mercia and disputes with the border line. A recognizable boundary will help solve this trouble. The project is of immense proportions, running south to north and surpassing Hadrian's Wall. I need good men to help oversee and get the wall built in record time. The more men I can put on my project, the less time involved, especially since I'm using a mixture of war captives and conscripted men to man the workforce. If necessary, the military will provide protection from any marauder trying to prevent its completion and help with moving materials. I want my overseers to be without family or encumbrances to hinder the work. Do these two sons have families?"

What could Alwin say? He wasn't interested in either of them being in the King's employ or whatever he had in mind. "No, they do not have families." He dreaded what was coming next.

"Then, I have need of them." He walked over and looked Dever up and down. What he saw was a muscular man in his middle twenties, long jawed with short, blond beard and mustache. "My daughter is pledged to the King of Northumbria. And as such, she and her maids need protection for her trip to the city of York. I'd like for this son to be her escort. That is, if you can spare him."

"Dever?" Alwin looked at his son, knowing he couldn't say no to the King.

"Of course, I'll go. You know wandering is in my blood." Dever made the best of the situation.

Of Alwin's four sons, the King had chosen the one his father would have selected if given the chance. Dever would be an excellent choice and worth the King's trust.

"How long will the trip take?" asked Alwin, wondering if Dever would be back for the fall harvesting and planting in the spring.

"The trip will be by water. In fact, the boat is at the dock now. There's just enough time for your son to go home and pack his provisions for the trip. He has no more than a week before the captain needs to leave. The arrangements are already made with King Æthelred. Your son will be gone two months at the most."

The King walked to Eggen and pointed at him. "I'd like for him to oversee a section of the dyke beyond Scrobbesbyrig. He can report to Andras. He's a Welsh warrior who is now loyal to me, and he knows the terrain. I'll see that your son meets him before you leave, and this one," he waved toward Dever, "will meet the Princess. Both can go home and come back together." The King dismissed the trio with a wave of his hand, telling his Steward to make sure his orders were carried out. An appointment was made for the young men to come the next morning to complete their introductions.

With those words, the immediate lives of Alwin's two sons were settled. Outside in the palace gardens, the three men stood talking amongst themselves.

Dever spoke first. "My task doesn't sound too bad. Running around the country with a bunch of women sounds like a plum occupation. I wonder if Offa's daughter is beautiful." He was grinning but shaking his head at the same time. "Brother, yours sounds harder."

"Yes, I agree that overseer may run some risks, and I'm wondering what this Andras is like. I thought all Welshmen were hard to get along with, especially if you are Mercian."

Alwin was still shaken at the last few minute's happenings. He'd brought two of his prize horses and given then to the King and in the process had his youngest sons taken from him! And, he hadn't or couldn't say a word in their defense! At present, he didn't feel like much of a man. "I'm sorry, boys. I should have protested. Maybe, I still can." He turned in the direction of the gatehouse.

"What!" said Dever, grabbing his father by the arm. "And become another dark spot on his floor? You did see it. We stepped over it as we went into his chamber."

"What are you talking about, Dever?" asked Eggen.

Dever explained. "The dark spot was a stain from the beheading of King Offa's soon to be son-in-law on the eve of his wedding to the King's daughter. Queen Cynethryth was jealous of her daughter's love for Æthelberht, King of East Anglia, and persuaded the King to lop off his head. *That's* why the dark spot."

"Guess that's one way you can eliminate the competition," Eggen said, shaking his head.

"Father, you know this story." Dever still held his arm.

"Of course, I do. I just don't like to carry gossip."

"Gossip! The courtiers all swear it's true."

"True or not, let's get back to the problem at hand. Can we refuse the King?" asked Alwin.

"No," both men said at once.

Dever continued. "We're both young," he nodded at Eggen, "and we can come home after our service to his majesty. It's not like you've lost us forever."

Alwin nodded and embraced his two sons. "Instead of staying two nights like we planned, I want to head home tomorrow afternoon after you've fulfilled your audiences with the Welshman and the Princess Ælfflaed. Eggen, we have something else to do while we are here. Let's head to the monastery." The three men turned and walked toward a stone building with steeples.

~

The monk was astounded at seeing a book in the hand of a common sheepherder. Seeing his amazement, Eggen stood awkwardly before the scribe at the monastery. He explained the history of the book in his hand.

"From one generation to the next, the oldest or youngest grandson receives this book. My grandfather couldn't read nor write, and neither can I. I would ask first that you read its contents to us, and because I have a head full of information to add to it, I ask you to include these words in the book. My father, Alwin," Eggen nodded toward his father, "will contribute an offering to the monastery for your efforts." He stood fingering the leather tooled cover of a ship with one sail.

"My son, please let me see the book." Eggen held the leather-bound volume toward the monk, who took it gently, looked at the ship, and turned the pages. Looking up at the three men, he said, "I have time today to read the message in the book to you, but no more than that."

There was more discussion, and finally the decision was made to read the words already inscribed in the book. When Eggen returned to start his assignment from the King, he would stay at the monastery, and at night he and the monk would record the memories of his grandfather.

"If we don't do this now, I may forget his words, or I may be injured on the Welsh border," explained Eggen.

"I do understand, my son. Shall we start now?" questioned the monk.

"Yes," said Alwin, sitting on a bench before the scribe. Dever and Eggen did the same.

This was the first time any of the men from Tybbington had heard the story of their ancestor's arrival in England.

He was named Tybba, and he'd lived on the coastal lands of Germania. His friend was Cassius Aurelius. They'd sailed across the North Sea and up the River Trent and headed toward the River Tame, so Tybba could find a new home for his family. The rest was firmly established in Eggen's mind.

Eggen said to his father, "Tybbington must have been named after him."

The monk answered, "Such was customary in those times." The aged man handed the book back to Eggen. "This is your ancestry book. Guard it well."

~

Back home in Tybbington, Eggen sat in the feasting area, turning the book over and over in his hand. He was in awe that a village could have been named after his family. Now, it didn't matter. He was leaving his beloved village. At twenty, he was going to help King Offa build a wall—a wall between the Welsh kingdoms and Mercia. But would the barrier protect the Mercian Kingdom from the onslaught of the different Welsh tribes?

Only years ago, these kingdoms had fought side-by-side. Was it tit-for-tat over territory? He didn't understand what had happened, and really it didn't matter. As he'd done in other villages, the King had demanded men to help. His father couldn't refuse. At the least, he would be an overseer and paid for his help. Offa would have conscripted men, the military, and slave labor to do the dirty work.

Eggen fingered the small pouch with the strange symbol in it. No one knew what the two intersecting arches meant. He would ask the monk when he returned to Tamworth.

What was the name the monk had called the book—the Ancestry Book—a very good name, he thought. He'd ask his mother to make a larger leather bag, because he was sure this one would soon not be big enough. He pushed the book back in its holder and placed it inside his larger bag to leave for Tamworth.

He and Dever would ride horses on the trip, covering the same route they'd taken a week before.

⚜ **Chapter 7** ⚜

Late 700 A.D *or Thereabouts*

Dever, The Princess, and Winflaed

Winflaed looked over the wooden boxes which were full of Princess Ælfflaed's clothes, including her expensive nuptial dress of light purple silk with purple trim. The garment was expensive because the dye was brought from the Phoenician city of Tyre and made from rare sea snails. The gown, made in Londinium, was fit for a queen, which her mistress would become after her royal union. The Princess was to be joined to King Æthelred of Northumbria at York.

Not happy with another maid's work, Winnae, as everyone called her, carefully picked up the dress to refold it. Using her hand to gently tuck the folds, she placed it along with the other wedding clothes into one of the smaller boxes. The Princess had emphatically ordered it placed by itself and not crushed with other items she was taking on her trip north. The maid closed the lid. Later today, someone would arrive to tightly secure all the box covers.

The young woman went to a window overlooking the busy River Tame. The small vessel they would take lay at anchor in the crowded harbour. The blue and yellow Mercian banner flew from a pole at the aft of the boat. This small ship was the same one King Offa used when he went on royal business down the River Tame. His royal quarters were built aft ship and mostly atop the deck, adding two steps down into an opulent hold, just enough to give more head room. The boat was not suitable for ocean going or even the large Humber Estuary where the waters were churned by winds during storms.

Winnae could see men standing by the railing, casually chatting and watching other riverboat traffic being loaded with bundles of cotton which were stacked high on the wharf or other goods to be transported down the stream to the River Trent. Occasionally, one would throw up a hand, point, and give instructions to a sailor in another craft, as if the other man welcomed his idea of how he should do his job.

Winnae pulled in a deep lungful of air and let it out through pursed lips. As a lady-in-waiting to the Princess, she didn't have a choice in the matter of going or staying. It was obey or die in King Offa's realm.

Even the King's daughter was subject to his demands. Being joined to someone she'd never met was weighing heavily on her spirit, and her servants were suffering the brunt of her unspoken anger.

A clatter from the courtyard below averted her attention. The King, dressed in his finest woolen cloak and tunic, was riding one of his beautiful black horses. Many times, during the week, he mounted the steed and rode through the village and countryside so his people could ogle at the splendid spectacle the whole entourage earned. He and his followers along with the noise disappeared through the royal gate.

There *were* advantages to being a good servant in the King's household. Winnae looked down at the linen dress she was wearing, very stylish with a belt around her slim waist. It fitted her youthful figure— showing off her womanly curves. She loved the multi-colored trim and the swish of the floor-length, beige skirt. All of the servants dressed the same, and each one had the services of the royal hair dresser. If the Princess had a major pet peeve, it was straggly hair, so the women in her immediate employ were well coifed and dressed.

Winnae touched her golden crown of hair. Twisted until it lay on top of her head and fastened with a metal pin, the sun danced among its tufts. Her eyes were olive green with specks of brown, and there was a touch of rouge on her lips. She was not ugly. Turning from the window, she went back to the task at hand.

In the afternoon, the escort for their trip to Northumbria would come and the boat would be loaded. Their journey would start in the morning.

Dever checked the load on the small ship's exposed deck, which was midship. Yesterday, he'd met the crew chief and supervised the loading of the Princess's personal possessions. They were brought from the palace, staged on the wharf, and loaded as to importance on the trip. Last night, when he'd found his bed in the boat's bow under the forecastle, he was exhausted but satisfied, knowing the ship would be ready to shove off the next day.

This morning there were more boxes with the initial D, which the Steward said was the dowry. Another pile included a bed and wooden chairs for lounging on deck. Not only that, but the King's Steward had said Princess Ælfflaed had specifically asked for a canopy and tent to be erected in the open air. She did not intend to sleep down below in the cabin. The servant had pointed to boxes to be opened with the necessary supplies to install the sleeping quarters.

After he left, Dever went over and kicked at one box, calling to the crew chief. "Gaius, get your shipmates. We need to rearrange some of the cargo already on ship and then put up a tent and canopy." Anxious to be off, several of the crew jumped to the task.

"The Princess isn't sleeping in the royal sleeping area?" Gaius asked.

"No, and I don't know why. I found my cot very restful and your snoring almost a lullaby." Dever was grinning at his new friend, whose temperament matched his own. This trip was going to be a pleasure.

The two men watched the tent go up, giving instructions to the crew on nailing stakes and pulling ropes. It took some doing, but finally Gaius and Dever could walk through the heavy cloth door of the ship's new portable cabin. The whole apparatus could be easily dismantled once the trip was complete.

"If it rains, all the ladies will have wet feet, they will be waddling around like ducklings," Gaius observed, tiptoeing around as if his feet were wet.

Laughing at his new friend's actions, Dever walked the gangplank to the wharf. He was sure he'd seen something in the boxes to take care of wet feet. He rummaged through the open containers and held up thick reed mats. "I think these will take care of the wet feet problem." He started slinging them over the gunnels until the box was empty.

With the tent, beds, and chairs installed on deck, everything was ready.

Gaius stood with his hands on his hips. "I hope that's the last of it."

Dever looked up at the castle walls, catching a glimpse of a female figure in the open window.

He motioned for her to come down.

She drew back and disappeared into the darkness of the room beyond.

The ship was ready for its journey. They were prepared to shove off.

"Do you think she'll come down?" Gaius was standing at his elbow, watching the empty window.

"No way to know, my friend. While we wait, I've been wanting to ask. Will you use the sail to go downriver?"

"No, we will row. Our river isn't deep, the curves are sharp, and it can have snags or sandbars if it rains hard. We can stop the boat's progress much easier if we row. Once we are past the mouth of the River Tame and on the River Trent, we can use the sail. It's deeper and there's not much chance of hitting a tree trunk or running upon a shallow place."

"And after the River Trent?"

"It's the River Ouse, where it joins with the River Trent to form the Humber Estuary. The water gets a little rough there — the current is strong."

"We don't go as far as the old Roman fort of Petuaria?"

"No. How do you know about Petuaria?" asked Gaius, looking at Dever.

"My ancestors came through there years ago."

"And you know that how?"

"We have a book with the information about the trip. They stayed at the old fort overnight before continuing up to the River Trent and on to the location of Snotta's village."

"Amazing!" Gaius looked at Dever with more admiration. "The village is still there, going by the name of Nottingham."

Dever headed for the wharf.

"Where are you going?"

"To tell the King's Steward that we're loaded." Dever jumped off the gangplank and headed up the dock area.

The minute Dever saw Winnae, he knew she was the woman he wanted as his partner for life. She was lovely, with sunlight dancing in her blonde hair as she held the royal Princesses' elbow, helping her walk down the quay. And in his eyes, she was more beautiful than the somber Princess — although, none of the ladies were smiling.

He stepped up to help the subdued Princess cross the gangplank to the ship. "My Lady, may I help you," he said extending his hand, stumbling at the plank's edge, and feeling like an oaf for being so awkward in her presence — and more importantly in the other lady's presence.

Princess Ælfflaed put her gloved fingers daintily in his palm and following him, carefully stepped onto the boat. She did not meet his gaze nor say a word but went quickly to the tent and disappeared inside.

In amazement, Dever stood watching her disappearing back and when he turned around, he looked into the beautiful green eyes of Winnae. She stood by his side. "Good morning."

"I hope so," she said, sucking in a lungful of air and sending it out in a rush, a faint smile on her tightly pulled lips. Two more women passed by her, heading for the tent. "My Lady is not happy this morning. She had an audience with her father before we left, and I don't know what was said. She's been silent since. She has those spells."

"Maybe she's sad at leaving Mercia," ventured Dever, realizing her eyes were the color of willow leaves or the soft, cool mosses which grew on the banks of the brooks running through and around Tybbington.

"She's not the only one," Winnae did sound unhappy. "How about you? Aren't you feeling a little sad? Oh, I forget, you can come back home." With that retort, Winnae followed the other women to the tent. No one in the entourage seemed in happy spirits.

Dever stood still, wondering what he'd said to cause the woman to jump at him. Yes, he did hope to return home, and for that reason he looked on the journey as a new exciting experience. He shook his head and looked at Gaius. "Where's the captain?" They'd been waiting two days for him to come onboard.

"Finally got news, he's *sick*." Gaius winked at Dever. Lowering his voice, he continued, "He's a big drinker. Guess I'm your Captain on this trip."

What else was going to go wrong? But, Dever was happy with Gaius. "Okay, Captain. Let's shove off." He watched as the ropes were thrown from shore and felt the movement of the ship under his feet as the oarsmen pulled into the current of the river.

There was sudden activity on the wharf. His brother, Eggen, came running down its wooden surface. "Hey brother, you're almost too late to see me off."

"Sorry," Eggen said. "I had an errand to run. Have a great trip."

"Don't get too many blisters on your hands digging ditches," teased Dever, acting like he was shoveling and knowing his brother would probably not touch a spade. The distance between them widened, and other boats intermittently blocked their view. He waved at his brother. Eggen waved back. The shore slid by. Soon Tamworth and Eggen were out of sight.

～

Dever and Winnae had been standing on the aft deck, watching the trees go by. Winnae had apologized after their rocky start and finally smiled at him. Her smile, like the sunshine hiding in her hair, came quickly and frequently. Dever had never seen green eyes. They fascinated him. He couldn't get enough of them.

Occasionally, the two waved at a shepherd on the shore, who came running to see the King's ship. These sightings became less frequent as they traveled downriver. Gaius pointed out trees, birds, and streams flowing into the main river, and occasionally they sighted a village, poking through the jumble of bushes and trees. Their rude houses positioned off the river's banks on distant hills because the river was a great flooder. He gave a running history of river happenings as he manned the helm or ship's wheel.

"The Princess wants to know how long you think we'll be on the water?" Winnae directed this question to Gaius, realizing that what her mistress actually wanted to know was when her freedom would be gone.

Before answering, Gaius put his forefinger to his lips and pointed to a solitary hawk sitting on a dead tree branch, intently eyeing something on the ground. The bird swooped down and came up with a rat in his beak. Returning to the tree, he held the squirming rat in one claw and tore at its flesh with its beak.

Winnae wondered if this was a warning for coming days. She was glad when the hawk was out of sight.

Finally, Gaius answered, "Three to four days and we should be on the river to York. The trip will go faster when we put up the sail."

"Will we put into shore for the night?" she asked.

"Yes, or anchor in the river. I can't take a chance of damaging the boat. At least, until we get on the River Trent. We'll make a decision then on whether to sail at night. If the skies are clear, we will sail by moonlight."

"I'm hungry," Dever realized he hadn't had anything to eat since morning and noon had passed hours ago.

"There's bread and meat. You know where it is."

"Come with me, Dever. I'll fix some of the Princess's food for you. I'm hungry, too."

Dever looked at Gaius. "Guess you'll have to eat your own fare." Turning to Winnae, he said bowing, "I'm your servant, my Lady."

On the first day, Princess Ælfflaed did not come out of her tent during the daytime. Winnae appeared again with the other two ladies at nightfall. The western sun's rays were sucking yellowish-gray streaks of moisture into the sky, until they bounced off clouds floating overhead. There were dark shadows under the trees, making misshapen figures on land and turning the water into a black, silky ribbon between its darkening banks. After the heat of the day, a sudden chill caused Dever to shiver.

"The Princess is already asleep," explained Winnae to him, disturbing the almost noiseless travel on the river. "I'm worried that she's going to make herself sick with worry over her approaching marriage."

"You kin bet on it," one of the older women said, nodding. Her grin showed a missing front tooth. "It's 'appened ta 'er afore."

"Yes. When the King gives orders and things don't go her way." Winnae took two steps away from the group and toward Dever. "We wanted to walk on deck and watch Gaius anchor the ship. Mostly, we just wanted outside in the fresh air." Winnae and the other ladies moved to the rail.

Dever followed, standing by her. "Enjoy it while you can," he said, pointing to the sky. "I've been watching the clouds. Tomorrow, we may have rain at some point. Better break out your head covers." Dever had never seen one, but he knew they existed. Made out of leather and painted with flowers or birds, they folded down for storage. Only the very rich and royal families carried them.

Winnae explained as she stood beside him, "We do have head covers. King Offa bought them in Londinium from a merchant who buys from a supplier coming from the Orient. When the Queen saw them, she hounded the King until he had his Steward get a supply. They'll be in one of our packed boxes."

"Do you know which one?" asked Dever, waving his hand toward the mound on deck, thinking it better to be prepared should the clouds open up and rain pour down.

Winnae looked at the other ladies, who threw up their hands and shook their heads.

"Guess that settles it. We'll stay under the lean-to."

"The King's Steward is a busy man," noted Dever, starting to yawn.

"I wouldn't want his job. The King trusts him and sends him on all kinds of errands. He works from dawn to dark and sometimes all night."

"And you don't," Dever grinned.

Winnae sighed. "Sometimes, we do too."

"Are you tired?"

"Yes," Winnae said, turning those green eyes upon him. He wilted like the greens his mother boiled in her iron pot.

In silence, the group stood watching the last rays of the sun as it set below the horizon.

At a sign from the captain, the oarsman started putting up their oak paddles, the noise of wood-on-wood and sandals scraping the deck, interrupting the quiet of the nightfall. Two of the crew headed aft to throw out the stone anchor. It had a hole chiseled in the middle and a rope looped around and through the opening. The cord was tied back to itself. The rock scraped the bottom of the river until something stopped it. This was their harbour for the night—the middle of the sluggish River Tame with the frogs croaking on either side and a lone dove cooing to its mate.

Dever put his hand over his mouth and yawned again. "Ladies, I'm going to bed. I'll see you in the morning." He touched Winnae's elbow, turned, and took several steps to the forecastle. Before he went to sleep, he heard Gaius set the night watch. He didn't hear his captain when he came to bed.

In the afternoon on day two, the ship came to the mouth of the River Tame and started down the River Trent. Before they got to Nottingham, it started drizzling rain. The further they went on the River Trent, the harder the rain poured from the leaden, gray sky, hitting the deck and bouncing back into the air.

Gaius and Dever stood under the cover installed to keep the rain from the helm, with the sound of the rain beating overhead and the force of the fall sending a light spray through the cloth and onto their heads. Occasionally, a puddle caught on the top and plunged in a deluge to the deck. The men saw its flash from the corner of their eyes and jumped to keep from getting splashed.

"We'll tie up at the Nottingham wharf for the night, and you and I will go ashore. We'll look for some hot stew for our night meal. I think I know exactly where to find it. I've been there before."

"I like your plan. Hot food will be a pleasure after this afternoon." Chill bumps popped up on his bare skin. He crossed his arms and rubbed his cold skin. "Dever, that lady-in-waiting is waving at you."

Dever turned toward the tent. "Yes, I think she wants me to come." He peered at the drops splashing on the deck and looked at his sandaled feet.

"Grab the lid off the water barrel. Might help keep you from getting soaked to the bone."

"Good idea." Dever pulled the lid off, put it over his head, and headed for the lean-to. He made a ridiculous looking figure as he balanced it one way or the other, sending splashes of water to the deck.

Winnae moved over and laughed at him as he joined her underneath the cover. He shook the water off the lid onto the wet reed mats under the lean-to.

"Very stylish, sir. I'll be sure and recommend them to the men at court." Still smiling, she said, "Seriously, we have a problem. The rain is coming through the tent cloth and everything is getting wet. My Lady wants to go to the aft cabin. The problem is, how do we get her there without her getting drenched. The barrel lid won't do."

Dever nodded, thinking. "Are your coverlets soaked, or are they dry on the bottom side?"

"I don't know. I'll check." She disappeared into the tent and came back immediately. "Dry."

"Then get one. We'll hold it over her head until she gets to the door leading to the quarters. The other women can help by opening the door and aiding her down the two steps. If we hurry, she won't get a single drop on her."

The move went off without a problem. When the women had disappeared into the room, Winnae asked, "Could we get the wet coverlets?"

"You won't need them. Look in the trunks and you'll find plenty of dry bedclothes. I'll see that the wet ones are aired out once it quits raining."

"I hope it isn't raining tomorrow," Winnae looked at him as if he could turn off the sky's leaky hole.

"We're going into the village later to get hot food. Would you want to go?"

"Maybe the Lady would like fresh food, instead of dry bread, cold meat, and apples. I'll ask and let you know." She eagerly responded, disappearing into the darkness of the room, and shutting the door.

As he turned to go, the door opened. "I'm going with you. The Princess will stay with the cold meat, but everyone else wants hot food. Let me know when you leave."

"I will," he said, and putting the water barrel lid over his head, he went back to Gaius.

The pouring rain caused more problems. In the afternoon of the following day, the River Trent was rising and the current much stronger. When the ship got to the mouth of the river where it joined the River Ouse, the wind was blowing, the waves high, and the waters were muddy. Over the water, here and there, a gray mist hung sullenly, obstructing sight. Observing the wide expanse of the angry rivers, Captain Gaius took one look and decided to shelter in a small anchorage on the northern side of the River Trent. He turned the rudder in that direction, while the crew adjusted the mast. There was one plus, it had stopped raining.

"We're not going across?" asked Dever.

"No. I'm not chancing it. In that mist, and with the waves kicking up such a fuss, we'd never find the mouth of the River Ouse. And, even if we did, everyone on board would be sick and there'd be lots of water below deck. I don't think our Princess would like that. Tomorrow, the waves will die down enough to make the crossing easier. We'll wait until the tide is fully in and starts to go out and that will help calm the water."

"The wind will blow us out of this sheltered harbour." Dever observed. The gusts were already pushing the boat back into the stream.

"Yes, it could, but we'll tie up to the bank. It's deep enough so we can get alongside." Gaius ordered the sail lowered. Then the oarsmen went to their posts, and with their help he steered the boat gently into the bank. One of the crew jumped onto land and tied a rope to a tree trunk.

With the boat's slight bump on the bank, Winnae came from below. Seeing land almost within reach, she asked, "What's happening? Did we run aground?"

"No. Come and look." Winnae walked a bit unsteadily to the aft deck and stepped upon its raised surface. "There." Dever pointed to the estuary ahead. "Gaius wants to wait until tomorrow to cross."

"I can see why. Is this the sea?" There was no land in sight, only waves white capping in the vast expanse of water. She grabbed at the ship's gunnels. The boat was rolling even though the craft was tied up to the bank.

"Gaius says the two rivers form the Humber Estuary which goes to the sea, so you might say it's a portion of the sea." Dever looked at Winnae. He wondered what she'd do if he put his arm around her — for protection from the boat's movement, of course.

"I'll tell my Lady Ælfflaed." She turned to go and stopped as the sun popped through the clouds. Closing her eyes, she raised her head, feeling the sun warm on her upturned face.

"Look! Winnae." Dever came quickly and stood by her side.

She opened her eyes to a sight she'd seen before — but not like this.

Brilliant colors spread across the sky as the dark clouds sped to the east. The enormous rainbow, riding on the moisture in the sky, stretched from the wet ground in an arc to the roaring river's surface and disappeared into the angry water. The sight was awe-inspiring.

Winnae put her hand on Dever's arm and they stood, watching the majestic display of nature's paintbrush. Neither spoke a word, but at that moment, they were joined together in sharing this singular moment in time.

Although the waters of the River Trent and River Ouse had abated somewhat, the crossing of the two rivers was not easy. The trip continued to be one problem after another. Sailing up the River Ouse was not unproblematic. The current as they neared York was stronger and more alarming. So were the looks they were receiving from the boats they were passing and the people on shore.

"Do you think we should take the Mercian banner down from its pole?" asked Dever after several hard stares and threatening gestures from the crew of a boat which came close to examine them. The Northumbrians were always at war with Mercia, but at present there was an uneasy peace. The people above the Humber Estuary were Angles, fierce fighters which King Offa couldn't conquer. Sending his daughter to this King was one way to assuage conflict—he hoped.

"No. Not yet. I'm trusting King Æthelred's representative is in the city of York. He's to meet us at the port and guide us to the palace. If we leave the flag up, he'll recognize the fact that we have special cargo on board. Just in case, will you tell the crew to break out the armour and be ready should trouble start."

Before Dever left on this errand, he asked, "Will this man speak our language?"

Gaius shook his head. "I don't know, but I understand he was the principal in the negotiations for the marriage." Leaving one of the crew to man the wheel, Gaius walked to the bow and looked uneasily upriver.

∿

When the ship pulled into a vacant slip at York, the King's emissary stepped on board and introduced himself as Cuthbert. He spoke the Mercian tongue. "Who's the captain?"

Gaius introduced himself. "I'm Gaius, Captain of King Offa's ship from Tamworth."

Cuthbert was waiting with more bad news. King Æthelred was not at the town, but at Catterick with the Archbishop of York Minister on the River Swale, several miles north of York. The two were awaiting the arrival of the Princess in expectation of the marriage. Their trip was not over.

"Anticipating that your vessel would be too big to navigate the river but a short way, I realized you would need to disembark and go by horse-drawn covered cart. The two carts are waiting, because I left them above York almost two days ago and caught a ride on a small fishing boat into the village.

Dever was heeding the conversation. Now he intervened, "How long until we get to Catterick? Are there towns or villages on the way? We need food and drink." Dever's statements came rapid fire. He noticed some men were beginning to gather, listening to the ensuing conversation and eying the ship's cargo.

Cuthbert turned to look at him. "Who are you?"

"Dever, King Offa's selection as the escort for the Princess and her entourage."

"In answer to your question, Dever," this said with sarcasm, "It depends on the roads and with all this rain—" Cuthbert threw up his hands to the cloudy sky. "There are no inns on the way, but I have provisions for the trip," he motioned to two boxes and a sack on the dock. "I have food. We'll place it on your vessel. But if the Princess wishes, there is food prepared in the Merchant House just within the city walls," he motioned toward the stone boundaries of York.

Dever felt tension building on the wharf. He wondered what kind of authority this Cuthbert had over the men standing around. Getting out of the waterfront was getting more important with each minute. He looked at Gaius and rolled his eyes, giving a little nod toward the gathering crowd.

Gaius understood. "Cuthbert, my question is, what do we do with the boxes—the clothes and dowry? You can't put all of these on two carts." He walked around the mound on deck.

"Our King doesn't intend to stay long in Catterick. We can offload them here in storage," explained Cuthbert. "Once he returns from the north, they can be taken to the palace."

"Why don't we take them to the palace now?" Gaius asked, although he wasn't sure if he wanted any of his crew on land. He did have secret orders to check out the castle and environs.

Cuthbert, who was older, almost bald, and had the bluntest nose Gaius had ever seen, answered, "Because they'll be safer here. I will leave them in the care of the Archbishop's staff at the Minster Church. And, here's something else you'll need for safe passage." He held out the purple and gold Northumbrian banner. Gaius sent one of the crew to change them. The tension eased a bit on the wharf. The hated and suspicious Mercian symbol was gone.

"Then her ladies will need to sort out the clothes she intends to take with her," responded Dever, heading for the royal quarters and Winnae. What a mess that was going to be!

Dever knocked on the door. When it was opened, he explained to Winnae the problem at hand. "We'll be bringing the boxes to the cabin. Sort the clothes she'll need for the trip north."

"What will happen to the boxes we'll leave here?"

"There's a warehouse where they'll be stored in care of the Archbishop—a dry place here on the wharf."

"Dever, I can identify those boxes with the nuptial gowns. You won't have to remove them from the boat."

"Come with me. We'll move them to another side, and you can point to the others for sorting."

Walking to the boxes midship exposed Winnae to stares from the men gathered on the shore and to Cuthbert's gaze. It was the look on the face of this man which made Dever the most uncomfortable.

∼

After they had all eaten and offloaded the boxes, those which were to remain in York, the ship's crew cast off the lines, and the boat headed north on the next stage of the journey. News of the Princess's coming had traveled fast among the people, and where the river flowed through the village, people lined the banks hoping to catch a glimpse of the Lady who was to be their queen. She refused to come on deck.

Dever stood on the starboard side, wishing he was heading south instead of north, but there was no way he was leaving Winnae by herself in the clutches of the men of these northern lands.

The River Swale, normally a faster flowing and shallower brook, was in flood stage, requiring the rowing men to dig their oars deeper into the muddy water and put much effort into moving the boat upstream. By the time the men reached the designated place, where the carts sat by the river, they were exhausted.

Ropes, thrown to men on the shore, were quickly tied to large trees to hold the boat's position. There was no wharf where the carts sat, and moving goods and people off the boat was dangerous in the swiftly moving, murky water and treacherous on the muddy bank.

Seeing the conveyances and armed men on the riverbank, meant the departure of Gaius and any protection the Mercian group had from his crew. Dever was the last off the ship. "Until we meet again, Captain. I hate to see you go."

"I dislike leaving you here." Gaius stared at Cuthbert who busied himself with helping the Princess and Winnae into the largest cart which was covered. Then he turned, leaving the older two to fend for themselves as they scrambled into the other. He didn't like this twist of events. He'd planned to travel to the palace at York and give King Offa his opinion of the place, but now this idea was impossible. "Be careful of that man," he nodded in the direction of Cuthbert and gave Dever a little salute. Then he turned to give orders to his crew.

Standing on the bank, Dever watched with misgivings as the gulf between shore and ship swiftly widened. When he turned around, Cuthbert was sending a man on horseback to Catterick to alert the King of their impending arrival, and he was climbing into the bigger cart.

The Princess, Dever, Winnae, and the other two ladies were at the mercy of their new escort. Dever mounted into the smaller cart with the ladies-in-waiting. Six armed guards on horses rode to the rear of their cart.

The Princess still wore a thick veil over her head and face.

All he could see was Winnae's backside. Once she turned to look at him, as if making sure he was coming along behind. She gave a slight smile. He noticed the emissary leaning toward her and touching her when the cart bumped in the path.

What kind of problems awaited his little band of women at Catterick? How would the King receive them? Dever looked out at the passing scenery. *I can't wait to find out!* Or could he? He thought quietly about the problems of the last few days. He looked at the bald-headed man in the other cart. Shaking his head, he returned to the passing scenery. He'd cross *that* bridge when he came to it.

～

When they arrived at Catterick, it was almost at midnight. But the manor, after the carriage passed through the main gate, was well lit in the courtyard's garden, revealing stone walls and cultivated gardens with flowers.

The King, notified of his soon-to-be queen's pending arrival, had stayed up to greet her. He recognized Cuthbert and was very welcoming to the rest, including his bride to be. He bowed to her and offered his arm, escorting her into the Great Hall of the manor, where he left the group with his Steward.

Dever felt relieved. Suddenly, he was tired to the bone. He followed all the women to their rooms, making sure the Princess was comfortable. "I'll see you in the morning," he told Winnae, touching her arm briefly.

Cuthbert led him to another part of the manor house.

"Is this one of the King's homes?" he asked as they walked the torch lit hall.

"No, the Lord of the Manor loans the King this house when he's away visiting in the Dales, and the King is always happy to get away from the city for a few days. Here is your room."

Dever nodded at Cuthbert. He went into the bed chamber, closed the door, and fell into bed.

∼

The sun was streaming through his window, making an elongated rectangle on his floor when he awoke. He jumped up as a young man came into his room with a basin of water and towels.

"I am your servant while you are visiting," the young man explained as he put the supplies on a stool in the room. "Here is the trunk with your belongings," he indicated with a wave of his hand and then he went to the door. "I will bring food," he said and disappeared.

From somewhere close to his stone-walled, sparse room, his nose detected the delightful and strong smell of fried meat. His stomach grumbled in response. His *servant* couldn't come back too soon. Later, he determined he'd find the cooking area—a nibble was always welcome.

Dever took off his tunic, wet a towel, and wiped his torso, cleaning his body as much as he could. What he would give for a dip in the creek near his home in Tybbington.

Suddenly, he felt homesick. Going to the window, he looked out at the landscape below. The sun had already burned off the morning's mist. Where was Tybbington? His present circumstances were a far cry from his home of wattle and daub houses in the Midlands. From the window, he couldn't see south because the manor house's walls were thick stone, but looking straight out to the east, there was a river, forests of tall trees, and across the water, sheep grazing in fields. The fields were separated by rock fences. In one green pasture, a shepherd with his staff and dog were moving the sheep along a rock wall, heading for the river bank.

He turned from the window. He needed to see Winnae. The sensation of aloneness or separation from home was strong. Seeing her would help. Was she feeling the same way? Could she be missing him?

The morning meal of bread and fried meat went quickly. After putting on a fresh change of clothes, he was soon striding toward the rooms designated for the Mercian ladies. Winnae stood outside the main chamber, entrapped by Cuthbert, who was speaking earnestly to her.

Dever picked up his pace. His sandals made almost no sound on the stone floor as he approached and said, "Good morning to you both."

Cuthbert, deeply engrossed in conversation, jumped and turned to greet him. Winnae rolled her eyes and grinned. Cuthbert did not smile. He spoke first.

"Good to see you. Did you sleep well?" His voice betrayed the fact that he wasn't the least bit interested in seeing Dever or in his welfare. The man had interrupted his conversation with this beautiful woman—one he'd immediately had designs on as soon as he'd seen her on the boat. His wife was old and fat. Since this one was alone in a strange country, she would be ripe for the picking.

"I slept very well. Our journey was stressful as Winnae can tell you."

"I was informing Winnae of my Lord's intention to meet in the courtyard for the ceremony since there is no church here at Catterick. This is where the Archbishop will bless the union of the King and Princess. Before this happens, I will come and get Princess Ælfflaed and her attendants. Afterward, there will be a banquet in celebration of their bond in the Great Hall of the manor. Several of the city of York are staying around the manor. They will be invited to the ceremony and the banquet." He bowed his way down the corridor and disappeared through a door.

"How's the Lady today?" Dever asked Winnae as soon as Cuthbert disappeared.

"She's much better. King Æthelred made a good impression on her. In fact, a very good impression, since he's not an old man but a young virile one. And, he *was* gracious on her arrival." Winnae said this without enthusiasm.

"But?" questioned Dever, wondering what was on Winnae's mind. "Is it Cuthbert that is bothering you?"

"Yes. He's very demanding. I'm not sure of his intentions, but he mentioned he has a large home close to the palace in York, and the walk is short and easy to wait on my Lady. I don't know why he thinks I care."

Dever was pretty sure he did. "Winnae—" but instead of continuing, he held his tongue. He hoped she felt the same way he did, but he couldn't be sure, and it was better to wait to tell her he loved her and wanted her for his own. He realized Cuthbert might precipitate those words with his continued advances.

~

Because of a sudden chill in the air, the blessing of the union of the royal couple did not take long. Cuthbert grasped Winnae's arm and with determined step, followed the King and new Queen into the warm banqueting hall. He sat beside her and motioned for Dever to take a place across the table. During the meal, he was constantly whispering in Winnae's ear, and at one point, his arm went around her in a possessive and intimate motion.

"Isn't that awful," said the woman sitting beside him. She had put her hand over her mouth and directed this comment to him in a whisper. He was surprised when she spoke Mercian. If he hadn't been so angry at the sight across the table, he would have asked her why. "And, he's got a wife," she continued.

At her comment, Dever wanted to get up and grab the blunt-nosed runt by the collar and —.

The woman was speaking again. "He's got no shame. And, she's not any better."

At that, Dever arose and excused himself. If he stayed any longer, he would embarrass himself and Winnae. He left the room and headed for the Queen's quarters. She would not be using them this night, but he hoped to see Winnae there later. If she didn't come, he'd look until he found her.

The other ladies-in-waiting greeted him. Could he draw them into his confidence? Realizing he didn't have any choice, he started explaining the problem, only to be interrupted.

"We know she likes you and you like her, and she's worried about the King's man. We don't like him either. We'll help."

~

Cuthbert was with her when she arrived. Whatever was on his mind was averted when the ladies appeared in the hall. He, obviously angry with his ego deflated, stomped off in a huff.

The women drew Winnae out of the hall and into the bed chamber, where Dever waited, and left the room. He came immediately to her side.

"Are you alright?" He didn't touch her, although his need to was strong.

"Yes. I now know what *that* man wants. He wants me." Winnae turned her teary eyes on Dever. "Are you heading back to Tamworth? Cuthbert said they expected you to return home soon." Tears welled in her eyes. Winnae touched his arm, and then hesitated.

That was enough for the man who loved her with all his heart. He put his arms around her, drawing her to his side. "I have no plans to return at present and anyway, I don't want to leave you here. I can't leave you here," he said with passion in his voice, looking at her longingly.

"Dever, if you go, I want to go with you."

"Are you saying what I think you are saying? Would you come with me and stay with me?"

"Yes," Winnae nodded. Two giant tears made wet paths down her face, followed by two more.

"Then, from now on, you will be mine, and I will be yours." Dever hugged her and kissed her forehead, hardly believing she was in his arms. "We do have a problem. Can you leave the Princess, uh Queen?

Because I think Cuthbert will not let you go easily. For that reason, we can't stay here. He could cause trouble for us. Let me think about the best way to handle the situation. I'll start forming a plan." He lifted Winnae's face to his and kissed her. "Don't worry, I'll think of a way. Meanwhile, you keep a bag packed and ready to go. Remember, you are mine, dear Winnae."

~

With his plans made to escape the manor at Catterick, Dever went to get Winnae. She like he had put on layers of clothing to keep warm through the cold nights ahead.

They would walk in the dark shadows within the walls of the building and open a small postern door, leading to the road they'd come on from York. No, they weren't heading back down the river, but west and north to the mountains and dales beyond. Once over the highest hills, they'd go down the other side until an opportunity to stop confronted them. He carried two bags—one with more of their clothes and one with food—mainly bread and cheese—from the manor pantry. Water they would drink from the mountain brooks they crossed.

~

Walking in the dark was almost impossible, but a dirt path and a full moon gave them some comfort as they avoided rocks in the road. A couple of times, they disturbed a sleeping dog beside a house. No one lighted a candle, so they continued on, until, because they were fatigued, it was necessary to pause and sleep.

"Winnae, we are going to rest against the haystack in that field." Dever pointed to a ghostly mound rising from the misty grassland. "No one's close, and we can use some of the fodder to cover the damp soil."

She followed him, as he made a resting place on the ground, and they sat down wrapped in their cloaks. She leaned back against the mound of grain and nestled in the round of his arm. "My feet hurt."

"Are you sorry you came with me?" he asked, moving his covering and placing it around her, so she would be more comfortable.

"Never," she said, leaning over to give him an unexpected and gentle kiss on the lips. "I'll never regret a minute of being with you. You've been my choice since we viewed the rainbow together at the mouth of the River Trent. I've watched you since. You're honorable, trustworthy, and handsome. I feel safe with you." She touched his beard, which was soft and his warm cheek. Running her finger over his mouth, she kissed him again.

He caught her hand. "That's enough," he uttered, never realizing she was such an ardent woman. "We can't sleep long. We need to start moving early in the morning."

～

Seven days later, they topped the ridgeline and looked down on a village of twenty or thirty houses. The small community was spread along a dale or open place at the bottom and along a small thread-like river. Up above the village and just below them, a small cottage with thatched roof, separated from the rest, caught Dever's attention. Something tugged at his heart, and he knew this was the place he and Winnae needed to go.

"We'll go there," he told Winnae, pointing.

"We'll go there," she repeated, smiling at him and nodding.

Two hours later, after picking their way through the rocks and heath on the hillside, they stood by a small barn where penned up sheep were trying to drink water from an almost empty trough. An elderly, gray-haired woman came slowly around the edge of the structure, struggling to tug a half-full pail of water over the fence for the sheep to drink. She poured the small amount of liquid into the trough, splashing most of it on the ground, and turned to head back to the trickling brook running down the hill.

Dever looked at Winnae. "Let's help her," he whispered. He didn't hesitate but went to the woman's side. "Please don't be afraid. Winnae and I will help you."

The elderly woman drew back in surprise and fear, sucking in her breath, and looking at him skeptically. "Who are you?"

"My name is Dever and this is Winnae. Let us help you." He took the pail from her hand and continued to the stream. With the pail full, he returned to the sheep and poured the water into the holder. Several trips later, the sheep had plenty of water and were crowded around the new supply to drink.

"Do you need anything else done? Should we give them fodder to eat?" He pointed to the sheep.

"An old woman always needs things done," she grinned, still being careful but warming up to these strange people. "Are you hungry?"

And this is the way the couple met Abi. After telling her their story, she took them in, and they became her family. When there wasn't anyone to bless their union, she did. And Dever and Winnae became one.

The couple worked hard, establishing a growing farm and supplying the needs of the blended family. Their first child was a boy. They named him Alwin, after Dever's father—a name they passed down through the next generations. Their second child was a girl they named Abi, and their third girl had green eyes just like Winnae's. Of course, they named her Winflaed.

When Abi died, the land became theirs because as she had said, "You are my son and daughter, and these are my little ones, and because there is no one else to claim it."

Winnae and Dever would never see Tamworth and Tybbington again, but they were happy in the York Dales.

❧ Chapter 8 ❧

Late 700 A.D *or Thereabouts*
Eggen, The Dyke, and Alina

Eggen stood on the wharf as the boat carrying his brother was rowed out of sight. He felt strangely sad as he glimpsed the empty river, where the ripples of the craft's departure still splashed gently against the shore. His thoughts said he'd never see his brother again. When the river's current erased the effects of the boat's passing, he shook his head to clear his reflections. But this strange cloud of sorrow hung over him the rest of the day.

Coming to Tamworth, he'd immediately reported to Andras. Andras was an impressive Welshman, muscular and tall, who put Eggen to work sorting a storehouse of supplies which would be used on the journey and the ensuing stay on the Welsh border. He was to keep a tally in his head of anything else the journey would require and report back each day. This was the first time in his life Eggen wished he could read and write.

When he got a chance, he visited the monk who had translated his ancestry history. The monk had offered to write the history Eggen had memorized on pages of parchment to place in the book. They would do this at night, when Eggen could not work.

Andras had taken him to a small, stark room in the palace next to his room as a place to stay. Eggen had declined, saying he already had one at the monastery with food in the pantry anytime he was hungry. Before sunrise each morning, Eggen went to prayers, something his family in Tybbington never did. He realized the monks had something—he couldn't explain it, but something different, something he began to think he needed.

On the fourth day, Andras came to the warehouse. "Come with me. The King wants to see us."

The royal horses were saddled and waiting in the courtyard. Eggen walked over and stroked the silky noses of the beautiful black horses he and his family had brought from Tybbington. Four horsemen with armour were positioned behind the royal steeds and the King's Steward stood beside all. "We'll wait here on his Majesty," he explained.

Andras and he exchanged glances. "Do you have any idea what he wants?"

"No, but here he comes. We'll soon find out."

As King Offa approached, the two men bowed. The Steward placed a step on the ground. The ruler of Mercia climbed upon his mount and urged the horse forward.

"Please," the servant motioned to Andras and Eggen, waving his hand toward their rides. The three climbed into their saddles with the Steward assuming his position beside the King.

With the King's kick to the flank of his horse, they were off and through the main gate. They turned north toward a less settled part of the village as people bowed and scraped the ground with their hats. The King did not say a word until they reached a stretch of the fortifications of Tamworth.

"We will stop here," he said, flicking his hand toward the dyke.

The Steward dismounted his horse and, taking the step, helped the King to the ground. Eggen and Andras followed suit.

The King was nodding at the dyke as the two came forward. "See," he said, taking his hand and pointing, since it was ill-mannered to point with a finger among the upper classes. "Ditches make boundaries and borders keep people from trespassing into territory where they aren't wanted. We have Roman stone and dirt ramparts built in England hundreds of years ago. They are still being used today to establish a territory—Hadrian's and Antonine Walls." The King waved his hand at the dirt ditch. "This is what I want." He looked deliberately at Eggen. "Come back tomorrow and have a good look—walk from one end to the other." With that, he returned to his horse, and the group went a roundabout way to the palace, where they dismounted. Before the King walked through the castle gate, he asked one more question. "What is your timetable, Andras?"

"Sire, we'll be heading out on the first of the week. Six or seven days should get us to the spot where Eggen's group will start—the area west of Scrobbesbyrig at Oswestry."

"How are the other groups fairing?"

"According to the last report from my overseers, I believe we'll finish the dyke before the date on your schedule."

"Great news! Great news! Remember, I'm counting on you. Please send a courier each week with information on your progress and let me know if you need anything." The King gathered his cloak and swept up the flagstone courtyard, disappearing into the dark corridor beyond. The Steward followed on his heels with the step.

Eggen and Andras were left to stare at themselves.

"Are you hungry, Eggen?" Andras didn't wait for an answer. He grabbed the young man around the shoulders and started toward the warehouse. On the way, they stopped to eat.

~

Eggen's group headed west, following an old track through the forests used mostly by residents of the area. Those in the company going to their new work area was not large. Besides Eggen and Andras, there were forty armed men, which were part of Offa's conscripted military, and several people from Tamworth, driving carts full of supplies.

Once on the worksite, Andras would move slaves and others from areas which were almost finished to start digging at the new location. When the older section was finished, the remaining group would either come and help Eggen or be moved elsewhere. The overseer and his armed men would go home. Their task was complete. Following a fight between two men, Andras had found out that one overseer in a location was enough.

～

At the head of the procession, Eggen rode his black horse beside Andras. He'd named her Beauty, because when Andras had first seen her, he'd said she was a 'black beauty.'

If he could have gotten a message to his father or his brother Chad, he could have met either of them on the march to his workstation because the groups trip west went close to Wodensbyri and Tybbington. Instead, Eggen waved to the empty forest from Beauty as the group passed north of both villages, heading toward Scrobbesbyrig.

"Eggen, we'll stop in a small hamlet about a half's day's ride and see if we can get a hot meal. I sent a messenger to tell them we're coming so they'll be expecting us."

Eggen had noticed one of the soldiers was missing and wondered where he'd gone.

And expecting them they were. A buxom woman in flaming red tunic came from her hut. "Andras, it's been too long!" she exclaimed, walking close to his horse.

As soon as Andras dismounted his steed, he was covered in kisses. And that's the last Eggen saw of him until daylight the next morning when he sat on his horse saying, "Let's go."

Three days passed until they arrived at River Tern. The stream was a tributary of the River Severn. Andras led the party to a shallow place to ford, and then on the opposite bank he and Eggen waited until the waggons and soldiers were through the rocky shoals.

As the last of the men on horseback cleared the river, Eggen asked, "How much longer until we get to Scrobbesbyrig?"

"We'll cross the River Severn twice before we get to Scrobbesbyrig. Its course is as curvy and meandering as our River Tame. Don't expect too much when we get there. Being on the border with the Welsh, it's inhabited by Welshmen and Saxons alike. It's bigger than the last village. The one where we stayed the night."

"Where is your home, Andras?"

The man waved his hand. "I'm from everywhere and no place in particular. I'm an orphan—a victim of the many bloody wars fought between our countries. I don't belong any place. The King picked me up out of the dirt in one of the villages he'd ransacked as he and his men went from hut-to-hut. My mother and father were killed in that raid—hacked to death in front of me." He paused—remembering and shivered. "He pays me well. So as long as I'm in his employ, I'm Mercian."

If Andras' allegiance depended on being payed, Eggen wondered how much it would take to break the bond. And he seemed to harbour feelings for his dead mother and father—and who wouldn't? For the first time, a smidgen of distrust for the man reared its head. "But King Offa said you knew this country."

"I do. Many times, I've been sent on royal missions as an emissary to my land and fought in skirmishes on this border dig." He could have said he'd never killed any of his countrymen—wounded a few. Instead, Andras pulled up the sleeve of his tunic, exposing a deep, ragged scar on his shoulder. "See the results of one of them — an arrow." He put the shirt down and they rode for several minutes until he continued, "I suppose if I were to be from somewhere in this country, I'd pick Bristol and become a seafaring man."

"Have you been there?"

"No, but I've sure heard a lot about the place. When we finish the southern part of the dyke, I'll be close. Might just hop a ship and sail away."

While they were talking, the distance to the River Severn lessened, and finally the first crossing appeared.

"Does the river make a large loop around Scrobbesbyrig?" Eggen asked, getting this impression as he sat on his horse, looking over the village.

"Yes, and, at this time of year, it is shallow enough to wade across." Andras explained, "There are two fords here called English Ford and Welsh Ford. We'll cross the English Ford first."

In the distance, positioned on the hill above the river and before the other leg of the loop, were several houses. Some were wattle and daub. Some were stone with thatched roofs. There was the vague smell of smoke and occasionally the distant squeal of children playing as they ran through the paths of the community.

∽

After crossing the second bend or Welsh Ford of the River Severn, the group had waded through marshland to a higher ground. The sun was past noonday and starting down in the west.

"We'll stop now and overnight," Andras called from his horse as he looked around the flat area. It was located a little north of the town and suitable for stretching their shelters. "We've camped here before," he told Eggen.

After making sure everyone knew his plans, he rode back toward the village and halted before entering or passing the first house.

"Do you know somebody here?" asked Eggen, reining Beauty up beside him and halfway expecting another woman to come rushing from her house toward the leader.

"Yes. Listen." He cupped his hand to his ear.

At first, Eggen couldn't make out any particular noise. When he did, there was the faint, unfamiliar sound of music being played in the distance. The haunting melody came from the highest and largest stone building in the village, covering and including those dwelling below with its sweet tune.

"What is that?"

"Alina on her lute," was all Andras said. He turned his horse back to camp and dismounted. While he unsaddled his horse, Eggen pursued him with questions.

"Who is Alina?"

"She and her father came by boat up the River Severn from Gloucester. I don't know the full story, but she plays music every afternoon until time to eat the night meal."

"What does her father do?"

"Basically, nothing, as far as I can tell. They seem to have money to buy everything they need, including servants. There's some talk about him being a rich merchant from Londinium or East Anglia who moved because he came into conflict with the ruler there. No one knows the real truth—not even I." Andras stood, looking up at him with his hand on Beauty.

"Will we see her?"

"We'll make a call on her and the reclusive father tomorrow as we leave the village. Can you cook?" With that comment, Andras went to help the men complete the temporary shelters for the night. This was just in case it rained and also to escape other questions about the other unknown woman.

Eggen walked to the supply waggon and started breaking out the food stock. Who was this lady who'd made a pagan like Andras stop and ponder her? Was it the music? And, what was the Welshman pondering? It was obvious even to him that something drew his supervisor to her. Eggen couldn't wait to meet her.

"Start a fire," he told the man driving the waggon. "I'll see if I can buy some meat from the village. Maybe we'll have fresh, roasted lamb."

~

Next day, before he and Andras could approach the town, they were delayed by a large herd of sheep driven by four men. The men threw up their hands and one called, "Andras, are you headed for Offa's Dyke?"

"Yes, at Oswald's Well this time," Andras called back, recognizing the men. "How about coming to help us work?" he teased.

"No, we'll stay with the sheep. We're moving them to a greener pasture to the west of town. Will you need some mutton, chicken, or pork while you're nearby? We can supply all."

"Yes. We'll be there for some months. Bring several of each and build a pen for them."

The men were familiar with Andras and his request. "We'll come in four days with all the supplies to build your pen and animals to stock it."

"That's suitable," replied Andras, continuing on, heading for the Welsh Ford. He crossed, halted his horse, and dismounted before the house where the music had originated. "Come, Eggen. We'll pay our respects to the lady of the house."

Before Eggen could alight, a woman in a beautiful, flowing orange robe with puffy yellow sleeves and tied with a yellow rope belt at the waist came out of the home's door. She had on an orange hat with ruffles around the edges which matched her sleeves. From where he sat, staring at her, he couldn't see much of her hair, but the few curls which escaped its confines were darker than the women he was accustomed too. She was plain and soft-spoken—gentle and welcoming. She smoothed her escaping curls with her hands, which she held out to Andras. "I see you have returned, my friend. Some in the village came to tell me."

"Yes, we'll be here until the section of the dyke is built at Oswald's Well." Andras turned and gave a steely-eyed stare at Eggen—a get off your horse look.

Eggen, embarrassed that he was caught staring at the woman, dismounted his horse and stepped to Andras' side. "This is Eggen. He will be overseer on this section."

Turning her eyes on Eggen, she acknowledged him with a smile and a nod of her head. "Will your work take long?" she continued with Andras.

"Depends on how well Eggen's crew works, and if the new overseer can do the job." Andras put his hand on Eggen's back, and the woman glanced his way again. "Alina, we may take a break from our labor and come into the village to rest and sleep. Will you have a room for us?"

Alina nodded. "You'll always have a room here, Andras. But I must go. There's a woman in the village who's giving birth. I need to check on her." She turned from the door and headed down the path to the lower area of the village section. The two watched until she was gone from sight.

"She seems to know you, Andras."

"Yes, she should. She tended me while the arrow wound healed, dug out the point, and kept it from festering by keeping the area clean. She's good at watching wounds and setting bones as some of my workers have found out."

"When did you get shot with the arrow?"

"Three years ago, on this dig but much farther south. You have to remember, the Welsh and Mercians are still at war, or we wouldn't need this ditch in the ground. Getting ambushed is still a possibility on any day."

"I'll keep that in mind. I can't believe this has been going on for three years and no one knew about it."

"King Offa wanted as much done in private as possible. But the secret is out now."

"How much farther to the work site?"

Both men mounted their horses. "If we don't dawdle, we'll get there this afternoon."

They crossed the Welsh Ford again, heading west.

~

After riding for several hours, Andras stopped to get water out of a spring flowing from a depression at the foot of a slight hill. The site was rocky with grasses growing in tufts between the stones. The clear water was cold. "Do you know the story of Oswald's Well?" Andras asked, after getting on his horse and kicking the animal into a walk. Eggen mounted Beauty and fell into step beside him.

"No. What is the story of Oswald's Well?"

"All Welshmen know of King Oswald. He was the ruthless King of Northumbria with a lust for power, just as was his nemesis, Penda of Mercia. Oswald desired the land below the Humber Estuary, and Penda sought the land above it—both never seemed to have enough land or control. As destiny would have it, a major battle needed to be fought, which eliminated one of the rivals. That slaughter took place here at Maserfield over a hundred years ago." Andras waved his arm over a field of beautiful wild flowers of white, blue, and yellow which grew on the rolling hills several miles beyond Scrobbesbyrig.

"I find it hard to believe a bloody battle was fought here."

"Yes, these flowers and hills conceal the field of a vicious battle. So many men died here that the area was covered with white bones, because the dead were left to rot and decay, while the ravens and vultures picked their bodies clean. Our Welsh Prince, Cynddylan, made the correct decision and joined with Penda. Here, he and Penda lived, and King Oswald died."

"So, the spring was named after King Oswald?"

"Yes, but that's not the end of the account. After King Oswald died, the story goes that he was chopped to pieces. His arms and head were put on stakes so everyone could see the great King was gone. One of his arms was not nailed very well. A bird grabbed it and flew to a tree to rest. The arm dropped to the ground and that's where water came to the surface. Everyone said this was a miracle."

"You mean where we drank the water was caused by a dismembered arm falling to the ground?" Eggen grimaced.

Andras laughed, "That's the story."

"Do you believe it?"

"Stranger things have happened."

"Name one," replied Eggen.

Andras couldn't come up with any.

After giving instructions for setting up camp at Oswestry, Eggen and Andras made a decision to travel south and meet the end of the dig. The section was almost completed and heading north. Standing on top of the new dyke, Eggen looked out over a land with an unobstructed view—of green pastures with occasional hills protruding from the ground. Anyone coming from the western side could certainly be spotted some distance away, except for large stands of beech trees in the hollows between the hills, where a small army could hide. Some of the forested areas were close enough for an excellent archer with good accuracy to launch an arrow and hit a target on the hill where he stood, and the Welsh were renowned for marksmanship with the longbow which they preferred.

To the south, the dyke stretched for miles, topping the tallest hills and snaking through the valleys. The ditch was an impressive site for friend and foe alike.

~

Several days passed before Eggen had a complete crew to actually start working. As the men were released from the completed section, he put them to work clearing brush, scrub trees, fallen tree trunks, and rocks from his area.

They built fires, burnt the dead wood, and grubbed stumps, burning the larger ones and digging out their roots. The crew worked north as the newly released workers started to dig with spades, haul dirt in wooden wheel barrows, and move large rocks on sleds pulled by horses. All this work was taken uphill to the top of the dirt-dig and positioned to make the mound higher. Ten to twelve feet of earth was moved to make the higher section where a wooden fence or rock wall was established. So many men swarmed the area that from afar they looked like ants, busily constructing a new home. Up and down, up and down, until in the end the dyke was at least twenty-five feet high. This included the hole from where the dirt was dug.

"Where does the dyke end?" asked Eggen one day as Andras was approving the first part of his dig.

"The work will continue north until it ends at the River Dee estuary, at least I'm proposing this as the end. When you finish here, we'll be way over one-half done."

"Why are we building an earthen boundary?"

"Has anyone built one like it since the Roman's left?"

"No. I can't think of one."

Andras continued, "Maybe it's a warning should anyone want to confront the Mercian might and maybe it harkens back to Roman ingenuity and the strength or power of Rome. King Offa may think he's attained their level of supremacy."

"Will he charge a toll to cross the dyke?"

"I'm sure that's in the back of his mind. If the King sets up checkpoints on the border, he can extract revenue from those wishing to cross—either way. This will add money into his coffers. King Offa never seems to have enough money," Andras laughed.

∾

Although Andras sometimes went back to Scrobbesbyrig to stay the night, Eggen decided to stay on his post at Oswestry. Going to see Alina was not on his list of things to accomplish, but tramping the hills of Wales was at the top. He didn't expect to be in the country again. When these thoughts ran through his mind, he thought of Dever. Where was he and what was he doing? Months had passed. Was his brother home? He grinned at his father's idea that his older brother was the adventurous one in the family, because he was the one walking in the hills of a foreign land.

Toward the end of his dig, one of these trips was almost his downfall. The late autumn day was full of sunshine, so he called a halt to work, preferring to let his crew have a day of rest. He'd proved to be a valuable and fair overseer, and his men worked hard to please him. They were ahead of schedule, working north of Oswald's Well, and Andras had left for Scrobbesbyrig.

A ridge of rocks poked their heads above the ground to the east—this time in Mercian territory.

Eggen had been eyeing the peak for a week. *A perfect day for a climb*, he thought.

After eating the noon meal and telling one of the military men the general direction he was going, he set off to explore the rocky mount.

"I'll be back before nightfall," he called as he walked away.

His first mistake was underestimating the closeness to the formation which protruded through the top of the hill. In the distance, the path looked smooth and easy, but soon he was threading, uphill and down, through brambles, rocks, and crevices, taking longer than he'd planned. The sun was on its path to sundown when he arrived at the rock peak, which was already casting long, dark shadows over the land.

After expending so much energy, he paused to enjoy the view of the sun, sending rays to the ground through distant clouds. He remembered his father's father telling him the streams of light were pulling water from the earth so it could rain on the morrow.

"Eggen, that's not a good thing to remember, since you'll either be sleeping in the rain tonight or walking in it tomorrow," he said to the silence around him.

Realizing he was too far away and couldn't make the work camp before nightfall, he needed to pick out an agreeable place to hunker down for the night. He shook his waterskin. He had a little water, but no food, or extra cloak for the chill which was sure to come after the sun disappeared.

He headed back the way he'd come, or at least he thought this was the way. After one hour of steady walking, he wanted to kick himself for not marking the trail. Coming to a large rock he didn't remember, he decided this was the place he'd stop and shelter. He'd curl up beside it and sleep until morning, letting the residual warmth of the rock and ground keep him warm.

Because it was dusky-dark, with myriads of rock shadows, he didn't see the crevice in the ground beside the boulder.

Although he flung his arm out to block his fall, he felt a distinct snap in his leg when he stepped in it, and his forward momentum pitched him headfirst into a boulder. His body rolled sideways, hitting his shoulder a glancing blow on another rock. He didn't feel the second blow, because the first knocked him unconscious.

∽

When Eggen came back to his senses, he was so cold his teeth were chattering. Every time he tried to move, a pain shot through his leg and his shoulder felt like it was on fire. Not only that, but when he put his hand to his head, he felt crusted blood in his hair, on his cheek, and in his beard. What had he done to himself?

The saving grace of the whole situation, since he lay on his side, was the hollowed-out place where he had fallen was not uncomfortable, and he dozed, off and on, in a semi-conscious state which meant he wasn't subject to pain all the time.

Finally, at daybreak, he could assess his situation. He was in pain. He was cold. His foot was caught in an awkward way in the crevice. He was hungry. He was thirsty—where was his waterskin? Moving his painful shoulder and craning his neck, he found it close to his head where it had fallen. Drinking a few sups, he put the bag under his head for a pillow.

He lay there thinking, *they will find me, but when?* What else could he do? Nothing.

He fell asleep.

When he awoke, it was fully daylight. The gray clouds overhead had started to drop a misty rain. Later, the drizzle turned into a downpour. Fear raised its ugly head, and for the first time, Eggen wondered if he would die. He began to pray—not to the god of his fathers, but to the God of the monks at the monastery.

After what should have been the noon meal, the rain stopped and the sun shone over the rocky outcrop, and Eggen started to warm up and dry out. If he was to travel at all, he needed to get his foot loose from the grip of the rock holding the appendage in its clutches. Using all the strength he could muster, he pushed himself up on one elbow and managed to get his hand under his hip, giving him extra space between the rock and the ground. Moving the leg caused too much pain. He settled back down, thought of another way and tried again. Exhausted, he lay still, listening to something skittering around in the rocks above his resting place. Then he fell asleep.

~

Was that voices? Eggen's eyes fluttered open. A face came slowly into focus. "Andras, it's good to see you. I got stuck in the rock."

"My friend, you look a mess. We're here to help you."

~

The trip back to camp was best forgotten. He endured being loaded on a makeshift stretcher and carried by four of his crew the whole way. At that point, a cart with straw in the bottom became his all-day ride to Scrobbesbyrig and Alina's house. The sun beat down on his shifting, prostrate body until it set in the west and the night chill made him shake. Constant pain was his unwanted companion. Eggen closed his eyes and passed in-and-out of the world he traveled through.

When the cart stopped, he heard a soft-spoken, female voice, and he was sure she was an angel sent from heaven, like the monks talked about. Her hand was cool when he felt it touch his forehead and gentle as she examined his damaged body. He vaguely heard her tell Andras, "He has a fever from his fall and being exposed to the cold weather."

"I'll leave him with you, Alina. How long until the leg heals?"

"Not before Yuletide season. If he survives until then." Alina stood by the bedside, shaking her head. "I need to tend to him."

"We're going." Andras looked at Eggen, whose eyes were closed. "Eggen, we'll finish the dig. Don't worry about the job getting done." He didn't know if his overseer heard or understood what he said. He turned and walked out the door.

The next days were a blur to Eggen. The angel who tended him hovered over the bed, raising his head to feed and give him some bitter tasting medicine. The soup was good, but the bitter tasting stuff, he tried to spit out. He heard the angel laugh and insist he would swallow or she would stuff the nasty brew down his throat. And he did — swallow — because he loved the sound of her laughter — and because he'd begun to love the woman who hovered above him.

Then the sound of music would float over his cot, and he would see his mother with her spoons, the ones she used in the pots on her hearth. She would take them and beat them together so her children could step to the rhythm of the music as she called the little shuffle they did.

Little did he know, how close the fever he had caught, brought him to dying, but his angel insisted he would survive — and he did. When he opened his eyes, Alina was there.

◇

During the next weeks, Eggen continued to improve. Several times she caught him sitting on the side of his bed.

"You're going to undo all the progress you've made," she chided him, wagging her finger. "You'll get up when I say you can get up." Then she would come and pick at the gash on his head, adjust his shoulder, and gently run her hand up and down his lower leg. "There's less swelling today," she would say and push him down on his back.

To soothe him she would pull out her lute and play for him. Her instrument was in the shape of a huge boiled egg, cut in two pieces, with a flat shaft on one end. A hole was cut in the middle of the oval's flat surface, and strings were mounted from one end to another to be plucked with her fingers. "I do this for my father. The afternoons are the worst for him," she explained, strumming a tune of her own making.

One day, when he woke up, a set of two sticks that looked like they had a yoke on top rested at the foot of his bed. On Alina's chair, a group of his clean clothes, cloak, and leather shoes were carefully placed for his use.

A servant came in to stoke the morning fire. "My lady says to put on your clothes. You are going for a walk."

When Alina arrived, he was ready and sitting on the edge of the bed. She stood with her hands on her hips, grinning at him. "When we get back, you'll be ready to crawl onto your cot," she threatened.

"Good morning to you, too," said Eggen, smiling back.

Coming to him, she bent over and put her arms under his. They were cheek to cheek. He took advantage of the unexpected moment to give her a quick kiss, turning his head enough to miss her ear. She didn't draw back or reproach him. Instead, he apologized, "I'm sorry, Alina. I shouldn't have taken the liberty to kiss you."

"You've been through so much in the last few weeks," was how she excused the action.

Then she pulled with all her might upward, until he stood upright. The shoulder had a few twinges, but the problem he felt the most was being dizzy. He put his hand to his head.

"Are you dizzy?" Alina asked, stepping back but still holding onto his body.

"Yes, a little."

"That's normal. We'll not move until you feel better."

So, they stood there, arms around each other, her head on his shoulder, with Eggen thinking maybe he'd never feel better—on purpose.

Noises came from the courtyard outside. "Where is Alina?"

Eggen's reverie stopped, jerked back to reality by the sound of Andras' voice. They heard his footsteps in the hall, as Alina helped him sit back down. "How's my overseer doing?" he said as he entered the room.

"We were attempting to stand this morning, but Eggen was dizzy," Alina said blushing.

"How did the leg feel?" Andras asked Eggen.

"I don't know. We didn't get that far."

"I have good news. Your part of the dig is almost done, and I'm heading back to Tamworth for a new crew. I was hoping you would be able to go with me. I could take you by Tybbington."

"No! He's not able to stand up, much less ride a horse," Alina interjected so fast that Andras gave her a quick look.

He drew back as if stung by a bee. "I wouldn't want him to go unless he could ride. Anyway Eggen, Beauty is outside. I brought her with me, just-in-case."

Eggen hadn't thought of Beauty or Tybbington for several days. "Thank you. She will give me a great reason to walk out of this room."

"Until we meet again, my friend." Andras raised his hand and was gone.

$\sim$

Several days passed before Eggen could support his weight on the broken leg, but finally with the wooden supports, he limped out of the stone house and to the horse enclosure. Beauty whinnied and headed his way. "She's such a beautiful horse," Alina said, rubbing the animal's nose. "I'd love to ride her."

"Why not tomorrow," suggested Eggen, thinking with some help he could mount her.

"We will try," was all Alina said.

The next day, Eggen was ready when Alina appeared. They went to the stone-walled enclosure which held Beauty. Today, there was another horse—both saddled and ready to ride.

"You *are* going to let me ride Beauty," she said, raising her eyebrows at him.

"What?" He drew his head back and furrowed his brow. He teased her, "It takes a very special lady for a man to let her ride his own horse."

"You said I could ride her yesterday." Alina insisted, grinning at him.

Eggen couldn't help but smile back at this very persuasive woman. She'd taken his words or maybe his thoughts and twisted them to her advantage. "Yes, you can ride Beauty, but you have to help me on the other horse first."

The rock wall became the best prop for getting on his horse. Alina brought a wooden bench from the side of the stone house. From this height and putting his hands on the top of the fence, he pushed upward until his belly rested on the highest part. He stayed prone until Alina brought the horse around. From there, he slung his leg over the horse's back and pushing sideways sat upright in the saddle. Breathing heavily from the effort, he watched her get on Beauty with the grace of a queen. She sat astride with her shoes in the stirrups.

"Are you ready to ride, my Lord?"

"You've elevated my position in life, haven't you?" he teased, again.

"That's what you are to me," she returned and rode out of the enclosure.

When Eggen caught up with her, he noticed her cheeks were rosy red. He decided to push an issue close to his heart. "So, I'm your Lord, am I?"

Alina kept riding — eyes straight ahead.

"Alina, you should know my feelings for you. If there was anyone else in the world I could pick as a companion for life, they wouldn't hold a candle to you."

Alina stopped Beauty and looked at him. "Is there — anyone?"

"No," he said, shaking his head. "Never."

Eggen said this with such conviction Alina instinctively knew he was telling her the truth. She sat for several moments in silence, head down and eyes closed, weighing her answer.

Finally, knowing this was a moment he would either hold dear or regret for the rest of his life, he said her name, "Alina?"

She turned toward him with tears in her eyes, saying simply, "Then I'm yours — your companion for life," she said, reaching her hand out to him, as if in support of her words.

Eggen turned the hand over and kissed her palm. "Do I get a real kiss?" he asked, looking down at her.

"Yes."

With that, their future together was settled.

"Eggen."

"Yes, my love?"

"There is a church not far from here, where I go to be alone and to kneel and pray. Would you go with me today? For me, our promise to each other is holy, and I'd like to say a prayer for our future union." Her voice was trembling with emotion as she addressed him.

"We will go. Lead the way."

Alina rode east across the English Ford, following a winding path just above the floodplain, and there alone in a field was a small stone church with a large arched window in front. From the outside, there was nothing about the building which was graceful or beautiful.

"What is this church called?" asked Eggen, who waited for Alina to help him dismount his horse, which he did very gingerly. Leaning heavily on her, he limped a few steps to the doorway, noticing the wood casing looked very old and some of the stone walls were overlaid with bricks. The bricks were interleaved in a strange way. "The bricks are very unusual. From an old Roman ruin, I suppose," he mused to himself, running his hand over the rough surface.

"The Church of the Holy Fathers is its name," Alina said on entering the door. "No one knows when the structure was built, but as you can see, over time, layers have been added. Shall we go in?"

The building was empty. Slowly, they went down front. Eggen eased his leg into a position where he could sit on a front wooden pew. His leg was stiff and would not bend properly to kneel.

Alina knelt at the wooden altar and prayed out loud at first, *"My Father, today Eggen and I have made a promise to each other to become one. Give us many days together, wherever we may sojourn, and healthy, happy children. Please bless our future union."*

Eggen could not hear the rest, as she lowered her tone to talk in a private voice to her Father in heaven. Instead, he stared at a symbol he knew well. The emblem was two double arches intersecting each other, exactly like the one with the Ancestry Book — the ichthys or symbol of God's son, Jesus Christ. This was the explanation of the monk at Tamworth. The ancient wood displayed more than one. How did the outline get here? What person did the carving in the olden wood? Where did he come from? Because there was no answer to his questions, he glanced one more time around the building's interior and joined his future companion in prayer.

～

During the ride back to Alina's home, the talk was of meeting his family and his desire to have his parents present when they pledged themselves together. Then he asked about her father. He hadn't seen this man since he'd been at Scrobbesbyrig.

"He does exist," Alina laughed. "But he's a recluse, almost a monk in many respects. After losing my mother, who didn't recover from my birth, he stayed in his room at Bamburgh in our manor for years."

"Was he a father to you?"

"As much as he could be."

They were back to the stoned enclosure. Getting off the horse was easier than getting on. As Eggen slid to the ground, his legs almost didn't hold him. He grabbed the saddle and waited for Alina to help him. "I want to hear the rest of the story when we get to my room. The cot will be a welcome sight." He was exhausted. He didn't notice Alina's quick smile.

Getting his wooden walking sticks, Alina helped him into his room and to his bed. "I'll get some water and something to eat."

When she came back, she asked, "Would you prefer to take a nap after you eat? We can finish the story later."

"No, I want to hear it now," he said, taking a sup of water and chewing on a piece of meat and bread.

Alina continued, "My father's father was a local and very successful merchant. He was also a trusted confidante of one of the princes of Northumbria. This was a time when there was much intrigue and unrest in the royal palace at Bamburgh with rumours of beheadings and reports of distant relatives wishing to usurp the ruler. You really didn't want to be a friend of the King."

"Things haven't changed much since then—with any King or kingdom," observed Eggen, nodding. "Sorry, I interrupted you."

Alina grinned and continued. "There was also a flourishing monastery at Lindisfarne, which my family supported monetarily. It was north of the royal town, and where my family had rooms, retiring there at times for safety and protection, especially in the worst periods of insurrection. Finally, the King, fearing for his life and monarchy, sent his oldest son to my grandfather with part of the royal coffers—chests filled with coins and jewels for safe keeping. After receiving the chests, which he had no desire to take charge of, grandfather stored them in the monastery in a safe place known only to him. During one of the many battles in Northumbria, the King and his sons were killed, and my grandfather, despising the new King, couldn't or wouldn't take the treasure to the new ruler, but transferred it in the dead of night to our family house at Bamburgh. Do you really want to hear the rest of this tale?"

"Yes, please go on." Eggen could picture each sentence she was uttering, and Alina's face was the most beautiful and animated as she smiled, gesturing at some points of the story to emphasize a particular detail. Her words were fascinating. Putting his bowl aside, he pulled up to rest his elbow on the couch and grimaced at the pain which ran through his leg and shoulder.

"We rode too long today. Tomorrow, we'll be more careful," she said, reaching out her hand to touch his tender shoulder, and gently pushing him back to a prone position.

"You know, I'm going to have to stand on the leg without the wooden supports sometime in the future."

Alina nodded, agreeing with him. "But not yet, Eggen. The leg isn't ready for all your weight."

"I realize the complete healing will take time." He pulled in air and let it go in a rush. "Go ahead and finish your story."

"The treasure went to my father when the older man died. This left my father with a tough decision. Take it to the present King or leave it in our home. So much time had lapsed, he had no way of knowing what kind of reception he'd get. Would the King believe his story? My father decided not to chance having his head severed from his body. So, the chests remained secreted at Bamburgh, until —." Alina paused, getting up at a noisy sound outside the window. She peered out at a herd of sheep being driven through the village. Raising her hand, she waved to the herders. "Good day," she called.

"Until what?" Eggen exclaimed as she returned to sit beside his resting place.

"Oh, let me see," she thought. "Until one day, my father was standing on the parapet of the town looking north. He often walked there in the early afternoon. What he saw made his blood run cold. He spied a fleet of ships—Danish war ships, heading down the coast of Northumbria. There were only two reasons for the feared Norse raiders to be in the country—to inspect potential targets or to plunder and kill. With the terrible dragon head on front and the tail end on the back, there was no way to mistake them. These long, slim ships sailed close to the coast, with so many oarsmen my father couldn't count them. He could make out an armour-clad man in front and the one steering the rudder in the rear. They didn't stop but continued south.

"He made a right guess. It wouldn't be long until they came back and attacked the monastery. At this sight he made up his mind. We were leaving our homeland. We loaded our goods aboard the next merchant ship in the harbour on the coast and headed south to Lundenwic, a Saxon trading settlement just outside the old Roman city of Londinium and under Mercian control.

"Was this during King Offa's reign?" The exertion of the day was catching up with Eggen, and Alina's voice was musical and soft. His eyelids were growing heavy.

"No, an ancestor of his. My father sold the jewels and traded for monies of currently used Mercian coins. But, Lundenwic wasn't far enough away for him. We went south and around the southern coast of England to the western side of this country, and because the captain of the ship was from Bristol, we ended up on the River Severn where we heard about Scrobbesbyrig. From there, we hired a boat and came north until we found this settlement. This was far enough away from Bamburgh."

Alina looked over at Eggen. He was asleep. At least, his eyes were closed. "Let him rest," she said, getting up, bending over and kissing him on the lips. "You're doing so well, my love," she whispered and left the room.

Eggen opened one eye a bit and followed her figure out the door.

∽

After sending a local sheepherder to his father with news of his return and pending marriage, and receiving a reply of welcome, Eggen, Alina and such of her many friends who wished to attend set out by horse and cart for Tybbington.

Although Eggen had met Alina's father, he could not be persuaded to go. The father suggested a trip by Eggen's family to visit him in the near future. He would be glad to receive them in Scrobbesbyrig, but he would not budge an inch from his home.

∽

Eggen sat talking to his father at Tybbington. "What's the truth about Dever?" This was the first question he'd asked after the normal words of welcome. They were standing near the sheep shearing shed as they spoke.

"He disappeared into the wilds of the north without a trace, so said Gaius, who captained the ship taking him and the Princess to York. And, they didn't stop at York, they got off the boat and went by carriage to Catterick where she was to be married to King Æthelred. The Captain hinted at an attraction between one of the ladies tending the Princess and your brother. I pray he's alright, and he's got something to remind him of his roots."

"I wondered if he'd returned." Eggen went to a bench and sat down. This presented a dilemma. "How will you get the harvesting and sheep shearing done this year?"

"Aren't you staying?"

"No. I'll be going back to Scrobbesbyrig with Alina. She needs to take care of her father, and I'm going to pursue another interest which has recently occurred to me."

"You're not going to raise sheep?" his father teased.

"No. Alina's father was a merchant in Bamburgh, and she thinks he will help me set up a market for several men and women in the area who are excellent at producing their crafts. I want to go to Bristol with their wares and see if I can promote their skills— pottery, metal and woodworking to start. Perhaps we might sell wool to merchants in the south, instead of carting it east. When going down the River Severn, I can think of several opportunities which might be available. I've even entertained the thought of setting up a store in Bristol."

"Bristol is on the coast?"

"Actually no. It's on the River Avon, but close enough to support a small market. I've had plenty of practice watching you bargain for the best prices for our wool and other harvested crops."

"Son, I think you'll do well in your new effort. Don't worry about us here at Tybbington. Godwin has already expressed a desire to come and help. Chad will be returning to Wodensbyri with his family. You will be coming back to visit, won't you?"

"Yes, as often as I can."

"Alwin," Aisley called to her husband. "We're ready."

Father and son stood, heading for the feasting area.

"The question is, are you ready, Eggen? Is she the right one for you?" asked Alwin, clapping his son on the back and winking at him.

"Father, was it fate that sent me to Scrobbesbyrig? I don't know. I've just been thinking how strangely our lives are woven together, then my mind gets bogged down in the maze I try to work through." Eggen shook his head. "And yes, I'm ready. I've been ready for months. Alina's exactly what I've been waiting for."

The two men walked together to the feasting area where Eggen and Alina exchanged vows to become one. One year later, little Alwin was born. He became the spitting image of his father's father.

In later years and with lots of patience, Alina taught Eggen to read and write Latin.

ॐ **Chapter 9** ॐ

Early 900 A.D. *or Thereabouts*
Æthelflaed, Battle at Tettenhall

King Offa died at Bedford Priory in 796. No one knows where he's buried. One hundred and ten years pass after Offa's death and Mercia's importance diminishes somewhat, while Wessex in the south, under Alfred the Great, rises in power and importance.

No one knows the final extent of King Alfred's territory or realm, because one factor halted his advance and exposed his weaknesses—the invasion of the Danish Vikings or raiders from the northlands.

For years, the Vikings from Scandinavia had been sailing the seas and delivering lightening raids in their dragon boats on the exposed villages and religious compounds near the sea and up the river estuaries of the European continent. These included Russia, France, the Mediterranean Sea, and the many isles found within their reach.

England was no different. The Vikings were sailing and attacking both the east and west coasts of the country, as well as the isle of Ireland.

At first, as at the monastery at Lindisfarne, the Vikings did not want land, but were satisfied to plunder, rape, and pillage individual objectives, taking their spoils and tribute back home to support their lifestyle. But as targets dwindled and their own population grew, they turned to land conquests, learned farming, and trading lifestyles—some intermingling peacefully in the countryside where they remained and established families.

∼

Alina and her reclusive father had just barely got out of Bamburgh before the monastery at Lindisfarne was ransacked by the Danish Vikings. In this newly Christianized country of England, the heathen and barbaric Norsemen went on a rampage down the English coasts, subduing Northumbria (York), East Anglia, most of Mercia, and then knocking on the gates of King Alfred's Wessex. Over the following years, the King tried bribery, treaties, fighting and retreating, until the lashing he gave the Vikings at Edington, stopped the Danish invasion and saved his kingdom.

The question causing Saxon King Alfred many sleepless nights was this: how could he keep Wessex safely within his grasp and establish a firm hold onto his expanding territory? What could he do to block the Danes from invading and retaking what he'd given blood and treasure to recapture? An idea formed. He would use King Offa's concept of fortifications and reinforce all the major villages by building or heaping up dirt embankments which would have vertical barriers of wood on top. These major villages were called burhs.

If there was a brook or river nearby, it would be diverted, adding a moat to cross. Although most burhs were too high in elevation for the water hazard, this could establish another hinderance to an enemy's approach.

Gates into the fortified villages would be manned at all times, and extra supplies in case of an attack or siege would be housed in the secured enclosure.

When raiders came, people from outside the walls (fighting men, plus women and children) could hasten to the village for protection and to help with fending off the intruders. Slowly, these fortified places gained in numbers in the countryside of Wessex, providing protection and safety for the countrymen, who, in return, manned Alfred's army and fought valiantly for their King.

There were times of peace and times of war. Ultimately, the land and people needed rest. King Alfred agreed with the Vikings to divide England into two territories. The Viking lands were known as Danelaw. This resolution or treaty gave Alfred time to build up his army and navy. He wasn't done with the fighting. But sadly, although he fought hard, he didn't live to realize the total liberation of the country he loved. When he died, he left a protected land containing thirty-three taxable and fortified towns or burhs in a territory called Wessex.

This kingdom was ruled by laws and a highly effective government with an established currency which could raise taxes to support a wide-ranging military organization. With a successful heir or leader, Wessex could continue to defend its territory and expand its borders.

~

Into this mix of over one hundred and ten years and not to be outdone, the Vikings continued their desire to rule the island, but with Alfred's death, his children joined together and continued his assault on the Vikings, nibbling at their strongholds, taking back land and fortifying the land they claimed. The siblings built more wooden castles, along with burhs on top of hills, which could be easily defended with minimal causalities.

Their armies or Fyrd consisted mostly of citizen soldiers known as thanes who were nothing more than well-trained farmers. Owning land, these freemen could be called on at a moment's notice to defend a burh or serve in the field army. They were willing to risk life and limb for their leaders, families, and for peace. They were not issued uniforms or armour by the King, so when called they grabbed a hodge-podge of helmets, shields, spears, swords, and knives—anything they had to fight the enemy. What they lacked in equipment, they gained in expertise, training in war tactics and fighting from an early age.

∽

After Offa's scheming and controlling wife, Queen Cynethryth, no other woman was called Queen in Mercia, but that didn't stop another woman's rise to prominence, because the Angles and Saxons had no problem with a woman in command. She was Alfred the Great's daughter, known as the Lady of Mercia, Æthelflaed, who was loved and respected by her subjects and who became a great warrior leader. Æthelflaed built wooden castles with burhs on Wodensbyri Hill and Dudda Hill which protected the lower valley of Tybbington. She rebuilt Tamworth and Chester which the Danes had destroyed, making Tamworth her principal residence.

Her brother, Edward the Elder, became King of Wessex after the death of their father, Alfred the Great. The two of them started wresting the control of Mercia and the remainder of the south of England from Danish control and blocked their further expansion. This did not make the Vikings happy. They were after the whole of England.

In 910, the Danelaw Kings planned a sneak attack from south of the Humber Estuary and East Anglia. They went toward Wessex. Meanwhile, a fleet of ships was assembled in Ireland to transport a Danish army up the River Severn, directly into the heart of Mercia and Wessex which they considered the most vulnerable area. When the two armies met, this would cut the country into two parts, making it easier to conquer.

The Viking's plans were brought up short by King Edward's army of freemen. The Fyrd slowed their rampage to the south and turned them north and west into the West Midlands and toward his sister, Æthelflaed. She expected them and waited with her army, consisting of other Saxons and Angles. These were the Mercians of Offa's kingdom. Tybba's descendants who were now native to this country and strong to defend the land of their fathers.

When the Danes realized the battle wasn't going as planned, because of new fortifications protecting the villages, and that they were mostly surrounded by hostile forces, squeezing them northward, the Danes took the way of least resistance, or so they thought. Heading for Northumbria and safer territory toward the Humber Estuary, they arrived at Tettenhall.

As the Danes moved north, the English military led by the Lady of Mercia slowly retreated. She'd used this tactic before at Chester against the Danes, and it had worked. This time there would be no walls to hold her enemy within, but she had something else in mind just as good. Her plan drew the Danish forces into the West Midlands, where they would be confronted by a mighty army which awaited at Tettenhall, just west of Tybbington and Wodensbyri with Æthelflaed and her brother in command. The trap was set!

❧ **Chapter 10** ❧

Early 900 A.D *or Thereabouts*

Æthelflaed, Battle at Tettenhall, King Edward the Elder, and Meta

Thirteen-year-old Briallen stood outside her father's shop on the floating wooden wharf at Portishead, England, where the River Avon flowed into the Severn Estuary. She looked northwest across the River Avon at the sea birds flying on the morning breeze, as they dove for minnows in the shallow sand banks to the side of the river's mouth. The only sound, besides the sea bird's song, was the splashing of water as she pulled in her fishing line and rebaited her bone hook.

Normally, her grandfather fished with her, but today he was busy. The worms, which she and he had dug from a neighbor's garden the night before, were placed in soil within a cracked pottery jar which the two kept for just such an occasion. She pulled a juicy worm out and, grinning watched it wriggle between her fingers.

It was early morning, and grandfather was in the building with her father and mother. They sorted through new supplies sent from Scrobbesbyrig, Gloucester, or one of the other smaller villages along the River Severn in the West Midlands. She had seen some from Bristol, which was up the River Avon, beyond the hills to the east of where she sat. In the afternoon, the goods would be loaded and shipped to the Londinium market place to a merchant who accepted the man-made goods of the area as well as wool from the midlands of Mercia.

A boat to take the newly filled, wooden boxes was anchored on the opposite side of the dock from where she stood. The ship obscured the view to the southern part of the large Severn Estuary and the open sea several miles beyond.

Unafraid of her sticky bait, she pushed her wriggling victim onto the hook. Dropping the line back into the water, she sat down on the wooden planks, swinging her legs over the area of slightly dingy water which flowed from the River Avon into the estuary. She could see the fish swimming below. They congregated here when they saw her shadow because she fed them scraps of food from the family table—she fed them and they in turn fed her. Briallen loved to fish and, with any luck she hoped to snag enough from the massive Severn Estuary to provide a fresh catch for the night meal.

"Are you getting any bites?" Her father, Elis, shut the door and strode from the store onto the dock, his steps echoing across the silently flowing water. He sat down next to her on the wooden boards, putting his arm around his young daughter.

"I don't think any of them are hungry." Briallen jiggled the line in the water, watching the fish follow her hooked worm.

"Have patience. You'll hook some," he offered words of encouragement.

Elis looked around the area. Behind them to the east, a line of steep hills poked out of the earth with a deep vee where the River Avon cut a path in their midst. The stream flowed into the Severn Estuary, leaving a light brown path of silt in the Severn's current from the downpour of rain in the far mountains which had raised the River Avon's height during the night.

Barely visible across the way was the coastline of Wales with its alluvial flatlands which swept back from the river's edge, until they met with their own share of hills to the west. There were no sheep on the coastal lands, because of the Severn's tidal bore and tendency to rise quickly and trap them in its floods. The flat land with its rich soil was planted in crops to harvest. Somehow, they managed to survive the countless moods of the waterway.

"Are you and grandfather finished with sorting your new collection of goods?"

"Almost. We are counting and sorting into bales, chests, and barrels for loading onto this ship." Elis looked around at the sea-going boat behind him. Sails would be unfurled when it reached the open sea on its way to Londinium. He loved the sight of a ship under sail—the white material bulging with the wind.

"Briallen, I've been thinking. Grandfather and I might make shipping crates. We could use them ourselves, and if we are good enough, we might sell them to other people who ship goods in containers. We need good tight chests and barrels for the trip to Londinium, especially in dangerous storms, and some of those we have are cobbled together. They aren't made well. This would mean more work for the men along the Avon and Severn, and we might even expand our building here at the wharf or start a new one in Bristol."

"Well, father, if you are going to make barrels, why don't you make ships too?"

Elis laughed. "You have a far-fetched idea there, little girl. But, maybe buying or renting one would do. Then we could sell our wool directly to the Franks, rather than go through other merchants." He sat for a moment considering his daughter's suggestion. Getting up, he said, "I'd better go help. Look, you're getting a bite."

Sure enough, Elis stayed long enough to help Briallen pull in her first fish of the day. It flopped around on the wooden dock until he caught it and put it on a stringer, hanging it on a post attached to the wharf. He returned to the store and entered under a sign saying, *Eggen-Merchant and Trader.*

〜

After fishing for several hours, Briallen needed one more fish to make a good meal for her family. It was hot, she was sweating, and the birds had given up in the afternoon heat. She tugged at the sleeve of her shirt, loosening it from her clammy arm. Her ears perked up when she heard the sound of splashing like multiple oars in the water. This wasn't unusual, because ships plied the river waters almost every day, so she didn't get up to check on the noise.

The sound came closer until the dragon nose of a Viking ship appeared behind the ship moored to the dock. Suddenly, the warm world turned cold. Chill bumps raised on her exposed arms. Her face paled. She sucked in her breath and froze in shock, sitting very still like the wooden figures she'd seen in the church at Bristol.

Would the ship head up the River Avon, within feet of where she sat? No. It went on north. Another ship passed. And then another. After five or six, she laid her fishing pole aside and rising, she walked slowly, deliberately to the store. With her hand on the latch, she turned to look at the malevolent sight on the river. The massive Severn Estuary was full of the hated Viking ships heading north.

Bursting through the door, she shouted, "Father! Come and look. The Vikings," was all she could get out as she entered, doubling over and gasping for air—not because she was out of breath, but because she was horrified at seeing the emblem of death and destruction she'd heard so much about. "There's a hundred boats!"

"What on earth child?" her mother exclaimed, observing her ashen face and coming to her. Surely, she was exaggerating. The two males rushed from the store.

Briallen burst out crying, tears running down her cheeks. "What's happening, mother? Why are they here? Are they going to kill us?"

"Can't be anything good," replied her mother, wrapping her arms around her daughter to calm her. "I hope your brother will be safe." She would naturally think of her son who was outside of her warm nest and who might possibly be in harm's way, depending on the intentions of the Vikings.

Elis and grandfather re-entered the building. "Looks like a major invasion. None of them stopped here. I wonder where they're headed?" Grandfather put into words everyone's thoughts.

"Is there any way we could get a message to the Mercian or Wessex rulers?" asked Elis.

"Not likely," responded grandfather. "The Viking's will be upon someone before we could get halfway there. What about Alric and Meta? They're with the Mercian forces at Tamworth." Alric was Briallen's oldest brother. Meta was a son of Elis's brother who lived in Scrobbesbyrig, manning the business there.

"Father, we don't know where they are at present. Hopefully, they're at Tybbington with our relatives for the after-harvest feasting," responded Elis, as the older man went to the window to check the river again.

"Surely, there's some way King Edward will be warned. Don't you think he has an alert system in place for just such a situation as this?" Elis's wife took her apron and wiped the tears from Briallen's cheek.

"The river's empty," noted the older man, as the last dragon tail disappeared from view. "The men who came down the River Avon last week said King Edward was already fighting a group of Vikings in Wessex. These may be heading to join them. They'll probably land at Gloucester, take the town, and move south and east. We can only hope the King and his sister will be ready for these barbarian heathens."

"Elis, what if they come back this way on their way home?" His wife continued, thinking the worst. "Maybe we should get on the boat and go to Londinium until this is over."

"You may be right. But for now, let's go to the Church and pray for the boys and our country. We'll decide on a course of action when we come back."

~

Æthelflaed sat with her brother, Edward the Elder, in the throne room of the newly restored castle at Tamworth. She had just given him permission to take Mercia under his control—all the territory, from Chester in the north and including Londinium and Oxford—the furthest cities under her rule. Her husband, the Lord of Mercia, was sick to the point of death, and she wished to save the area that they'd fought for and won back from the Vikings. Also, she was anxious to talk to Edward about news which had been whispered in her ear this morning. "Is it true that the Vikings have entered the River Severn with a large contingent of boats and fighting men?"

"That's what the spies who arrived this morning say."

"Where do you think the invaders are going?"

King Edward got up from his chair and started pacing the floor. "Where else but into the south, to Wessex, to join the others we're fighting and take back the parts of the Danelaw they've lost. For sure to divide our kingdoms, yours from mine, and make us weaker."

She watched him as he continued to walk. "What will you do?"

"I'll head on south, once our meeting is done. I have already sent messengers to call up some more of the Fyrd, and we will engage them before they can cause much more destruction in Wessex. I have many hundreds of men in the southern villages besides those who are already fighting who will be ready to take arms and fight. The few men I have here will join them. We'll go around beyond Dudda Hill and stay inland. I don't want to alert the Danes before I'm ready. Maybe we can push them back to the Severn and send them on their way home."

"When you do that, there's only one way they can go." Æthelflaed looked at her brother with a knowing smile.

"Why?" he asked, wondering what she knew that he didn't know. He stopped pacing in front of her.

"Because the men I have on the border of Mercia at the River Severn have orders to scuttle or burn any empty Viking or suspicious boats left on the river. There's no mistaking a Danish ship. They won't be able to leave by boat, so to access a safe territory like Northumbria, or get to the western coast and hopefully escape to Ireland, they must come northeast right into our hands — that is if you and your army can prevail against them and send them this way." She couldn't help but needle him, although fighting a war was a serious and deadly business. "Once they leave the Severn, you'll need to send part of your army to block them. This means they can't go back to the river, find other boats, and sail away."

Edward smirked, "Dear sister, get ready. We'll drive them right into your worthy hands. What's the rest of your plan?"

"I have more, but I'll need your help. My plot is one I've been contemplating for some time, ever since they started this latest rampage. If it works out, the Danes' back will be broken and their hold on Mercia and Wessex will be finished forever."

Æthelflaed reduced her voice to a whisper and proceeded to tell her brother the basics of her strategy.

King Edward kept nodding, agreeing with her words. Finally, Edward said, "I think our father would be proud of his two children."

"Yes, and we should be proud of him. He was a man of courage with a strong sense of duty, a lover of books and the Church, and one who understood the necessities of war, although he hated to fight them. Without his system of burhs and his building of our army and navy, where would we be today? We wouldn't have much of a chance against the marauding Danes."

"Then let's implement your plan," Edward nodded again. "I'll leave Tamworth in the morning at daybreak, if you can spare a guide who knows the area — go east of Dudda Hill. You get ready. The Danes will be here before you know it."

In the July heat of early morning, Æthelflaed stood in the courtyard of the palace at Tamworth. Her brother mounted his horse to leave. "Remember, Sister, make haste to execute your plan," he called.

Edward spurred his white horse, turned, and trotted it to the main gate of the castle, waving as he rode through.

Æthelflaed walked across the courtyard grass to the open portal and watched as he crossed the bridge over the River Anker, the clatter of his horse's hooves sending a loud but firm noise from its surface. "God speed, Edward," she mouthed the words, sending them along as a prayer for his safety.

～

As he crossed the bridge, King Edward pulled in a lungful of air. *Another battle. When will my country be one of peace? Why can't the wars end?*

Miles to the south, beyond the marsh and the woods, beyond the southern hills, the valiant men of Wessex were fighting without waiting on him. They would willingly die for him and he for them in battle. What lay beyond for the Fyrd, for Wessex and Mercia? From this morning's report, he had no way of knowing. He urged his horse forward, joining his chief officers for his ride to the southern Kingdom and his army beyond Warwick. Once he knew the enemy's strategy, the battle would continue with England's greatest rival. He and his sister had a plan, and God willing, he intended to keep his part of the scheme.

～

Æthelflaed walked back to the castle and up the steps into her audience chamber. Calling to her Steward, she gave him orders to send riders for the closest ealdormen and reeves of these western Midlands. The men were overlords of areas of the Kingdom or the heads of towns. This is how Tybbington and the descendants of Tybba became involved in the Battle of Tettenhall.

～

When the order came to meet the Lady of Mercia at Tamworth, Alric and Meta were at Tybbington enjoying the end of sheep shearing season and feasting with their extended family from Wodensbyri and the surrounding area. The harvest was in full swing, with carts of food for humans being deposited in communal, underground root cellars and animal silage in grain storage or haystacks in the fields. For one of the two young men, this was a time when he could flex his muscles and show off for the young girls and his relatives.

"Meta, do you see the young girl tending the children while their mothers work at preparing tonight's feast?" Alric discreetly pointed to a beautiful girl with dark curls in a short, sleeveless tunic which showed more curves than her shapely legs and arms. She and the children played hide and seek. They ran between baskets and tall stacks of other supplies, the children squealing with sounds of delight when caught. Since it was hot, she was taking a break, vigorously using a fan she held in her hand, which caused her curls to wave in its rush of air.

"She's got a hot way to have fun for the month of July," was Meta's comment, noticing her pause to cool off.

"No, Meta. I wasn't even talking about her actions. Don't you think she's the loveliest girl you've ever seen?" Alric moved his hands in the shape of a woman's curves.

Now Meta gave her the once over. "Beauty *is* determined in different ways by different people, Alric."

"I should've known not to ask your opinion," Alric said, shaking his head and throwing up his hands in disgust. "I don't need a lecture on how people think, feel, or act. Save that for your scholarly buddies."

Alric walked off, mumbling to himself, and thinking about his cousin.

Meta hadn't been around much since they'd arrived at Tybbington, preferring to travel to Tamworth, where he had a letter of introduction from the Prior of the monastery at Scrobbesbyrig to the Abbot of the monastery at Tamworth. He was warmly welcomed and immediately given a bed in the dormitory. It took only one week for the Abbot to realize that Meta was an exceptional young man, high in morals, and skilled in writing both Latin and English. The Abbot had taken him to the castle where he'd been presented to the Lady of Mercia, who was asking for someone who could read and write both of these languages.

"Alric, where are you going?" Wilfred, the village chieftain, coming toward him interrupted his thoughts. He was waving a piece of parchment in the air.

"Any place away from Meta," a disgusted Alric exclaimed to his relative.

"You shouldn't be so hard on him. He's a little different from you, Alric. Just realize it takes all kinds of people to make up the world, and he's needed as much as you."

"What are you waving around?" asked Alric of Wilfred, not interested in an explanation of his actions, which he knew were wrong and lacking in patience toward his relative. At times, Meta just rubbed him the wrong way.

"This is a summons to Tamworth and into the Lady of Mercia's presence. It specifically asks for Meta to come and bring his cousin. I assume that's you and, of course I'll accompany you as the head of Tybbington. Let's go tell Meta."

With that, the two turned and headed back where Alric had just departed.

After discussing the letter and its contents, Meta asked, "When will we leave?"

"Is tomorrow good for both of you?" asked Wilfred.

"Tomorrow it is," responded Alric, while Meta nodded in assent.

❦ Chapter 11 ❦

Early 900 A.D *or Thereabouts*
Æthelflaed, Battle at Tettenhall, and Meta

Meta stood in the room he was sharing with Alric in the hall at Wodensbyri. The Lady of Mercia had moved from Tamworth with her entourage and soldiers the week before to this recently-built wooden castle.

Wodensbyri would be closer to the area where the actual battle would take place. That is, if everything worked as she and King Edward had planned. And so far, it was. This time, she would orchestrate the battle from where she would be standing and fighting. She would have the advantage of terrain, positioning of men, and numbers. Between her brother's army and her men, they should outnumber the enemy, unless there were more Vikings coming from the River Severn to change the totals. When the time arrived to fight, she would be at the forefront of the charge, leading her army, and Meta would be alongside.

Meta was appointed her official scribe. His duties included being the communication between Æthelflaed, King Edward, and her field officers— anything requiring correspondence or orders written down on parchment, which was keeping him quite busy. This necessitated a table be set up in her presence. In this way, she had immediate access to him at all times. Because her father had insisted on it, the Lady of Mercia could read and write, but at this moment in her life, she had other more important challenges to consider, and she was consumed with them.

Alric, his cousin, was appointed as one of the runners, between the men in the field and Meta, taking the most important messages back and forth. Meta realized this wasn't Alric's dream job, and he really wasn't sure what was. So far, no major squabbles had risen, and his cousin had accepted the job as an honor.

Meta walked to a small window where a table with stool was positioned. Several goose feathers from the tip of the bird's wings rested atop the wooden stand along with some small hollow reeds. He sat down and took out his small pen knife. Meticulously, he removed the feathers and left the hollow quill. Cutting the nib or point at an angle using his knife, he carefully split the end from the nib upward to the precise location he preferred. When he dipped the pen into his inkwell, the cut would wick the black iron gall ink onto the nib, just in the right amount.

Holding the quill up to the bright rays of the sun, coming through the window, he could barely see a tiny shaft of light in the slit. Taking another quill, he did the same—angle at the end and slit upward until he had them all ready to use.

"Cousin' are you going to make pens out of the reeds? Aren't they outdated?" asked Alric, who had come into the room and now stood by at his table.

"Yes, they are, but if they worked for the Romans for hundreds of years, I can still use them in a pinch," returned Meta. He took the little hollow reeds and prepared them to look the same as the goose's quills. They would be kept as backup to the feather pens which were more resilient and those he preferred.

Alric stood watching Meta test his work on the quills and reeds. "When do you think we'll move camp and go into battle?" He knew the scribe would know the answer to his question. He was privy to everything going on in the Kingdom.

"Our Lady hasn't said a word, and even if she did, I couldn't tell you," said Meta, gathering his new quill pens and carefully putting them in a leather pouch, one-at-a-time.

"I sure wish there was something to do. Standing, sitting, and eating is a tedious and dull way to spend the hours in the day." Alric was kidding his cousin, of course. "Speaking of eating, I think I'm hungry. In fact, I'm sure I smell food." Alric winked at Meta and left the room.

"You might find someone and practice your fighting skills," Meta threw after him as the door closed. He shook his head. *Alric never changes*, he thought. With his quills ready to use, he gathered the rest of his writing tools, ink stand, and the bottle of ink which was sent from the monastery at Tamworth. Getting prepared ink was easier than making his own, which required time he didn't have. He headed for Æthelflaed's throne room. The Lady had sent for him.

⤳

When Meta entered the room, Æthelflaed was bent over a rough map of the area and in a deep conversation with the chief officer of her royal army. She motioned for him to join them. "Here," she pointed to a place on the large parchment before her. "This is where I want most of the army to hide on the western side, on the hill above Smestow Brook."

"But, my Lady, that's just not a good place for our men to be. They'll be caught between the brook and the marshland below and unable to move. We'll be slaughtered." The man was dressed in his mail with a long knife on his right side and his beautifully etched sword with gold hilt in its gilded scabbard which was attached by a wide leather belt on the left. He carried his matching engraved helmet with gold trim in his hand. A gold cross with jewels hung around his neck and swung loose in the air as he bent over to peruse the map. One way to tell an officer's importance in the army was the amount and quality of armour he wore and carried. This man looked the part of high rank.

"You don't understand. Here's my hope, sir." Æthelflaed, who was dressed simply in a loose-fitting, knee-length tunic and sandals, drew back from the map, straightened to her full height, and looked pointedly at her officer. "If Edward confronts them where I think he will, the Danes will be headed north on the western side of the plateau. They'll probably not want to cross the plateau but follow it until they reach a good place to go directly northeast toward safer territory in Northumbria. The River Stour, running on the western side of the plateau, is ideal for them to get water and, as a directional guide, it will funnel them straight into our hands. I want to hit them at several points along the Stour and retreat to ensure the army comes here.

She bent back over the map and put her finger in the place she'd indicated before. "The ones caught in the marshland will be them—not us. If I remember correctly, this area has a flat field with less undergrowth. The hills aren't as pronounced as they are to the north or south and another small stream flows into the Smestow here," she pointed to a new black line indicating the stream bed.

"In fact, if it's possible, we may dig trenches and divert some water out of the area, making the marshes appear dryer and easier to traverse. Once King Edward is sure the Danes are headed toward safety in the north, he will send messengers to us, come from the south, and position himself on the east bank facing us on this high ground." She pointed to the east bank of the brook, tapping the area with her finger. "Both armies will seem to disappear into the trees. Our soldiers will be on dry ground on either side of the Smestow Brook. We will meet the Danes in the middle."

"How will you ensure they come up the River Stour?" the officer relented a bit.

"At this moment, Edward has stopped them on their rampage south and he's got men to keep them from returning to the River Severn, where hopefully my men have burned most or all of their ships. Once Edward sees they're headed north, he will slowly squeeze them in this direction and specifically toward the River Stour. This is all a matter of timing, and we've been good at that in the last months."

She continued, "The Vikings aren't the only ones who can make sneak attacks. So, we will give them a taste of their own medicine, through a variety of sneak attacks — not with our full army, but with a contingent on fast horses for just such a purpose. Secreted on and riding off from the hilly plateau at different points along the river, they will attack the front lines and retreat quickly, always heading north, following the stream and harassing the enemy. I'm hoping to keep the Danes off-balance and confused, thinking we Mercians are weak and afraid to stand and fight, drawing them further into our trap." Æthelflaed kept moving her finger until it rested on a place near Tettenhall and Wednesfield. "Our horsemen will continue in this direction, which will lead the Danish to this clearer lowland area, and to the major battle we've planned for them here."

"The Danes will be caught between our two armies," he agreed. "Do you want me to go and check out your battle plan?"

"Yes, exactly. You have a day-and-a-half to report back, because there's much to be done. If there's any complications before then, you'll get written notice from Meta." She nodded her head toward her scribe and continued, "We intend to keep everyone up to date on the plan, especially if it changes." She dismissed the royal officer with a wave of her hand. "Go, for we don't have much time to get ready."

"I understand, my Lady." He nodded his assent and bowed as he backed away and left the chamber.

Meta had witnessed this whole conversation. He was amazed at how fast the officer went from doubting to agreeing. With new admiration, he turned to look at Æthelflaed. She was skillful and decisive with her officer. She also understood the aggressor her army would face and spoke with authority about her battleplan. Meta's respect grew for his Lady, and he realized as many said, she was definitely like the late King Alfred, her father. He was privileged to do her bidding.

Æthelflaed turned to him. "Meta, send a message to King Edward. Just to make sure he remembers, spell out the plans you've just heard and inquire of him regarding his progress in the battle. Send your fastest horseman to deliver it, and the messenger is to tell my brother we need a reply straightway as to his progress." She started to walk off. "And, I need one to the armourer. Tell him to come to me at once. I want him and his men to get supplies ready to move at a moment's notice, and to set up camp above Tettenhall immediately. He's to return here once they are finished. When we receive news from my senior captains as to the viability of my battle plan, which I think will work, we'll all go to our field camp, and we won't come back here until the battle's over. With God's help, we will prevail."

As the Lady turned and went to her private chapel to pray, Meta sat down to write her orders, sending the first one by her Steward to the armourer. When it was on the way, he started with the battle plans to King Edward.

~

Alric turned his horse southward, giving a wide berth to the possibility of confronting Vikings on his route. He rode toward the last known position of King Edward's army, knowing this could change, because the last rider had left there two days ago. The letter to the Wessex ruler was in a pouch slung around his neck. His orders were to die rather than let it get into the Danes' hands. He doubted they could read it anyway, because it was written in Old English instead of Latin or any other writing they might understand.

~

The message Alric returned from King Edward said the results of their strategy was going according to plan. His army was almost at a point where the Lady's plan of attack and retreat could start. In three days, he would pull back part of his army and head north to position himself in the area on the east side of Smestow Brook, toward Wednesfield. She was to keep him posted on any further movements he needed to make.

~

"My Lady, they're coming," said Meta, pointing to movement as he looked south toward the brook. The tension was high as Æthelflaed, Meta, Alric, the senior officers and the Lady's personal guard of ten men crowded themselves into a blind made by cutting and piling limbs from trees in a U-shape around them. The brush was high enough so that they could see out, but no one could see inside. The rest of the army was enclosed in the thick forest immediately behind, awaiting orders—some had horses, some were on foot.

"You have good eyes, Meta. I can't see them at all."

Meta stood on the ground, peering through a hole cut head-high for that purpose. His horse's reins tied to a limb in the enclosure so he could freely move around the tight area. "Yes, I do," he agreed, looking up at his leader and then back to his assignment. The writing materials were gone and his armour on as he waited like the rest of the army. "The movement seems unorganized and slow. They seem uncertain as to their path. Some are climbing above the banks of the stream."

For a second, the woman felt a stab of anxiety. Were they going to turn the wrong way and thus thwart her best plan? Handing the reins of her horse to Alric, she dismounted and went to stand by Meta, needing to see for herself — watching the Viking's uncertain movement.

"See, my Lady. Down by the willows along the bank." Meta pointed and Æthelflaed followed his line of sight. The break in the hills to the south had, as she hoped, funneled the Vikings straight up the brook toward them.

"Yes, I do see, and someone who must be in command is riding a horse to the front and pointing this way. Oh, there's another rider who's pointing east." She held her breath as an obvious argument ensued, watching to find out the direction of the moving crowd of men. The easiest way for them to travel was straight ahead up the brook, but quicker territory lay to the right or directly east across the Mercian hills and through a more hostile territory. "I wonder which leader will win and where they got their horses," murmured Æthelflaed. The Danes were almost always on foot.

Either way, the Danish Vikings would face the wrath of the combined Mercian and Wessex forces, because Edward was in place across the brook on top of a hill. But the plan would work perfectly and be executed swiftly if they headed up the brook. Instead of days of tough fighting, the battle she'd planned would only take hours.

The second rider threw up his hand in disgust. The first Dane had won the discussion. "They're headed up the brook," she told everyone. "Remember to tell me to thank him, if he still has a head at the end of the day," said the Lady, with a thin, grim smile to no one in particular. She went back to her horse. "We wait until we're sure most of them are in the area." She waved her hand toward the now drained marshes and the stream directly ahead.

In her early forties, Æthelflaed took the reins of her black horse from Alric. The animal was one of the descendants of the horses given to King Offa by the Tybbington's. She made an impressive figure when she sat astride her saddle — the reins held lightly in her gloved hands. Her back straight. Her head high. She was just at that stage of maturity when her face revealed the hardships she'd been through and the experience she'd gained through making difficult decisions. Not necessarily a beautiful woman in appearance, but a stunning leader for Mercia, she was in the prime-of-life. Her beauty lay in the unknown mystery behind the determined expression on her face. What was she thinking? How did she feel?

She was dressed in a coat-of-mail with a sword and knife on her belt. Her lower legs were swathed in layers of leather held on with tightly laced straps which were crisscrossed, front to back, to keep the material firmly in place. Leather boots covered her feet for protection against being injured in battle. The gloves went to her elbows. Since most of her army did not wear helmets, neither did she — her dark hair fell in waves down her back. Helmets were hot and cumbersome and made turning your head to give orders much harder—she needed to be seen and heard. Her shield, made out of thin metal with engravings of birds and trees, was lighter than the wooden ones carried by her men. This was her only concession to being a woman and their leader. As a great communicator, she was also known as a "peace weaver," or negotiator. She could also plan a battle and, today, she would show the Danes she could fight.

In the elongated valley before her and along Smestow Brook, she watched breathlessly as the Vikings with their dreaded battle axes moved slowly toward the marsh. Draining the water from the area had worked like a charm. The Mercians had built up the edge of the Smestow so water could not run into a low area where it had been caught in a pool. They dug another channel for the pool at the lower end, letting the water run free. For five days, the sun had beat down on the emptied area, causing a crust to form on the surface of the soil. Underneath was an unwelcome surprise—sticky, sucking mud. And the farther a person walked upstream, the more the ground gave way because the water was not as well drained, and the path became marshland again. This happened on the other side of the brook in another low-lying area, making both sides a walking nightmare.

The fact that it hadn't rained in England for five days was a marvel in itself, and Æthelflaed hoped this was a good sign for the imminent battle.

The Lady watched the advance of the Vikings. At first, the path was dry, but as the raiding army advanced, the crust broke and walking became harder.

The ones who could walk faster over firmer ground soon piled up behind the first ones who were becoming stuck and slowing down in the deepening mud. Tempers flared, arms waved, and shouting voices carried up the hill to the waiting army of Mercians. Æthelflaed thought, *like rats-in-a-trap*. Then she sighed. Like her father, she did not like killing people.

Nor did she like sending men to their death. That was one reason she led her army into battle. If necessary, she would die with them and for her country. What other death could be more glorious?

She mounted her horse and pulled her sword from its sheath. "What can you see now, Meta. Is there an end in sight?"

"No, my Lady. Not yet. But the line is thinning and narrowing, mostly stragglers I would venture to guess."

The Lady of Mercia turned to her officers and said, "With God's help the battle will be ours." She waited another moment and shouted, "Mount up! It's time to go." With that comment, she rode out of the blind with her sword held high, "For Mercia and Wessex!" she shouted, loud enough for the men in the trees to hear.

She was followed by everyone but Meta. He had to mount his skittish horse, which the quickness of the riders' leaving had startled. After calming the animal down, he rode hard to catch up with the others, joining the fight just after it had started.

Chapter 12

Early 900 A.D *or Thereabouts*

The Battle at Tettenhall, Meta and Alric

All was pandemonium when Meta reached the battlefield. Æthelflaed, who had ridden down the hill from the west of Smestow Brook followed by her army of Mercians, was already in the midst of the battle. Her sword flashed in the sunlight. Meta headed for her. He had decided she was his responsibility.

The Vikings who were stuck in the mud and those who weren't turned to fight the approaching army. Normally very organized, their ragged lines spoke of the battle plan's effectiveness. With their red and black colored shields at the ready, they stood and fought, even though the outcome was now in some doubt. The stragglers coming up the rear gave a loud scream and started running to help those already fighting, the dreaded battle axe raised to strike.

Unbeknownst to those already in the melee, King Edward sat on his horse, waiting, watching until the Viking stragglers were all in the area of the fighting.

"Sire, the laggards are there."

King Edward turned to look at his chief officer. It was time. He nodded in acquiescence. "Then let's go help Æthelflaed." He urged his horse forward and appeared in the open field — sword raised. "For Mercia and Wessex," he yelled and spurred his horse again.

When the Danish men realized what was happening, it was too late. The trap was sprung. The King and his men first fought the ones closest to them, and then they crossed the brook to fight the ones engaged with Æthelflaed's men. Hundreds swarmed the area. Swords and battle axes flashed in the sun. Wounded and dying cried out in pain. The area was filled with bodies — bodies stacked on each other. The smell of blood, open wounds, and urine was prominent and sickening.

After several minutes, the water in the brook turned bright red with the mingling of the blood of both armies and flowed toward the River Stour, making a path of pink and staining the clear water of both streams. A mile downstream, the meandering water was clear. No one would guess that an epic and deadly battle was taking place upstream — one that would bring an uneasy peace and the beginning of the end of the Danish invasions into Mercia and Wessex.

~

Meta guided his horse toward Æthelflaed, slashing with his sword as he went. Suddenly, he couldn't see her. Her horse had tripped — something on the ground. He watched as she went over the animal's head.

He reached her just as she was likely to be killed or badly wounded. A Viking was engaging her from the front while one ran quickly toward her from the rear, battle axe raised. "My Lady," he yelled in the din of battle around him, trying to warn her. The noise of the fight drowned out his words.

The Lady of Mercia would be a prize kill — one full of glory for the person doing the deed, and it was a certain end to the battle. The hopes of the Saxons winning the day would be destroyed.

Meta's horse lunged forward as he kicked it violently with his foot. He gave another blood-curdling yell, which scared him as much as it did the fighters around him, and swung his sword at the combatant.

Æthelflaed, whose assailant had fallen to the ground, turned just as he hit her attacker.

Meta stared. The Viking's hand and battle axe fell to the ground. As the blade dropped, it grazed his Lady on her forearm.

The Viking stood looking in shock at where his hand had been. Blood gushed from the wound onto another dead fighter — the one Æthelflaed's horse had tripped over.

Meta knew he should finish the man off, but he was saved the task when Alric appeared with his sword.

The soldier fell to the ground. His helmet struck the foot of another downed man and came off.

Meta, Alric, and Æthelflaed looked on in astonishment. The person who'd almost killed the Lady of Mercia was a woman.

∾

The battle did not rage much longer. In the end, the fight was a clear victory for the Mercian and Wessex forces. While Æthelflaed and King Edward returned to Wodensbyri to rest and recuperate, others of their army were left to mop up the battlefield, taking anything of value—an act which was expected of the winner. They would finish off any Danes lingering on the edge of death.

Meta stood on the hill above the brook below, looking at the carnage scattered across the field and stream. "Wolves of slaughter," he murmured, going over and stroking the nose of his horse.

"What did you say?" asked Alric who stood with him, surveying the dead and dying.

"Wolves of slaughter," repeated Meta and then he explained. "The Vikings are sometimes referred to as people who love to kill and kill without mercy—like wolves. It's really interesting that the wolves who kill will be eaten by the very wolves which are their symbol."

Alric looked at him and shook his head. What was he saying? He'd never understand his cousin.

"And, the wolves will *feed the eagles.*" Meta grinned at Alric, knowing what he was thinking. "We don't want to come back here for a long time. The area will be full of wolves and birds who feed on carrion. There will be another fight. One over who gets the choicest parts of the corpses strewn over the field."

"I'll never understand you," stated Alric.

"My dear cousin, did it ever occur to you that you don't have to? We only need to understand what is common between us. The rest is better left alone." Meta's attention was directed toward a rider on horseback. "Is that someone coming for us?"

"Meta, the Lady would like for you to come back to Wodensbyri," the man said as he drew near.

Meta mounted his horse and looked down at his cousin. "Alric, I suppose you stay here. I'll send for you if she needs you also."

～

Meta hurried to his room to change from his bloody clothes, and then he went straight to the Lady of Mercia's throne room. King Edward was not there, but the captains of the army were, along with several other people. Most he did not recognize except for his relative, Wilfred, who smiled quickly at him. Æthelflaed stood in the center of the room. Seeing him, she called him forward.

"My Lady," he bowed to her, noticing that her arm was bandaged from the axe's fall during the battle. He waited for her to speak.

Æthelflaed did not delay but said, "Meta, you saved my life at Tettenhall." She was holding her sword in her hand as she talked and walked.

"My Lady, I just happened to get there at the right moment." Meta was embarrassed to be called out specifically by her in front of the others in the room. He preferred to be in the background and not noticed.

"No. If you hadn't gotten to me when you did, I would have more than a binding on my arm. Because of your bravery, I'm giving you my sword to commemorate your deed." She came and stood in front of him, holding out the metal blade which flashed in the sun streaming through an open window. "May it save you in battle, as yours did me." She smiled at him, her eyes saying, "thank you."

Meta was astonished and humbled. He took the sword and said, "Thank you, my Lady. I'll treasure it always."

Æthelflaed turned, saying she was going to the chapel to give thanks for their victory. As she walked away, Wilfred came up and gave his relative a quick embrace. "You are honored, Meta. When will you be coming back to Tybbington?"

The Lady of Mercia stopped as she heard the question. "He's much needed here, but I'll see that he goes home to Scrobbesbyrig soon, and he can use some of that time to visit you, Wilfred."

"Thank you, my Lady," said Wilfred, bowing as she turned and left.

Later, in the quiet of his room, Meta examined the sword. It was unusual because it had a crossguard which protected the user's hand in combat. The Stafford knot was engraved on the slightly curved guard, but words in Latin also appeared on both sides of the blade. He went to the window and read, *'Strike Hard'* and on turning the blade over he discovered the words, *'We Are Bound As One.'*

~

Alric headed down Smestow Brook toward the River Stour. Two days had passed since the end of the Tettenhall battle. His mission today was checking bodies and making sure no one survived. The farther he rode, the less he had to do, and he hadn't found anyone alive all morning. He was about to head back to Tettenhall when one more suspicious shape caught his attention.

As he had ridden downstream, the edge of the brook had become a tangle of willows and alders with roots growing down the steep bank. The depth had increased the more distance he covered and now it was four or five feet to the bottom. Because his vision wasn't clear, he couldn't tell for sure if the object was a person, but whatever the thing was, it was entangled in the roots or holding on to them. Suddenly the man coughed and with one hand, he grasped the root of a tree while floating in the water.

Alric rode close to the river bank and looked across. The warrior, still dressed in his coat-of-mail, coughed again. There were no obvious signs of other military equipment. Assessing the situation and realizing that the Danish Viking was perhaps dying, Alric almost left him in the stream, but he'd been charged with not leaving anyone alive. He prodded his horse off the bank through the brush and into the water, letting it swim down to the floating man, who turned his head to look at him.

His horse found footing, and Alric raised his sword to put the wounded man out of his misery. He stopped. Something in the young man's eyes said to him, "No." Alric almost dropped his sword in the creek. Why this one? What explained his reluctance to dispatch this one as he'd done with the others?

"What is your name?" Alric asked, knowing you never asked an adversary their name. This personalized the victim, making them harder to kill.

The young man started coughing again. Finally, he was able to say faintly, "I am Alwin. Alwin of the York Dales."

~

More than one problem was solved at the Tettenhall battle in 910. The Tybbingtons now learned what had happened to Dever after he departed from Tamworth with the daughter of King Offa for her marriage to King Æthelred I.

And young Alwin did survive. Years later, when it was safe, he returned home with a wife he'd chosen from his extended family at Tybbington.

Along with the loss of hundreds of men at the battle of Tettenhall, two of the Danish Kings, Healfdene and Eowils, were also killed with several other leaders of the Vikings. Their defeat meant the last great raiding army of the Danes was annihilated. There would never be another even close to this size, even though there would be other battles.

Æthelflaed's husband, the Lord of the Mercians, died a year after the battle in 911. Æthelflaed took complete control of Mercia. She and Edward conducted more successful campaigns into Danish territory. Finally, the leaders of York (Northumbria) pledged to her their loyalty. Before she could go to York and accept the homage of the people, she died — seven years after the passing of her husband. She was buried at St. Oswald's Priory in the town of Gloucester on the Severn River below Scrobbesbyrig.

In the end, she became more influential than her brother King Edward of Wessex, developing into one of the most trusted and respected women to wear a crown in England.

After having a daughter, she took a vow of chastity. But then, she raised a foster son, King Edward's illegitimate child, Æthelstan, who succeeded him to become the King of the united Mercian, Wessex, and York kingdoms — known as England.

❦ Chapter 13 ❦

The Next Years, After 1050 A.D
William of Normandy and The Following Kings of England

Even though Æthelflaed, Edward the Elder, and Æthelstan conquered the Danish Vikings and sent them scurrying north above the Humber Estuary on the English Isle, this did not keep the Vikings from invading and fighting wars with other countries such as France. Ironic, that in the end, the descendants of these four would fight again. This time the results would be reversed, and this change would last.

The King in England, January 1066, was the recently enthroned Earl of Wessex, Harold Godwinson. His ascent to the throne, on the death of his predecessor, King Edward—known as the Confessor—was marred by promises of succession from the former King to others, some on his deathbed, and the assumed rights to the throne by these three men.

Almost immediately after becoming the monarch, Godwinson had to defend his Kingdom.

In the summer, Harold Hardrada, King of Norway, joined with Godwinson's own estranged brother, the Anglo-Saxon, Tostig. Hardrada sailed up the Humber Estuary and the River Ouse to capture York. The two conspirators became the first threat to Godwinson's reign.

While Hardrada and Tostig rested from this battle victory, Godwinson, to defend his territory, marched his army north on a hard journey which covered one hundred eighty miles in four days.

The two armies met in September on a flat field at Stamford Bridge in Yorkshire.

The battle was hard fought until Hardrada was killed by an arrow to the neck. Later in the fight, Tostig also died.

After possibly hundreds of men lost their lives, Godwinson prevailed. But his victory was short lived. In late summer, ominous news came from the south of England.

Another threat to his Anglo-Saxon Kingdom was taking shape from an unexpected area. This danger was not from the northeast, and not in the direction of the sunrise, but from the south and across the English Channel, and it changed the country forever.

From France, William, Duke of Normandy—the illegitimate son of Robert I, Duke of Normandy— invaded England in 1066, claiming the throne had been previously promised to him by Edward the Confessor, the last Anglo-Saxon King and his relative.

William was one of the descendants of Rollo, a Viking of the late ninth century, who invaded France in 911—the year Aethelflaed's husband, the Lord of Mercia, died.

William, as claimant to the English throne, sailed his ships from Normandy in France to Pevensey in Sussex (southern England seacoast). After landing on English soil with seven thousand men, he headed for Hastings.

Godwinson rushed back from York to confront him. His troops fatigued from the confrontation with Hardrada and the difficult journey to London, he stayed in the city for a week to recuperate. This weariness may have been one reason for the final outcome of the Battle of Hastings.

William's forces suffered great losses but managed to oblige Harold Godwinson's army to retreat. The fight seesawed back and forth for a day. Part of William's army included excellent archers—noted for their deadly aim.

Finally, the duke of Normandy prevailed when Godwinson was shot by a well-aimed arrow to the eye and died.

After William's victory, he marched on to London and the city submitted to him. Westminster Abbey was the site of his coronation on Christmas day, 1066.

The Battle of Hastings was the definitive fight which determined the descendant line which would rule England from this time on. The Anglo-Saxon chapter of English rule was finished, and the Normans took over.

Within twenty years, the English ruling class was almost entirely dispossessed and replaced by Norman landholders. They dominated all senior positions in the government and the Church and conducted business in the French language.

For twenty-one years, William I of Normandy ruled England, although he never spoke the language and was illiterate. Every succeeding King and Queen of England is his descendant.

~

Many changes took place in King William's reign. He introduced the feudal system of government, revolving around who you knew politically and militarily.

The head of the feudal system was the King. Directly under him were overlords or barons who owed allegiance to the King and governed certain larger areas designated by his majesty.

Under the overlords were the Lords who owed allegiance to the overlords and the King. The Lords were apportioned smaller tracks of land called manors from the overlord or baron.

Then the next in the pecking order were the vassals.

The Lord, a large land owner who never physically worked the land, provided his vassals, some of them Knights, with landholdings in return for their assistance in military reinforcement. Hence, we have the Knights practicing military maneuvers as well as managing their fief or estate for the Lord who was over them. This was also the level where some of the Lord's vassals maintained the kingdom's roads and other public works within the landholdings of each Lord.

In the feudal agreement, the Lord swore to protect his vassal and the vassal was provided with a plot of land.

To continue this arrangement, the estate could be inherited by the vassal's heirs, which gave the vassal tenure over the land or fief. If the Lord had several fiefs, his collection was called a fiefdom.

Who actually did the work in the feudal system? The two lowest humans on the feudal totem pole, the peasant and serf. The peasant's labor included back-breaking work, and it followed the seasons—plowing in late autumn, sowing in spring, and harvest in late summer.

Everything a peasant or serf needed was contained within the village where he lived. He made his own clothes, cobbled his own shoes, and grew everyone's food from the King on down. The difference between these two classes of people—the peasant could move freely about the country, own land, and make money, but the serf was bound to the land on which he lived.

If the harvests were of plenty, the peasant and serf ate as well as the Lords, although not prepared to the level of a chef's expertise with spices and condiments which would have been expected in the Lord's residence.

The peasant and serf ate meat stews, leafy vegetables like cabbage, spinach, and leeks, butter, and cheese, along with dark rye bread and oats which were used to thicken the broth of the stews. They drank weak ale, which they brewed, and water.

If the harvest was poor, the peasant and serf were the ones who died first, starving to death.

Under William's authority, the Church was supported by tithes or one-tenth of the population's yearly profit. Some of the current elders of the Church were removed and Normans put in their place. The Church soon owned two-thirds of the English land from which the King, at this time, did not collect taxes.

Did William the Conqueror bring peace to the English isle? No. The fighting continued as he strove to contain the land's Anglo-Saxon natives.

Norman despots and greed soon started bringing unrest to his subjects, resulting in revolts breaking out all over the country. Although his Norman barons were guilty, William burned and slaughtered the Anglo-Saxons into total submission.

Following the brutal onslaught called the Harrowing of the North, large areas of Yorkshire, Cheshire, Shropshire, Staffordshire and Derbyshire were left ruined.

This included Tybba's old home in Staffordshire.

Another action of William was the 1085-6 Great Domesday Survey of England by the Normans. The study was carried out to compile a list of the entire population, their lands, and property for taxing purposes.

13,000 towns were surveyed. The family of Tybba or (Tybbington), listed as Tibintone in the survey was included.

Four hundred years had passed since Tybba's arrival on the River Tame. Not many Tybbington's were listed—only five families.

Where had they gone? Had they moved to other villages? What had happened to them? Did they fight William's forces with honor for their property on the River Tame and perish? No one knows—but, the family did survive.

When the Romans were living on the English isle, Latin was spoken. When the Anglo-Saxons arrived *en-masse*, the West Germanic tribal language soon called Old English (very different from modern English) was brought to the country.

With the arrival of the Normans, French was spoken in the highest echelons of society, but the lower classes, peasant and serf, still spoke the Anglo-Saxon tongue.

The future English language was to become a combination of these three dialects.

One other change was the appearance of motte and bailey castles. Several hundred of these were built by the Normans for their protection. Picture a hill selected for its conical shape, built up with more dirt and rocks, flattened on top where the wooden keep or castle was constructed.

This was where the Lord of the castle lived with his family.

At the bottom of the hill, a small community, which supported the castle occupants, was often established. This included some of the military, under the Knights. It was called a bailey with a deep ditch around it (sort of like a burh). Beside the ditch and surrounding the bailey was a wooden palisade or fence. The ditch or moat could be dry or filled with water.

A drawbridge accessing the whole fortification led to the gate or entrance to the bailey and keep. For 200 years, these motte and bailey castles were immensely popular until the wood started to decay.

Those opposing William soon found out one well-placed, flaming arrow easily destroyed a wooden castle during times of conflict.

Limestone would become the construction choice in the future.

During his reign, King William spent much of his time in France, trying to secure his part of Normandy, protecting it from his overlord, the King of France. He died in France as a result of falling from his horse.

The Plantagenet line of Kings started with Henry II, who became King in 1157. His son was Richard I, the Lionheart, who conducted the Crusades in the Eastern Byzantine

Empire. At Richard's death, his brother, John I, became King of England.

King John had problems with just about everyone.

His levy of taxes to fight losing battles in Normandy and elsewhere caused a rift within the English monarchy—with the barons and the bishops of the Church. Because of these disagreements, the Magna Carta was written and signed. This agreement limited his power and gave the people a "bill of rights" which they could enforce.

The King was a leader who loved the law, but rarely won a battle, giving up much of the English territories. His country was torn by civil strife which ended with the first Baron's War.

John is also remembered for his many illegitimate children. One of whom, Joan, was the wife of Llywelyn the Great, Prince of Wales.

King John's reign was unsteady to say the least. His attempts to add territory on the mainland of England started with the three Welsh Kingdoms. One known as Gwynedd was a particularly prickly thorn in the flesh.

❧ Chapter 14 ❧

1281 A.D

Anthony of Tybbington

The morning was chilly as Anthony of Tybbington walked his horse up the curvy road to Dudley Castle which sat on the top of Dudda Hill—now known as Castle Hill. The nippy air caused him to pull his cloak and arms closer to his body. The farther he climbed, the clearer the humid air became as he left the smoke and smell which hugged the valley from the wood and coal fires below.

Coal was becoming increasingly the heating trend of choice for the inhabitants of Tybbington and was struggling at being the preference for most of England.

The people found it was easier to dig coal than to cut trees, and the black energy lay just beneath the surface and sometimes on the surface of this southern portion of Staffordshire.

The potential to become a rich and successful shire lay a few shovelfuls of dirt away. Boats were starting to haul coal as far away as London and other areas where wood was becoming scarce and expensive.

Upon reaching the bailey of the castle, the gate keeper who was a man from Tybbington recognized him and opened the entry. The entrance squeaked on its iron hinges, as it swung inward, allowing Anthony to enter into the courtyard where he dismounted. He handed his horse's reins to a servant and turned toward the stairs leading to the stone stronghold atop.

Scaffolding, rising to the cloudless sky, meant serious rebuilding was taking place. The first wooden building, a motte and bailey castle type, was torn down by orders of Henry II, because the inhabitant during his reign rebelled against the King.

"Anthony, how are you?" the Constable of the castle called to him. The paunchy, bald-headed man, a distant and older relative of the man he addressed, ambled toward Anthony with a definite limp and waved his hand in welcome. It was his job to oversee the security of the castle grounds and keep the palace operations humming along.

"Wondering why I've been summoned into the baron's presence," responded the uncomfortable Anthony to the Constable. It was almost unheard of for a peasant to be bidden into a nobleman's company.

"I'm not sure, but I have an idea. I'm supposed to go with you."

"Do you have any inkling of why me?"

The Constable grinned at his companion's unease. "Don't worry about this. I can tell you my Lord wanted someone he could trust and who showed a head for detail and figuring, and I recommended you because you are young and literate."

"So, *you* are responsible," stated Anthony.

"I suppose I am in a way."

The two men walked across a courtyard and into the Great Hall of the castle. After entering, the baron's Chamberlain approached. "I'm to take you to one of the smaller chambers toward the living quarters." He turned to the Constable. "I'll call you when Anthony needs to leave. Thank you for escorting him here."

The Constable raised his eyebrows at this statement. "You don't want me to stay?"

"No. That's the orders from Baron Dudley himself."

The unhappy Constable bowed out and Anthony stood in the room with the Chamberlain.

"This way, Anthony."

As he followed the Chamberlain, Anthony looked around at the room.

They passed a huge fireplace at one end of the Great Hall, feeling the heat of large oak logs burning on the hearth as they went by. On another wall was a raised dais with a chair which looked like a throne. It was flanked by two smaller stools.

"What happens there?" he asked, pointing with his hand.

"The Baron administers justice and takes care of the business of the barony with his officers of the court. The tables and chairs," the man waved in the direction of several pushed back to another wall, "are pulled out on feast or ceremonial days."

They continued to walk in silence. The echo of their footsteps sounded against the high ceilings in the room. "We're here."

Anthony followed the Chamberlain into a small room off the main living quarters of the castle. He looked around. The room appeared to be storage for future construction. There was no window and only the one door. Recently lit and glowing candles on stands emitted enough light to see. Two stools, which matched the ones from the Great Hall, were conveniently placed for the conversation which would take place.

Anthony's thoughts were going in circles. *What has the Constable gotten me into?*

Noticing his interest in the items in the room, the Chamberlain explained, "Those are the tapestries which will adorn the Great Hall once all construction is done," the man pointed to several large rolls stacked along the back of the room. "I will tell the Baron you are here."

Anthony was left alone. The longer he waited, the more edgy he became.

Finally, the door opened. Baron Dudley entered the room — alone. He waved some papers in the air and motioned for Anthony to sit down. The baron was clothed in a blue, belted tunic which was short enough to show his black hose and pointed shoes. The shoes were not practical, but were becoming the rage among the nobles of the country. A round, furry black hat which looked like ermine sat atop his head.

"You are Anthony of Tybbington?"

"Yes, Sire. I am."

"Please sit down," the Baron motioned again toward one of the stools, sat down, and pulled his fur-trimmed cloak around him.

Anthony sat, too.

"I asked the Constable for someone I could trust, and he recommended you. You are the caretaker of several acres of land in my local fief and, according to the Constable do a wonderful job of maintaining your fields and animals. Is that right?"

"I do own and manage my acres and animals, understanding what you expect of us who have your confidence, my Lord."

"I have something I want you to do. This is to be done in the *utmost secrecy*. You are to take no one into your confidence, including the Constable. If the real reason for this undertaking is found out, I will deny it to any and all." The baron paused, expecting a response.

"I understand." But did he? Anthony could hardly breathe by this time. The chamber was cold, and he started to shiver. He wished he could get up and leave the place. What was coming next?

"I've always trusted the men who supervise my numerous lands. But the last two or three years, I've had reason to doubt their honesty, or at least, the men they control. Something may be going on underground — well, let's just say I need to know, and I've sent for you to help.

"To cover up the real reason for your mission, this is what I want. The first thing you will do is visit each farm, do a total of individuals and ages, evaluate the operation of the overseer, check and number his storage facilities, and do a counting of the animals which you find in the pastures and the villages." He handed Anthony a paper.

The baron's holdings were extensive and far-flung.

While Anthony looked at the names on the list, the baron continued, handing him several sheets this time. "Here is the listing of the places you will visit, with each sheet pertaining to one property." The baron pointed to one of the papers. "The page contains the kinds of animals which should be raised at each place.

You will write your numbers out from the type of animal. As you can see, we won't cover all my holdings, only certain ones."

The baron leaned toward him and continued in a lower voice, emphasizing his words. *"This is what I'm mainly interested in — the totals on their herds and whether or not there are coal pits being dug on their lands."* The baron paused and then added, "The rest of the survey is just to cover up my real interest."

Anthony looked up from the papers and spoke his thoughts out loud. "The lambing season should be over and the calves already born." He nodded his head at the baron, understanding why he wanted the animal count done at this particular time. "Coal is becoming a money-making operation and expanding rapidly — hard to keep up with if you live on a hill in a castle."

"Yes, exactly," agreed the baron. "As soon as you are done with the list and evaluations, and this may take some time, come back here and turn it in. In six months or so, we will do this again and compare numbers. Here is a letter explaining your reason for being on my lands."

Anthony received another paper. "It says you are inspecting the Baron of Dudley's fiefdom and compiling a list for future reference. You are checking herds for disease and general health. Coal digs are not mentioned, because you will ascertain this by observing, while you complete the survey."

The baron paused a minute to let Anthony look through the papers. Then he continued, "Most of the people you will be dealing with cannot read, so they will accept word-of-mouth and this." The Baron pulled a ring from his hand and gave it to Anthony. "They should recognize my seal because they've seen it before when I visited them and on official documents. Please be careful. There's always danger on this kind of expedition. Take along someone to protect you of your own choosing—someone you trust, but do not tell them the real reason for your task. And in addition, you may need a scribe. Do you understand?"

"Yes, I do. I understand the danger, and I'll start immediately."

"Good, and oh, yes. Here's a pouch in which to store your information and a purse so you can buy food as necessary. Keep them both safe." The baron pulled a leather bag from his shoulder and placed the purse inside. He stood and Anthony stood with him. "You and anyone who helps you will be well compensated for your trouble. Remember, I'm trusting you with something I feel is very important."

The baron started out the door. He turned and said, "Oh yes, when you have laid out your plan, please return to the castle and give the Chamberlain a copy. In this way, I can keep up with your progress should I need to contact you."

Anthony nodded and the baron left the room.

Carefully putting the batch of papers into the pouch, Anthony walked out the door. The Chamberlain came toward him. "The Constable is outside the Great Hall. He will escort you to your horse."

∽

The ride back down the hill was almost as difficult as the one up the hill. Anthony wasn't sure if it was the pouch slung over his shoulder or the heavy responsibility, he had been given which seemed to weigh a ton. He wished he could have said no, but he couldn't.

Protection, why did the baron use this word? Was it because the people who lived on the high hills of England weren't trusted by the people in the lower lands—and if he kept thinking about it, the nobles or elite didn't trust the people who served under them?

How often had he heard his fellow workers in the field say, *"Miserable am I and not free, and I work the field with a heavy heart."* As the baron's chosen emissary, he was a prime example of the mistrust on both sides. When he looked up at the castle, it was always with unease, but he had to agree with the Constable, he was honest in his dealings with the hierarchy living above him.

As he rode toward Tybbington, he was thinking about someone whom he might ask to go with him on this journey. One man stood out in his mind. He made a detour and headed south for his place of abode, passing the priory of St. James where he'd learned to read and write years ago.

John of Tybbington, who was older than Anthony, stood outside his grain mill feeding his chickens when Anthony rode up on his black horse. Recognizing his distant cousin, John waved, placed his wooden bowl on a stool, and strode toward the rider grasping the reins of his horse.

"Anthony, get down and rest." John indicated the stools outside the building in which he lived and worked. Inside, the stone wheels which ground grain into a finer material were at present idle and used only when someone needed to increase their supply of flour for the different kinds of bread they baked.

"I think I'll do just that," said Anthony, as he dismounted. "Your mill wheels are resting today, I see."

"Slow time of year, my friend," commented John, running his hand through his partially gray hair. "Give it two or three more months, when the first cutting of the grain fields is over. Did you notice, the fields are starting to green up even now."

Many millers had ovens and some baked bread, but since John's wife had died, and he didn't have daughters to carry on, he'd moved the ovens out of the building, and now he supplied other women the material they needed for their household bread baking.

The excess of their labor was sold and distributed in the immediate area to those who had no time to make it, being busy with household chores, children, or their own money-making arrangements based on their individual talents.

This was the start of small, entrepreneurial efforts on the part of the community to use each person's abilities to start a commercial society.

"Then, I have a proposition for you."

John led Anthony to the stools, eager to hear the young man's suggestion.

The men sat down amidst the clucking chickens who scratched at the earth for another morsel and fought each other for bits of grain found in the dirt—wings flapped and dirt flew in all directions. One rooster stood out from the rest.

Anthony grinned. Like his country, the chickens even had a serious pecking order.

Behind the men the sound of dropping water which ran the mill was heard. A long, thin U-shaped mill race, carrying water, ran from a higher elevation on Castle Hill and dropped the liquid into the cups on the mill wheel. The weight of the full cups caused the wheel to rotate, and the gears attached to the wheels located inside the building to turn the grinding stones and grind the different kinds of grain grown in the peasant's or serf's fields. Depending on the stones he used, John could make the grain coarse or very fine.

Today, the mill race was closed off. No water poured from the wooden, moss-covered mill race and the giant wheel did not turn.

Usually John was covered with a fine flour dust, but today his clothes were not dusty. "So, what's on your mind?" he asked after the two had settled down.

"I've been up to the castle and—" this was as far as Anthony got.

"What!" John's eyebrows shot up and his eyes swung upward toward the limestone rock castle. He had been in Tipton all his life and had never been invited to the castle. Of course, he even knew King Edward I, because that's how he got his work as miller, so a trip to the castle might have been appropriate. The King had ordered the mill built by Baron Dudley as a project for his vassals, those of his highness's men who were designated to work on building and repairing bridges within the shires and keeping the roads passable.

When John went on the Nineth Crusade to the Holy Land with Prince Edward, he was one of the

King's personal bodyguard, and he'd been wounded protecting his Lord. While they were on the crusade, Edward's father had died, and he'd become King. As King, he hadn't forgotten John's service and ordered the position of miller be given to John for his assistance and protection. He'd been the miller for several years.

"How did that happen?" asked the miller.

Anthony grinned and proceeded to explain the situation and give the reason for his being chosen. "Guess he doesn't trust his closest confidantes so I, as a total unknown, was designated."

"Maybe he *doesn't know* who to trust, but I have to agree with the Constable. He chose wisely." John sat nodding at Anthony's comments. "Now, what does that have to do with me?"

"I need a bodyguard and, because you have experience in this position, I wanted to give you the opportunity to help me as you've done in times past. You will be compensated by the baron."

John thought about Anthony's words all of one second. "I'll help. There's nothing I can do here at present. I'll let my ladies know of my intent to be gone and that way they can have extra grain ground to cover their needs. My, what an adventure!" he exclaimed. "I can't wait to get back on my horse and see the people and lands in the baron's fiefdom."

"Can you read and write?" asked Anthony, even though he was almost sure John could.

"Yes. I know my letters."

"Then I think between you and I we will not need anyone else to help."

"When do we start?" asked John.

"The first day of next week, be ready to ride out of Tipton. I'll map out our journey and this will be our guide for the next period."

"How about your mother?" asked John.

Renaee was not Anthony's real mother, but his aunt. She was blind and required some of the family to assist her with her household work and food.

She was not blind at birth. When she was twelve years old, she'd fallen from the housetop of her neighbor's hut and hit her head on the ground. From that time on, she hadn't been able to see.

When Anthony's own mother died in an epidemic which had swept over England, he'd moved in with her and by all accounts, she had become his mother. He loved her as such.

"I'm sure some of the immediate family and neighbors will help take care of her."

"Does she know of your assignment from the baron?"

"Not yet," responded Anthony, getting up from the stool and walking to his horse. "That's where I'm headed now." He mounted to the saddle, and John handed him his reins. "We'll talk again soon."

John stood and watched Anthony until he rode out of sight. He threw another handful of cracked grain to the chickens and headed down the path to his first customer with the news of his impending break from milling.

∼

Anthony rode on toward Tipton, passing other kin and helloing to them. He didn't come to this area often, preferring to stay around Renaee's home on the Summerhill near to the church of St. Martin, tending their small garden on the edge of the Glebe or Church lands. Besides working his own land, which was part of the open fields of his village, he helped an elderly neighbor with his sheep in return for meat to eat each year.

As he rode, he was amazed at the amount of bell-pit mining which was going on out from the base of Dudley Hill. Some holes weren't very deep, but some shafts were so deep he couldn't see the miner, who used a pickaxe and shoveled coal, removing it with a bucket and pulley out of his pit. Obviously, coal mining was a trade which was becoming very important. No wonder the baron was interested. He wondered if coal was beneath the home where he lived, or on his mother's fields, where he raised produce to be sold in the market at Sedgley or Wolverhampton. He nodded — something to check on later.

∼

Renaee heard Anthony coming. She got up from her chair and walked slowly the ten steps to the door of her house. Opening it, she waited until he rode up to the door. She heard him dismount and then his footsteps as he closed the distance between them.

"You left the house very early this morning," she said as he hugged and kissed her on one cheek after the other.

"Yes, I had official business to attend to with Baron Dudley at the castle."

Renaee was shocked but didn't raise her voice as she continued, "What on earth did the baron want with you? Official business, you say?"

"Come, let's sit down. I'm tired from this morning's experience." He led her to her favorite chair by the fire and collapsed opposite her on his stool, letting the pouch slide off his arm to the floor. The smell of cooking food on the hearth caused his stomach to say, *I'm hungry.*

Renaee heard his stomach growl, and she heard him sit heavily on the stool. Then he sighed, pulling in a lungful of air and letting it out quickly. "Must have been a very intense meeting," she agreed, knowing she should get up and fix them both a cup of the stew which was cooking on its spit over the fire.

"What's troubling you?" She realized from the sound of his voice something was bothering her Anthony, and finding out what it was seemed more important than eating. He gave her a reason to live and, without him life would be tedious and hard. When he adopted her as his mom, he became the warmth in her lonely heart.

Anthony told the story for the second time. She kept nodding at his comments, urging him on. "I am going to leave the first day of next week and John of Tybbington is going with me as my body guard. With him to help, we should get the whole survey done quickly, barring no complications or resistance from the men over their farms being examined."

"I'm glad John's going. You can help each other. How do you think you'll be received?" she asked, troubled at the word 'resistance.'

"I'll soon know."

"Are you hungry? I have stew and bread to eat for our morning meal." Renaee rose from her chair. Walking six steps she turned to her cupboard and pulled out bowls and spoons for the mutton stew she'd been cooking all morning.

Anthony watched her come to the fireplace with its chimney. She pulled an iron spoon from its holder on the rock wall along with a cloth to keep from burning her hand. Following a thin leather strip he'd run from a nail next to the spoon, she ran her hand along it until it touched the metal rack which held the pot over the fire. Wrapping the cloth around her hand, she swung the iron pot toward her and removed its lid, putting the cover on a small box by the hearth. Deftly, she dipped the soup, two scoops for each dish, from the kettle hanging from its holder, and turning, presented Anthony with his full bowl. She did not spill a drop.

Although the fireplace and chimney were in use at Dudley Castle, it was unheard of in the peasant homes in the valley of Tybbington. This one was the result of Anthony's friendship with John.

While John was recuperating in Europe with King Edward, he'd seen many fireplaces and chimneys in the houses they'd stayed in, and when Anthony was casting around for a solution to Renaee's problem with cooking, he'd suggested they build one. She used coal for her fire and a lid on her pot to keep the coal smoke taste and sparks from her food. Once she got accustomed to the distance and swinging pot hanger, she made cooking look as easy as walking to the door to greet visitors.

After eating, Anthony got up from his chair. "Do you need water from the spring?"

"Yes, to wash the dishes."

He went out the door to get the wooden bucket full of water.

Chapter 15

1281 A.D

Anthony and John of Tybbington

When Anthony and John of Tybbington left the village to survey the Baron Dudley's lands, they took with them two of the baron's soldiers who had the Dudley crest on their surcoats. This addition to their entourage was unexpected. The two Tiptons had belted on their swords and knives just in case there was trouble, but evidently some suspicion on the part of the baron had made protection from resistance to their presence in his fiefdom a real possibility.

"Why do you think we need extra protection?" asked John as they rode side-by-side on the path southeast of Castle Hill. Anthony had decided to start with Dudley and Rowley Regis and circle Castle Hill, ending up back at Tipton before going northwest to the sister villages of Wolverhampton and Tettenhall and northeast in the direction of Tamworth. Most of the baron's lands were concentrated in this area. The far-flung ones weren't on his list to survey.

"I don't know, and the Constable didn't say. Do you feel safer with some of his fighters with us?"

"Makes our group look more impressive and imposing, doesn't it?"

Anthony replied, "We might need to look official, since surveying the baron's lands isn't a normal activity. Here's our first stop. Wonder where the overseer is today?"

"I'll check with the woman in the doorway." John got off his horse and walked to greet her. She did not seem happy. He hoped walking to her seemed less threatening, than riding up the path to the entrance and towering over her.

Anthony watched as the woman pointed to a meadow in the distance which was lined by a stone wall. She continued to wave her hands and was obviously irritated at something.

Anthony watched the exchange and waited until John returned. "What did she say?"

"Meadow, there," John held his hand in the direction she'd pointed and started his horse toward the stone wall.

Anthony caught up and rode beside him. "And?"

"She's upset because she fixed the morning meal and her husband didn't come home to eat it. Or, it seems, last night's meal either. She wanted to know if I was married."

"What did you tell her?"

"I told her yes with six children." John shook his head and continued, "I don't know what that had to do with it."

Anthony couldn't help but laugh. Their first survey included a spat between a husband and wife. He noted it on the survey paper. He hoped the baron had a sense of humor.

Eleven days later, they finished the circle around Castle Hill. More than one manor required two days to inspect the property, and that was because the herds of cattle were in large fields and mixed in with the sheep. One other factor which slowed them down was the rough, heath covered hills, where it was impossible to see the herds. Even swine milled through the valleys and on the hills, looking for food. When this happened, all four men flushed the animals into an open area where they could be numbered. This took time, because they didn't want to rush the sheep or herds, causing them to get hurt in the process.

Anthony was astonished at the large numbers he was writing down on his survey sheets. If an overseer of his land was just guessing at the numbers of the flocks and herds—because the animals spent part of their time in the brush and woods—there would be a serious opportunity to cheat in large numbers on the taxes he owed the barony.

"Anthony, I would wager the baron's tax chest is fuller this year," John said after looking at the numbers and riding herd on the animals at another large manor.

"I'm with you. Can't imagine these overseers went to the trouble we've gone through."

As far as the coal mining, Anthony soon found that smaller and shallower bell-pit mines accounted for most of the digging for the expanding energy source, especially around Castle Hill.

"As we're going north on the west side of Castle Hill, we're seeing more bell-pits," observed John, who hadn't asked the question he wanted to ask. Why are we recording them? John wasn't stupid. If the baron wanted to know the extent of the animals grown on his fields, why wouldn't he want to know how much coal was being mined? This would certainly change the amount of revenue coming into his coffers, maybe more than the animals. Although Anthony hadn't told him the reason for the figures he was assembling, he knew without it being voiced.

"Yes, we are." Anthony was beginning to realize that estimating the amount of coal being mined was impossible, but the number of mines could be recorded. He wondered if the baron, standing on the parapet of the castle, could see the mines being worked below him. One thing was for sure, the baron was going to need an inspector or overseer of mines in the future. He wrote down the suggestion.

They were approaching Gornal, a small manor to the north-west of Castle Hill between Sedgely and Dudley Castle. It was here Anthony stopped his group to ask some pertinent questions.

Still in its early stages in other parts of south Staffordshire, mining coal was more prolific at Gornal with many pits being worked — most of them occupied by a single person. Anthony stood near one hole in the ground and watched the peasant miner use his pickaxe to loosen the black rock. Black chips and chunks flew in all directions.

The man's clothes and skin were covered with black coal dust. Only his eyes looked strangely white in his face.

"How long have you been digging in this hole?" asked John, peering into the bottom of the dark pit where several dirty bags of dug, lumpy coal were piled to one side.

A ladder leaning against the shaft wall was the only way the miner could get out. He looked up at

John with his white eyes, "Maybe three months," he said. "I've made good progress on this hole. The last one caved in — almost took me with it." He was a little more than head deep and pointed to a depression in the ground several feet away.

"So how do you know where to dig?" asked Anthony, coming closer to the edge.

"Coal's on the surface," he said, laughing nervously at being the center of attention. "Look around you."

John took the toe of his shoe and scraped the ground. The dirt turned to hard coal as he grazed the surface.

The miner continued, "I start at the top and work straight down until I run out of coal. Then I start following the seam sideways, wherever it takes me, and usually that's along the surface of the ground. I can work in all directions until I run into dirt or it isn't safe to dig anymore." He picked up a shovel so he could start bagging the loose coal in the bottom of the pit.

"So, since you're digging parallel to the surface of the ground, you run the risk of the dirt above collapsing on top of you."

"Yes, that's exactly what happen to my last pit." The miner rested his arm on the shovel, wondering where this was going.

"Why don't you brace the top of the mine?" asked Anthony. "Then it wouldn't collapse on top of you."

"Aw, there's so much coal, I just dig another pit. Bracing takes too much time and trouble. Coal means my family is well-taken care of and we are assured a steady supply of coins — until the coal runs out," he said, grinning, his white teeth and eyes showing in his coal-dusted face.

"So, how many people around here are mining coal?" This was a loaded question and Anthony knew it, but if the man gave him the information he wanted, he'd know exactly where to look, and this miner was open and forthcoming — even bragging.

~

Later, John and Anthony discussed what they'd been told.

"I think we may have missed some of the mines as we came through the area." Anthony made this statement as they ate the evening meal at a place where they would stay the night.

"No reason we can't nose around for a couple of days," suggested John.

"One other question, John. How many bell-pit mines do we have in Tybbington?"

"I don't know about Tybbington, but we counted four or five where I live, and just about everyone's using coal, so there's always a supply nearby. The only ones who don't use coal have vast forests to supply them with wood, including your baron, who has workers to cut his."

"Then, I'll need to determine how many are at home. We'll start there tomorrow as we pass through on the way north to the baron's manors in north Staffordshire."

"You mean I can sleep in my own bed tomorrow night?"

"Don't get used to it." Anthony thought better of his statement. "Really, you might as well stay with mother and I, since we'll be on our way bright and early the next day. There's no reason for you to ride south to Dudley."

~

It took two more weeks to travel to the rest of the Baron's estates—the ones he wanted counted. These overseers were farther away and not happy with the intrusion into their lives. News of their coming preceded them, traveling faster than they could finish each assessment. Complaining and snide remarks, the men could handle. Only once did some serious resistance materialize. This was on the western side of the River Tame, across from Tamworth.

But when the baron's two armed men rode up, and drew their swords to give an impression of authority, the overseer and his men stood aside, grumbling at their intrusion, and eventually helped in getting the figures Anthony needed. John whispered to Anthony, "I heard one of them say, 'the sooner they get their numbers, the sooner we'll be rid of them.'"

Anthony nodded in agreement. "Absolutely right," he said. He'd be glad to get his numbers and leave the whole area, too.

Mining was non-existent in the area, leaving Anthony and John wondering if the seam of coal came this far north. There was evidence of coal. It was being sold by vendors driving carts through the area.

~

Anthony breathed a sigh of relief. "I'm glad that's over with," he said to John.

He had released his protection to head for home, telling them to tell the Constable he'd be right behind them.

"I'd like to go into Tamworth and look around. I haven't been there in ages. I hear the market has expanded. I wonder if there's anything I need to take home with me." John jingled pennies in his pocket.

"If we head that way, we could spend the night in that fair village," said Anthony, feeling the euphoria of a job finished.

"Let's go." John turned his horse east, heading toward the old Mercian home of King Offa and Æthelflaed.

~

It was early morning when Anthony and John rode into Tybbington. The older man had decided to speak to Renaee before riding on home. Tied on the back of a packhorse, resting opposite of each other, were two chairs that rocked. One was a surprise gift for Renaee, and the other John intended to take home with him.

Renaee's sensitive ears heard them coming, and she opened the door. "Do I hear John?" she asked, grinning, putting out her hand in greeting.

"Yes, you do, Renaee," he answered, getting off his horse and striding quickly to the door. Catching her hand, he gave her a big hug and kiss on the cheek. "How are you?"

"Much better now that Anthony's back. I always worry about him. How did your trip go?" She heard Anthony walk past her into the house and strange movements coming from the fireplace hearth. What on earth was he doing?

Anthony came back and grasped her by the arm. "Mother, come sit by the fire while we talk."

"Child, what are you doing?" He'd not taken her by the arm to her chair in years. He knew she could find her own way. But his hand was insistent, and she followed his lead.

"Be careful when you sit down," cautioned Anthony.

When Renaee sat down, the chair moved. Startled, she grabbed at the air for support. "What—?" she exclaimed.

"A gift for you, my sweet Mother—from Tamworth." Then Anthony kissed her on the cheek. "It's a chair that rocks. Try it for a moment." Anthony stepped back and pushed the chair to make it move.

"Well, I'll be! What will they think of next?" With that she sat and rocked the whole time John stayed to visit, a delightful smile fixed on her face.

During a break in the conversation about their trip, she asked, "Have you heard that King Edward is planning to take an army and go to Wales?"

"No. When did this happen?"

"The castle Constable came by after you left and stayed awhile. He said the Prince of Wales was supposed to pledge allegiance to King Edward, but he hasn't done so. This angered the King. He's planning on forcing the Welsh Prince to pay him homage or they will go to war."

John looked at Anthony. "King Edward Longshanks will do exactly like he says. Get ready to go and fight. The Welsh won't be easy to conquer unless the King raises a large army. If he does, he'll include young and old men." With this bit of news, John rose to go home. "I need to tell my ladies I'm back," he explained, winking at Anthony. "Renaee, when you cook a pot of your good stew, I'll bring the bread. Let me know." He said his goodbye to Renaee and headed for the door.

Anthony walked him to his horse. "Thank you, John, for your valuable help."

"We may see each other again before long. I hope it's not under the circumstances I'm thinking about." With that, John rode toward home, with the awkward chair and the packhorse.

While Renaee cleaned up the dishes with water Anthony carried from the spring nearby, he went to place the shoulder bag with its completed surveys on a peg in the wall. Tomorrow, he would take them to the castle, deliver the pages to the Chamberlain, and ask questions of the Constable about King Edward's plans.

He walked out into the sunshine, pulled a stool up to the side of the house, and sat on it. Leaning back against the house wall, he let the sun's warmth relax his body and soothe his spirit. That's where Renaee found him. His heavy breathing meant he was sound asleep.

She walked back into the house to her new chair. Kneeling down, she took her hands and felt every piece of wood, feeling along the rockers, the seat, and rungs of the back. She touched it, making it move. Two tears ran down her cheeks. Touched to the bottom of her heart, she got up, sat down, and started to rock, smiling as she did so. Without her Anthony, she would have been a lonely woman. He made her happy, and when they attended St. Martin's Church, she always thanked God he'd chosen her to be his mother.

≈

Renaee stood at the door of their home. Her arms wrapped around Anthony—her head on his shoulder. "My son, please be careful."

"Don't worry. I'm coming back, and hopefully my absence won't be long. We'll fight this battle, and for sure peace will reign again." Anthony tried to be as convincing as possible, but he was not a seer or fortune-teller who could predict the future.

He knew Renaee had paced the floor for most of the night. He hadn't slept much himself, and she did not look well this morning, stumbling a little as she busied herself with the morning meal, knowing this goodbye was coming.

Renaee didn't want to make a scene, but she just couldn't let go. How could she go on without him? She didn't want to cry. That would make his going even harder. When he left each morning for his chore of the day, she knew he'd be coming back. This was different.

Anthony untangled her arms. Putting her hands together, he leaned over and kissed her on the forehead. "I see John coming. We need to join the other forces of the Constable as they head west."

"Anthony, I—" that was as far as she got. He interrupted her intended words.

"Mother, I intend to come back," he said as forcefully as he could. "Say prayers for me at church."

She heard his footsteps as he walked away. "Take care," Renaee called after him. "God speed, and may the Lord protect you," she whispered to the sky.

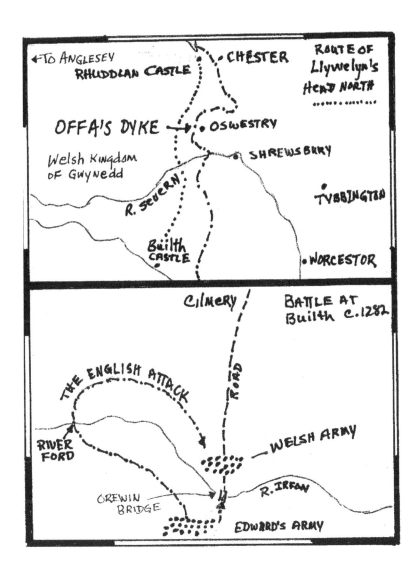

❧ **Chapter 16** ❧

1282 A.D

Anthony and John of Tybbington,
King Edward I (Longshanks) and Prince Llywelyn
the Last (ap Gruffudd)

Prince Llywelyn ap Gruffudd became the sole ruler of the northern Welsh territories by fighting and overpowering his brothers, participating in a chain of brilliant military successes, and forcing the capitulation of the other native Princes in the northern Welsh countryside. He started his rise to power in the Welsh territory of Gwynedd, which was one of the three main Welsh Lordships and was about as far removed from England as one could get, being north and west of the English lands and bordering the Irish Sea.

Known for conducting merciless raids on people who did not surrender to his wishes, he finally declared himself Prince of Wales, although he did not rule the southern Welsh territories. He joined Simon de Montfort of Leicester, an English baron in the Second Baron's War against King Edward, therefore becoming a traitor in the King's eyes.

As a reward for his help, Simon de Montfort betrothed his daughter, Eleanor, who was a child of five to Llywelyn, even though she was King Edward's cousin and was much admired by the King. After the Baron's War, with Simon the father dead, the rest of the de Montfort family fled to France. After ten years, Llywelyn, who had had many liaisons and children out of wedlock, decided to marry Eleanor. This was done by proxy.

At seventeen, Eleanor set sail for England to formally marry Prince Llywelyn.

At Bristol, King Edward's fleet overtook her ship, and Eleanor and her entourage were detained and imprisoned at Bristol Castle. Even though the two countries were at war, letters flew back and forth from the Prince to the King, asking for her release.

During this time, Llywelyn suffered a defeat in battle—the first Welsh War. In the Prince's weakened condition militarily, King Edward thought it safe to release Eleanor to marry the Prince.

In 1278, Edward and his wife, who was also named Eleanor, attended the wedding at Worcester on the River Seven.

Releasing and allowing the marriage of Llywelyn and Eleanor was a kind gesture by the King. She set about writing letters to him to obtain the release of her brothers and others in her household still detained at Bristol. This was finally given. And much like Æthelflaed of Mercia, she became a negotiator with King Edward on her husband's part, because misunderstandings continued to occur between the Throne of England and the Prince of Wales.

In June 1282, she died in childbirth at twenty-four.

It was Llywelyn's younger brother, Dafydd (David), who brought about his downfall when he attacked the English King's forces at Hawarden Castle on Palm

Sunday, 1282, precipitating his older brother's entry into the fray.

⁓

After signing a treaty to become a vassal of King Edward, at the conclusion of the first war of 1277, the stubborn Prince of Wales refused to come to court and pay homage to the English King, thus earning the King's ire.

Five years later, it was this atmosphere and the confusion surrounding the Prince's many actions that King Edward's army would encounter when they crossed the border and entered Wales. Marching or riding, they headed toward Gwynedd in the summer, fall, and winter of 1282.

The King decided to attack the Welsh on three fronts. He would go north, following the same path of the former war in 1277. The King found little resistance from Chester to Snowdonia. As the English advanced, the Welsh combatants faded into the forests and rocky hillsides of the north country—not gone, just waiting.

Having easily secured, the King thought, most of the northern lands of Wales, he sent armies south and into central Wales.

In June 1282, Gilbert de Clare, Earl of Gloucester was given the responsibility, to lead the southern fight. He attacked Carreg Cennen Castle and ransacked it.

The castle was built on a spectacular limestone cliff, with precarious drops on all points but one. This victory for the English soon turned into an embarrassing defeat. The Welsh attacked them on their way back down to safety and basically annihilated this segment of the English army.

After this disaster, de Clare was relieved of his command, which was given to William de Valence. Valence picked up the pieces and retreated.

In November 1282, another crushing defeat for the English occurred at the northern Isle of Anglesey, just off the mainland of Gwynedd. Anglesey was the breadbasket of Wales, a very fertile island, supplying food for the mainland inhabitants and Llywelyn's army—an important stronghold to control.

The island was separated from the Welsh mainland by the Menai Strait, a small isthmus of shallow water.

Depending on the time of day, the rising neap tide rushed north through the Menai Strait and then, as it ebbed, or lowered, the water went swiftly south. At one point, when the tide was changing, the water was slack or not moving. The slack water between Anglesey Isle and the mainland of Gwynedd tends to occur approximately one hour before high tide or low tide.

One of Edward's officers, Luke de Tany, known for his impetuousness, who'd accompanied Edward on his crusade to the Holy Land as an Admiral in his fleet, had taken the island, approaching from the sea. On the day of the mainland attack, the English planned to cross at high tide, when the sea would be calm.

A boat bridge was quickly built from the island to the mainland, and at noon the army started across with de Tany in the lead, bent on joining King Edward in the north.

Unbeknownst to de Tany, the Welsh, who had been pushed west by Edward's army, waited concealed in the hills. The Welsh tarried until the English army, horses, and equipment touched the beachhead.

Sweeping down from the hills, the Welsh with blood-curdling yells attacked with such force that the

English turned around, retracing their steps across the bridge. Under the weight of so many men, the boat bridge failed and broke apart.

With the tide running south at almost full force, and the men in full armour, de Tany and many of his men drowned. History records that sixteen English Knights, another sixteen squires, and three hundred footmen died that day—washed out to sea.

Prince Llywelyn, puffed up with pride at these two victories, unexpectedly headed south with his army to garner support among the other Welsh Lords of Wales who were subservient to him.

Edward stayed in the north to ensure Llywelyn didn't return.

In December 1282, the Prince approached the English castle at Builth and stopped in the hills before a bridge over the River Irfon. At this time, the Welsh forces numbered 7,000 infantry, with Llywelyn's personal bodyguard of 160 mounted, fully armed men.

The English force commanded by Edmund Mortimer, John Giffard and Roger l'Estrange had only 5,000 soldiers. The English advantage was 1,300 heavy cavalry—well-trained men on horses, protected by coats of mail and carrying an array of weapons, including the crossbow.

~

Anthony and John of Tybbington sat on their horses, discussing the turn of events during the past week.

"It *was true* that Llywelyn had headed south to stir up trouble in central and south Wales," Anthony stated to his cousin. Rumours had flown all week that the Prince was in the area.

Only yesterday they had arrived to the south of Builth Castle, riding the black horses for which the Tybbingtons were famous. They were dressed in mail with shields, helmets, swords on their belts, and lances—part of the cavalry attached to the central attack group. Others, on the ground around them, carried crossbows and swords.

"Yes, I saw the Welsh on the northern side of the River Irfon myself." John nodded. "They weren't trying to hide their presence—almost daring us to cross." He'd spent the morning riding with the Dudley Constable and a group doing reconnaissance for the leaders of the central group of Edward's army. John was always in the know, for he made friends easily and along with the Constable hobnobbed with the leader's closest men.

"Daring us to come across, is he? Do you think we need the King to come and lead us into battle? Where is he anyway?"

John answered, "I heard he's at Rhuddlan Castle—north, on the coast of the Irish Sea, making the territory there secure."

"Do you think the Lords Mortimer, Giffard and l'Estrange can take us into battle against Llewelyn? I've heard some murmuring about them."

"After de Clare and de Tany, I'm not surprised, but we'll find out soon enough. It's pretty obvious that they've got some of the best fighters in their command. They have us—men from the heart of England." John waved his hand over the closest group surrounding them—Knights, squires, and ordinary men who could fight from Lord Dudley's manors. "One thing's for sure, we can't go riding across the bridge. I wonder what they'll come up with to handle that situation?"

"Here comes the Constable now," said Anthony, holding out his hand because he thought he felt raindrops. The two Tiptons were under his command.

The Constable strode toward Lord Dudley's men — some were on horseback, some afoot. Standing at the front of them, he gave the first part of the battle plan. "We move out in the morning at dawn. It seems there's a river ford maybe one mile upriver. Our foot soldiers and part of the archers will go there, cross the River Irfon, giving the Welsh on the other side of the bridge a big surprise. At least, that's what we're after. This group will attack the Welsh on their right flank."

John leaned over and whispered loudly to Anthony, "Guess that answers my question."

The Constable looked at John and scowled. "If they keep their normal straight line of war tactics, bunch up several deep, and turn with their shields intertwined toward our first group, this will leave their left flank wide open to our archers. After the Welsh adjustment to our first thrust, the rest of our archers who will remain here will be given the command to proceed to the river bank. You'll advance close enough for your crossbow bolt to reach them, but, hopefully, not close enough for them to see you. This advance should give you a range to start shooting arrows in the backs of the Welshmen. Once this happens, we'll see what the Welsh do next."

"You will be here to lead the charge in the morning?" asked John, unperturbed by the Constable's stare, knowing the Constable liked to sleep-in, especially since he didn't have a whole castle to maintain.

"Yes. I'll be here," he said as the water from the sky fell harder. "Everyone should get comfortable and have as good of a night's rest as possible in this infernal rain, and we should all pray to God to be with us on the morrow." With that the older man brushed rain from his forehead and limped away toward the officer's tent.

John sat on his horse, watching the man leave. "I never could get *a good night's sleep* right before a battle. Too much to think about — like dying."

"John, maybe we should go and find a supply of dry wood for tonight's fire. I have a feeling it's going to be wet, cold, and miserable." Maybe gathering a stock of fuel for the fire would take their minds off the impending battle tomorrow.

"I'm with you, Anthony."

Mobilizing thousands of cold, stiff men was not easy the next morning. At least the rain had stopped in the night.

Because they would not be called on until later, Anthony and John were up early, fixing the morning meal for their group of men. This could be the only food they'd get all day.

Other teams amongst the army were doing the same. The smell of fried Welsh mutton taken from the nearest village was strong, and slices of bread dipped in the fat drippings was washed down with water out of a water bag.

Leaving the dirty pans with the camp servants, the squires made sure the Knights were ready to go. After putting on their armour, Anthony and John mounted their horses. The intention was to find a high hill and watch the progress of the battle until they were ordered into the melee.

After crossing the ford upriver, the fight proceeded just as the Constable had explained. When the archers were given orders to start shooting their bolts (short arrows used in a crossbow) into the exposed backs of Llywelyn's men, the Welsh dropped like flies with the first wave of wicked arrows being shot from the English crossbows.

Llywelyn's close-quarter combatant stance made his men a possible hit each time a bolt was strung in the crossbow. The Welsh broke ranks and headed for a hill far away from the river and bridge. The English pursued.

Mortimer gave the order for the heavy cavalry to charge across the bridge and up the hill. For a brief second, Anthony and John looked at each other.

"Where is their leader?" asked John of Anthony. "They don't seem to be coordinated at all. Stay close to me, and we will fight this battle together." He kicked his horse and the two men headed for the bridge with the rest of the group on horseback.

The three fronts of the English attack had caused the Welsh to scatter in all directions. They were obviously beaten. Waving to Anthony, John took off north after one Welsh soldier on a horse.

Anthony did the same but headed in the opposite direction. Turning south, he and the Welshman soon galloped over the bridge the English cavalry had just used to enter the conflict. Anthony didn't have time to wonder why this man was headed in a southernly direction.

The horseman kept looking back to see if he was making progress away from his pursuer.

Anthony's black mount was steadily gaining on the other one. Reaching a woodland, the horseman, realizing his steed could not outrun the black one, pulled back on his horse's reins, stopped dead in the path, and turned with his lance at the ready.

The fight did not last long.

Both men lost their lances, after a bone-chilling thrust at their mail. Then they reverted to swords on horseback. The other horse spooked at the sound of clashing blades, danced around, exposing the rider to Anthony. With a lucky blow, Anthony pierced the man's mail under his arm, and the Welshman fell mortally wounded to the ground.

Anthony got off his horse to check on his victim. Blood pooled on the ground next to the body. The vacant and fixed stare of Anthony's assailant meant he was dead. Anthony's sword had pierced through a flaw in the man's mail straight to the man's heart.

Anthony cut off a piece of the man's tunic and wiped his sword clean. Chill bumps rose on his arms as he saw the Stafford knot and the Latin words, *Strike hard*. "My Lady, your sword saved my life," he said as he stood above the dead man with the silence of the forest around him. Would the other words on the sword be true once the costs of this war were counted? Would England and Wales be united? Would they be bound as one? He certainly hoped so.

Putting his sword carefully in its scabbard, he leaned over to search the man's body for anything of value.

He found papers stuffed in the man's underclothes. They bore the seal of the Prince of Wales! Could it be he'd just killed the ruler of Wales? The man wasn't dressed as such.

Anthony sat down to wait on the army to return. He knew they must come back this way. He was sure someone would know the answer.

~

"I'm absolutely flabbergasted that you killed the Prince of Wales, Anthony." John patted him on the back. "Wait until King Edward hears about this. I'd like to be the one to tell him." John was grinning from ear to ear, shaking his head, and running his fingers through his sparse hair, something he did when he was excited or nervous.

"I think you may get to do just that."

"What? Why?" exclaimed John.

"The Constable and Mortimer are deciding on who'll take the head to his majesty. I volunteered your services," said Anthony.

"Thanks for asking." John feigned being indignant.

"We'll both be going if it happens."

~

A storm swept across North Wales, as if the heavens wept for the dead prince. Strong winds and squalls raged around the diamond-shaped fortress of Rhuddlan Castle. Outside the walls, the River Clywd threatened to breach its banks.

The two Tybbington men took off their wet cloaks, shaking them above the stone floor. Spreading them to dry on wooden benches, they waited in the antechamber outside the Great Hall. The head of the Prince of Wales rested in a leather bag between them. Roger Mortimer, Edmund's brother who had accompanied the two men on the way north, had gone to relay the news of their arrival to the King.

"Seeing our Lord King will be one of the highlights of my life," Anthony assured John as they waited for Roger Mortimer's return.

"I wonder if he'll remember me? I was a handsome young man on the crusade." John said, and both he and Anthony laughed at his comment, relieving some of the tension the men were feeling at their pending audience before the King.

"He was very kind to you."

"Yes, he was. Are you going to pull the head out of the bag for him to see?"

"No, I thought you would do it," responded Anthony.

"Guess we'll let him decide. Here's Sir Roger with the King's Chamberlain."

"Anthony and John, come with me. Our Lord, the King, is waiting." Sir Roger and the Chamberlain led the way into the Great Hall with its carpeted runner leading to a man who sat in a large, padded chair and not a throne. Many of the noble Lords of the Realm of England stood around and behind the Monarch, who was wrapped against the chill of the room, in a cloak with a collar and hem of ermine.

The two men bowed and knelt before a man with dark-blonde hair who most women would classify as ruggedly handsome. His eyes bored into your soul as if he could read your very life.

"Which one of you is Anthony of Tybbington?" King Edward asked, talking with a slight lisp.

Anthony opened his mouth to speak and for a second nothing came out. Finally, "I-I am Sire." Anthony ducked his head again and looked back up.

The King turned to John with a frown. "You look familiar. Who are you?"

"John of Tybbington, Sire. I went with you on the Nineth Crusade."

"Yes. I remember. You were wounded there in battle." This was a statement not a question. "Stand up, men, for I hear you two have something for me to see."

As they stood, Anthony glanced at John, who averted his eyes. Lord Roger helped hold the leather bag as Anthony grabbed a handful of hair and pulled the head of Llywelyn into the castle's candlelight.

In the soft light of the candles in the room, the head was gruesome and the smell ferocious.

As the head was displayed, a gust of wind blew down the chimney into the fireplace, the gust sending ashes and smoke into the room, causing the nobles to cough and sputter.

"Come a little closer?" ordered the King, delicately putting a cloth to his nose. Anthony approached the King, who, taking a closer look, scowled and nodded. "It is Llywelyn—henceforth to be known as the last Welsh Prince. From now on the Prince of Wales will be an English Prince."

The King paused only a moment. "You can put it up," he said to Anthony, while grimacing either at the smell or sight. He addressed his Chamberlain. "Take that disgusting foul-smelling thing from my presence. Put it in the courtyard under guard," he commanded. He motioned to his Chamberlain with a wave of the hand and turned back to his visitors.

The King got up from his chair and walked toward the Tybbington men. "You, Anthony, will tell me what happened?"

As Anthony recited the setting and actions of his battle with the Prince, the King walked to a wall full of armour arrayed for display. He picked a sword and came back. "Anthony, you've accomplished something I wish I could have done myself. You've been a great servant of the crown."

Anthony glanced quickly sideways at John. What was the King going to do? He was soon to find out, as the King continued speaking.

"For that reason, I intend to bestow on you a Knighthood of the realm. I firmly believe in honoring those who serve me well, disregarding their rank or lineage."

The King motioned to his Steward, who brought a low stool and placed it between the King and Anthony. "Will you kneel upon the stool before me?" This wasn't a question. It was a command.

"Sire, I will be honored to accept the Knighthood, but could you, I pray, use my sword? It's special to me and my family."

The King handed the sword he was holding toward John. "Take this sword and hold it for me."

Anthony pulled his sword from its scabbard and carefully handed it to the King, hilt first.

Edward looked at the old weapon, ancient but lovingly cared for, and noting the detail etched upon the blade smiled as he showed it to his courtiers saying, "This is the Saxon sword which sealed the fate of the last Welsh Prince.

The King was smiling as he asked, "Anthony of Tipton, tell me the tale of how this sword came into your possession."

As Anthony related the story, the King nodded his head. Hadn't the storytellers of his court related the story of Mercia, the Battle of Tettenhall, and the great Lady warrior, Aethelflaed?

When Anthony finished, the King stepped from his dais. "Anthony of Tybbington, I command you to kneel before me now."

Taking Anthony's sword, the King tapped the kneeling man on the right shoulder and as he did, he started uttering the French words, *"Sois chevalier, au nom de Dieu."* (Be thou a Knight in the name of God.) After saying those words, he continued with a tap on the left shoulder and added, *"Avancez, chevalier."* (Arise, Knight.) Reversing the sword, he handed it back to Anthony, who rose and put it back in its scabbard.

"John, bring the sword you are holding to me."

The King took the sword and turning to his new Knight said, "Anthony de Tybbington — Knight — keep your old sword safe and use this new weapon in the service of the Realm of England."

The Steward, hovering nearby, handed a purse of coins to the King, who passed the leather pouch to Sir Anthony.

Anthony bowed, took the sword and pouch, and backed to John's side.

King Edward turned to Roger Mortimer. "How shall we get Llywelyn's head to London? I want his head on one of the points of the gate at the Tower of London, with a wreath around his brow."

The rest of the conversation revolved around how the head would leave Rhuddlan Castle and arrive in London. Finally, the King said, "What better way than to let my recently Knighted Sir Anthony and his cousin, John, take it with a letter to the Constable, explaining what I want done with it.

Everyone in the room nodded in agreement.

"I will write the letter today. Meanwhile, you two men are invited to stay overnight here at the castle. Tomorrow we will provide you with provisions and money from the coffers of Llywelyn to start your journey." With an aside to his Chamberlain as to the men's housing for the night, King Edward called on Sir Anthony, his newest Knight, to take wine with him and to tell the rest of the court the story of the Saxon sword that was his family's prized possession.

Later that night in the privacy of the palace rooms, John said, "Guess I'll have to call you Sir Anthony de Tybbington from now on."

"If you even dare to call me Sir Anthony, I shall call you Sir John. No, cousin, I'll always be only Anthony to you.

~

For all intents and purposes, the fight to attach the Welsh homeland to England was over. Only one other problem needed to be solved. In 1283, Llywelyn's brother Dafydd was captured. Parliament was convened at Shrewsbury, and Dafydd was the first noble to be convicted of *high treason*.

As a special punishment, to send a message to others unhappy with the English rule in Wales and other parts of Edward's monarchy, the King decided to use a particularly cruel method of getting rid of his aggravating opponent. Dafydd was drawn through the streets tied to a horse's tail, hanged until he was almost dead, revived, and then he was disemboweled, and his body quartered. His body, cut into four pieces, was sent across the country. His entrails were burned.

There would be small skirmishes in the future, because the people were stubborn with a pride in their country to match, but major wars in the Welsh countryside were over.

∾

After helping Sir Anthony deliver the head to London, John of Tybbington came back to his milling operation. John was a prudent man who saved his earnings in a pottery jar hid amongst the gears of his mill. He died ten years later, leaving a sizable amount of money, which he willed to Anthony with instructions to distribute the sum evenly amongst his young children. This Anthony did immediately, because he wasn't in good health himself. Some of John's coins came from Baron Dudley, who used his services from time to time and some from his milling operation.

Because of King Edward and his generosity, John never wanted for anything. He, too, was given a small purse of coins from the Welsh gold mines at Dolgellau in recognition of his service in the Crusades. The King hadn't forgotten.

When John examined the coins in his purse, he found some were minted in the rule of the Roman Emperor Hadrian.

He never married again, preferring to remain celibate and enjoy his singular life. He did travel within England, visiting York, and then Shrewsbury and Bristol to see relatives—sometimes with his cousin, Sir Anthony.

❧ Chapter 17 ❧

14th Century A.D
Henry, Margery, Roger of Tipton
Ralph of Stafford

The subsidy rolls of 1332-33 include the names of those more affluent members of society who were eligible to pay taxes. The nine Tipton families, who are included on the list, indicate the people's relative prosperity compared to the other villages around. Out of ten communities, Tipton is listed at fourth from the top in wealth or movable goods, even though most of the land is forest or hunting area for the nobles.

After eight hundred years, Tybba's original lands include other families who aren't his relatives who reside there. Tybba's descendants are scattered around the area—east and west of the original Tybbington area. Some are positioned east beyond the original green, towards Summerhill where the church of St. Martin was built on the highest ground.

In the future, circumstances beyond his offspring's control would change the rest of his family's position in England, but for now, a few of the Tipton's still live on his original land near the River Tame.

The weather in England started fluctuating before the start of the 14th Century. In 1313, the wind blew with such force that roofs were ripped from buildings and falling trees and flooding made traveling the roads hazardous. The storm was called the Great Gale. Three years passed, and nature's elements hadn't let up. These included snow, ice, and hail.

～

The Festival of Christ had passed.

The whole community had attended the service. Everyone stood, including the old and infirm, during the worship celebrating the birth of the Christ Child. The celebratory goose was eaten along with mincemeat pie, which for the Tipton family, was made with the addition of a small amount of expensive spices bought from the market in Dudley. And even though the weather was terrible, some in the community managed to go door-to-door, cheering people up by singing carols of the Christmas season. The Catholic Church had out-lawed singing carols within its walls — too much merriment and dancing.

Henry of Tipton came into the house, carrying the full coal bucket, shutting the door quickly behind him. He was dressed in layers of clothes, a long cloak lined with wool, and a woollen hat with mittens. "Phew, it's cold outside," he reported to his wife, who stood beside the fireplace, stirring the porridge in the iron pot which hung over the coal fire burning on the hearth. During the last few years, with constant storms, the fire never went out.

Margery turned to look at her husband. "Did you get the roof patched on your brother's house?"

Yesterday, during the wind storm, a big piece of layered thatch had blown off, but not so that you could see into the house. Enough was gone that should there be rain, water would go through to the living quarters.

Henry came to the fire and sat the full bucket on the side of the hearth. He hugged his wife, took off his mittens, and put out his hands to warm them. "Yes, we think it's in good shape. Looks like more rain outside, so we'll soon see."

A commotion, mostly giggling, from the children's bedroom, which was up the ladder and under the rafters of the house, meant they were awake. Because the warmth from the fire went upward, his wife encouraged them to stay in the loft and sleep. This let her accomplish her morning's work and fix food for their morning meal.

Ten-year-old Roger and his younger sister, Anne, came scrambling down the ladder to the main room of the house. "Is it snowing, father?" asked Roger, coming over to the fire where his foot coverings were warming. He sat down on a low stool, pulled and pushed his feet inside, and laced up his leather shoes. His sister, who was a copycat of her older brother, sat on her low stool and did the same.

Henry laughed. "No. Not yet, but something's on the way. The sky is black over Bilstun and the clouds look heavy—drizzling rain or snow we may have before the day's out."

"Have you fed the cows? And has Bossy had her calf?" asked bright-eyed Anne. Bossy was her pet cow who often mooed at the sight of the young child.

"No, I haven't fed them. I'm waiting on you, sleepy-head." Henry went to his daughter and ruffled her blond, curly hair. "Waiting on you to get out of bed and help." He raised his bushy eyebrows and grinned at his only daughter.

Margery, smiling at the interaction of her husband and children, turned to add, "Go on and feed them now. Our morning meal will be ready when you return." She bent over the pot to stir it again, knowing a secret that she hadn't even told her husband.

In a few months, she figured early fall, there would be another mouth to feed in the Tipton household. She touched her stomach, where fluttering signs meant she was right, although there was nothing else, at present, to indicate her condition. She looked forward to another baby, even though growing crops was getting increasingly hard with yields down and the weather had caused some loss of livestock. Margery frowned at the thought. If the cold continued, what would this mean for her brood? Surviving was hard enough in the normal English cold.

Behind her, the children put on warm, wool-lined coats and mittens she'd made out of cloth bought from the market place at the Sedgely autumn fair, which the family attended each year. Turning, she smiled and watched as they went out the door. A chill draught of wind entered before Henry could close the opening. She shivered at its touch.

～

Outside, Anne sang in her high child's voice:

> *"Jesus our brother, strong and good*
> *Was humbly born in a stable rude*
> *And the friendly beasts around him stood*
> *Jesus our brother, strong and good."*

The muffled sound came through the walls as Margery smiled at hearing her daughter sing. But her thoughts rapidly returned to the weather. How long had it been since the Great Gale had ransacked Staffordshire and the rest of England—almost three years. Yesterday's wind hadn't caused as much havoc, but enough to send the men out in freezing weather to repair damage to several houses in the area. "Thank goodness, it wasn't ours," she said to the warm coal fire burning on the hearth.

Straightening up from her stance stirring the morning meal, she saw two swords hanging in their position of honor on the stone chimney. The house her family lived in had belonged to Henry's father, Sir Anthony de Tipton and his adopted mother, Renaee. The oldest sword had been in the family for hundreds of years and had been used by King Edward I to Knight Anthony for bravery at Rhuddlan Castle in Wales, and the more modern sword had been given to Anthony by the King on that very day.

Such a long time ago, she thought, reaching out to touch the ancient sword and bending forward to see the Staffordshire knot on its hilt.

Once Anthony was Knighted and Renaee had died, Sir Anthony had married. He lived long enough to have four children. Unable to pay the expenses associated with being a Knight, he'd let the title go, along with all privileges associated with it.

Leaving his home behind, he'd gone to live at Wednesbury (Wodensbyri) on the manor of Lord de Heronville as the Master Hunter, supplying the Lord's table and his guests with wild game. He told his younger son, who had just recently married, to enjoy this home until he returned. Anthony wasn't very old when he died—only thirty-seven. He'd never returned to his ancestral home in Tipton.

Roused from her musings, Margery sighed as she heard Anne singing again.

> *"I," said the donkey, shaggy and brown,*
> *"I carried his mother up hill and down;*
> *I carried his mother to Bethlehem town."*
> *"I," said the donkey, shaggy and brown."*

~

Anne continued to sing the song's refrain as she skipped toward the barn where Bossy was housed.

Henry had stepped aside to let his children pass. Two years ago, he'd built a large addition to the house his father had left him, and because of the cold weather, he had stabled his dwindling herd of cattle and sheep inside—sometimes including two horses and a pig. The area was crowded and required cleaning on a daily basis, which he did with the help of his children and sometimes his wife. The animals were a family affair because they were important to their survival.

He followed his giggling children toward the entrance of the newer addition and past a mound of coal. A stack of wood chopped as kindling, placed close to the entrance of the living quarters, served to start the fire and light the coal. Plus, Henry kept a pile of slack, small bits of coal and coal dust, which they put on the fire at night to keep it lit. There wasn't much warmth coming from the main house into the stable, but it was enough to keep the animals from freezing.

"Father, I like this next verse," said Anne, with glowing red cheeks like the cheerful child she was.

"I wonder why?" Henry responded, knowing exactly why. He listened as Anne sang.

> *"I," said the cow, all white and red*
> *"I gave him my manger for his bed;*
> *I gave him my hay to pillow his head."*
> *"I," said the cow, all white and red."*

"But Father, Bossy's not white and red. Are there white and red cows?"

Henry threw back his head and laughed. "There must be since the song says so. I've seen solid reddish-brown and solid white. Of course, I would say Bossy is brown."

They'd turned the corner. Anne continued to sing as his neighbor and cousin, Richard of Tipton, helloed from the path which cut through at the side of Henry's house, to reach the main track. He stopped to talk. "Do you think it's going to snow, Henry?" he asked.

Henry glanced up and checked the sky for the tenth time this morning. "I'm not a good predictor of the weather, but if it doesn't, it sure will miss a good chance to."

"Was it two years ago we had those two weeks of frost in April, and even after that snow and freezing hail? The snow and rain dried up toward summer. We had no rain, and I could hardly get a plow into the hard soil."

"Yes, and we had heavy rains in the autumn, just like last year, the harvest was poor. We couldn't do our fall plowing because the ground was heavy with mud. The rain didn't let up."

"It'll be like that this year since we couldn't plow in the fall. The ground didn't lie fallow to freeze and thaw for planting in the spring."

"I have been hoping this year won't mirror that year, but I have to agree with you," said Richard, shaking his head.

At that moment, Anne ran from the cattle enclosure, stopping further discussion. "Father, come and see. Bossy's had her calf and the poor little thing's trying to stand up." She grabbed her father's hand an pulled him toward the open door.

"Do you need help?" asked Richard, making Henry wonder where he was going and if he had a definite destination in mind. He decided not to ask since Anne's hand was insistent and pulling him hard toward the entrance where Bossy was stabled.

"No. I think we can handle it, but thanks." Henry waved at his friend who continued on to the road and let Anne guide him inside the room.

"See Father," Anne was practically jumping up and down in excitement.

Henry went over and helped the still wet calf stand on four wobbly feet. "What are you going to name your new calf, Anne?" he asked as they stood watching its awkward movements.

"I told Roger he could name it, because I named Bossy. If she has another calf, I'll name the new baby."

By now, the calf had made enough unsteady steps to its mother to nurse. "How about it, Roger? What's the new calf's name?"

Roger stood thinking. What did his family need at present? "How about Sunshine? Would that be alright, cause right now, we could use some."

"A very good suggestion, Roger. Sunshine, it is," said Henry. "Let's get out of here and leave Bossy with her new baby to get acquainted. I'm hungry."

Anne took him by the hand, and looking up at him with her beautiful brown eyes, said "Father, is that what you did when I was born—leave me with Mother to get acquainted?"

"You know, Anne. *You* are my sunshine and no, I couldn't wait to hold you in my arms." Then he added, "And your brother also."

As they left the stable, snow started falling. Beyond Castle Hill and the ridge line to the west, the dark, gray clouds mounded up like mountains. Henry realized they were in for a terrible snowfall. It seemed the rest of the winter was going to be a bad one.

The children ran ahead to tell their mother the snow had started to fall. "Wipe your feet," called Henry. He paused to look up and down the muddy road. Richard had stopped to talk to another bundled up neighbor. Henry waved to them both.

~

The years, 1317-18, saw the rains and freezing cold continue. People started to die all over England due to food shortages. The cloven-footed animals developed hoof-and-mouth disease, and their recently born offspring died in large percentages from this scourge, causing difficulties in plowing the fields and a scarcity of meat. Summer all but vanished, and with its disappearance grain prices rose—grain now being imported from Egypt, Africa, or other areas where the cold didn't paralyze the economy.

The Tipton family survived because of John of Tipton and their inheritance from him. They had money to buy grain for their animals and other produce which became expensive from the local and foreign markets.

Margery often cooked more than the family needed, with Henry taking food to those of their neighbors who had less. Clothes became ragged because of dwindling supplies of wool and high prices to buy it. Shoes had holes in the bottom and men carved wood, added leather, or lined the inside soles with any item which kept the water out and warmth in. A runny nose became the forerunner of a high fever, with no way to medicate the person back to health. The graveyard on the ridge at Summerhill, next to the church of St. Martin, rapidly filled with new graves. Being happy was hard with so much unhappiness in the village.

The difference was in the children, who were never down—they played and sang no matter what was happening around them. They buoyed everyone from the old to the young.

~

Twelve-year-old Roger came running into the house with Anne close behind. His baby sister, who'd just passed one, paused just long enough from nursing to look, wave her hands in the air, and grin at the racket.

"Father, I saw rabbit tracks in the snow. Can we go tracking?"

Henry looked up from his whittling project of the day—a small spoon for his wife to feed the baby.

"I'm almost finished," he paused. "Sure, let's go. I can finish this when I come back."

Dusting off his pants, he looked at his wife. She looked back and stared at the wood shavings on the uneven stones in the floor which were edged with river sand. "Anne, would you get the broom?" he said.

Instead of Anne racing to get it, Roger beat her. He started sweeping and his sister brought a piece of flat wood with an angled edge (an invention from Henry's active brain) to remove the small pieces of wood. "Henry, you can put those in the fireplace," said Margery, not wanting her daughter to get that close to the fire.

After getting rid of the shavings, Henry donned his cloak and other warm clothes. "Come on you two, let's find that rabbit."

"Henry," said Margery, "You need to stop by Richard's home and see how he's doing. His wife said he keeps going outside to cool off. He won't let her touch him. So, go talk to him and see what you can find out. She thinks he's sick—maybe with a fever."

"A dutiful husband always does what his wife wants," he said, bowing. But he smiled at her as he followed his children out the door.

"Where's the rabbit tracks, Roger?"

Roger, who was already out of sight around the side of the house called, "This way."

The three traced the tracks several feet through the snow until they disappeared in the road where horse hooves obliterated them.

"Look around and see if you can pick them up."

The two children searched the muddied snow, but the look was futile. The tracks were nowhere to be found.

"Why don't you two go home. Tell your mother I'm going by Richard's. I'll be home soon. And Roger, if it doesn't snow tonight, we'll ride over to the Coneygree Fields tomorrow. We'll go early so we can set the traps and have fresh rabbit stew tomorrow night," his father promised and started in the direction of Richard's dwelling.

When he arrived at his neighbor's house, Richard was wandering around outside in the freezing cold — without his cloak.

"Richard, have you lost your mind," exclaimed Henry, looking at his friend whose face was red. He looked like he was sweating. Droplets of water stood in beads on his forehead.

"No! That confounded woman keeps the house so hot! I have to get outside to cool off." Richard reached down and took a handful of snow, spreading the white stuff over his face and arms.

Henry started laughing. So that was it! Or was it. Henry kept plying his neighbor with questions. Do you have a fever? No. Do you feel sick at your stomach? No. Are you dizzy? No.

"Why are you asking so many questions?" asked Richard.

Henry thought about making up some kind of tale, but decided to tell the truth. "Your wife was concerned. She asked Margery to ask me to ask you."

"What's that woman thinking? Why didn't *she* just ask me?"

"My guess is she knew the truth and didn't want to give up her warm house, or maybe I should say her hot house. Why don't you tell her your problem? You have a tongue, too."

"I think I'll do just that. Good to see you Henry." Richard turned and with a determined step started toward his door.

But Henry noticed as he got closer to the entrance his step became more hesitant. He doubted the man said anything after going inside. He shook his head, gave a chuckle, and walked home.

～

Although it wasn't far to the area where the rabbits were raised, Henry put a saddle on his horse and, with Roger, sitting to his front, started toward Coneygree. The air was cold with a slight wind blowing. The brook, which wasn't very wide, was frozen over with ice and would be slippery to cross, but Henry had been here many times before and had his own way of crossing. Approaching the frozen stream, he dismounted his horse. He continued on toward the brook and stopped where several rough wooden boards lay next to the frozen surface.

"Father do you want me to help?" Roger started to dismount the horse.

"No. You stay mounted. I'll get them."

Kicking the wide boards loose from the ground, he turned them over and picked them up one-by-one. Walking gingerly on the ice, he pushed and pulled them into position side-by-side, making a bridge across the frozen stream, distributing the weight of men and horse. Then, he led Roger who was still on the horse across safely to the other side.

Henry was in charge of keeping the man-made pillow mounds of the warren in good order. This area was situated on a knoll where the rabbits lived and bred, ensuring a good hunt for the nobles, and a bad outcome for the rabbits. Tunnels lined with rock were embedded into the hillside with dirt mounded on top in the shape of a pillow, making it easy for the rabbits to use as the entrance of their Coneygree or burrows. Grass and other forage grew atop for the rabbits to eat.

Once Henry and Roger gained the slight mound of earth, there would be another ditch to cross, which was the water-filled moat he and others had dug around the mound to keep the rabbits from leaving. Water was no problem to fill the moat, because plenty of brooks ran through and around Tipton Green where Henry and his family lived. When it poured rain, they often flooded.

At the moat, there was a bridge and a gate, and along the outside of the moat a fence to keep foxes, who loved rabbit meat, and other predators out. The rabbits would stay on the confines of the knoll, because they did not like to swim.

Henry tied the reins of the horse to the bridge and dismounted. No one rode their horses onto the mounded area. He reached up to get Roger. "We'll walk across into the field." Then he made another observation and pointed. "Tracks of someone who's entered and none leaving." He stood still a moment and looked around the area. There'd been no new snow for two days. These tracks could have been made the day before.

"Who do you think is here?" asked Roger.

"I don't know, but if they're still here, we'll probably find out."

The field had cleared areas and places where scrub brush grew—a perfect place for rabbits to hide and eat. "How will we catch a rabbit?" asked Roger, knowing that they hadn't brought a bow and arrows.

His father pointed to a box attached to the other end of the bridge. The box was locked, and his father pulled a large key out of his pocket. "Who does that key belong to?"

"The Baron Dudley." Henry pointed up to the castle which overshadowed everything in Tipton and for miles beyond. "This is his hunting ground." He unlocked the box.

"Do you have permission to hunt here?"

"*We* have permission to hunt here," his father replied, taking a smaller wooden box out of the large one. "This is a trap. Let's get two and go set them up. Surely, we'll catch one rabbit with two boxes. Here, you can carry one. Look for a burrow entrance."

Burrow entrances weren't hard to find, because the distinctive rabbit's tracks were everywhere and more evident at the holes being used. "How do the traps work, Father?" asked Roger, looking at the rectangular, wooden boxes with the removable doors which raised up and down.

His father would know, because he'd made them. Henry demonstrated the door and the slim piece of wood which was attached to a wool string running to the back of the open box. The piece of wood propped the door open. "The string goes through this hole at the back of the box and it's tied to a piece of food the rabbits love to eat. When the rabbit nibbles the food, it pulls the string which moves the prop holding the door up and it falls."

"Oh, I see. The rabbit is trapped and can't get out."

"Exactly."

"Where's the bait?"

Henry pulled two carrots from his tunic pocket, handing one to Roger. "Why don't you set the second one? Remember to break it into two pieces and tie both onto the string."

"Why two pieces?"

"Because the carrot's smell will be more pungent, and the odor will spread farther."

The traps were set and the two went back to the bridge to wait.

∼

Not long after daybreak on the same day, thirteen-year-old Ralph of Stafford had snuck out of the castle on the hill under the watchful eye of his mother and the Constable. Pretending to be pursued by an enemy, he dodged, evaded, and hid among the castle's trappings, until finally he was without the walls of the massive stone edifice. Escaping from his mother's presence was the most fun he'd had since coming to Dudley Castle. He intended to enjoy his jaunt from the Castle Hill confines to the fullest.

Last night's talk in the Great Room of the castle was of hunting rabbits and deer in the vicinity. This had piqued his interest. He'd taken his crossbow and some bolts (arrows made especially for a crossbow) and asked directions of one of the maids in the castle.

"There," she'd pointed, "the Coneygree Fields are there," she continued, stopping her movements with a broom to answer his question. The companion to her broom, a wooden piece with an angle on one side rested on the window sill the two looked from.

His eyes had followed her hand's direction to a grassy area where he could barely see a bridge and what could be a moat filled with water.

"Is it the area to the far right of the church steeple and the village of Tipton where I see a small bridge?" he'd asked.

"Yes," she'd replied wide eyed, observing his heavy clothing and hunting equipment. "You surely aren't going there, are you? It's cold outside and the wind's blowing. I can't imagine your mother letting her children out on days like this."

He leaned over and whispered to her. "I'll be all right." Never one to back down from a challenge, he was determined to get there at all costs.

He knew from experience he might be looking at a rabbit warren, so he set off like a worthy Knight in search of it.

Ignoring the winding road down the hill, where he would be easily seen, he went slipping and sliding down the dangerous hillside in the snow. The white stuff coated his shoes and got into his mittens when he grabbed at sharp rocks or scrub bushes to slow his downward progress.

Starting down the limestone hill, he'd stayed as much as he could, in places where he couldn't be seen from the glassed windows, towering over him. Once he thought he caught a glimpse of the maid of which he asked directions, and he almost slipped on the steep, rocky slope with the treacherous ice covering it.

At the bottom of Castle Hill, he ran into trouble — the first frozen brook he needed to cross. Testing the ice with the toe of his shoe, he decided it was thick enough to traverse. So gingerly, he stepped on, listening with concern to the cracking and popping sounds as he advanced, and without sliding he crossed over the frozen stream.

Ah, very good, he congratulated himself, *a clever Knight I'll be*, and immediately wished he had a partner to share his adventure. Ralph was basically a loner. He didn't let many people into his life, adults or young ones his age, preferring to handle things his way.

This exasperated his mother who tried desperately to change him. Lately, she'd had another baby to occupy her thoughts, so this left Ralph more time to use his imagination — to escape her presence.

The wind had abated somewhat off the hillside, but the valley air seemed as cold without it blowing very hard. He noticed his feet were cold inside his shoes and his mittens weren't thick enough to keep his fingers from becoming stiff with cold. He decided to walk faster so he would stay warm. When he got to the warren where the rabbits lived, he crossed the bridge over the moat, opened and closed the gate. On the other side of the field, he found a burrow to watch, and a place he'd be concealed from view to hunker down in the snow and wait.

Before long, two people showed up riding a horse. He watched as they set traps and went to rest next to the same bridge he'd crossed when he arrived. The older man wrapped his cloak around himself and the young boy, making his body warmth work for both. Ralph felt a touch of envy. His own father was dead and his mother married again. He was sure having a foster father wasn't the same as having his real one.

When a rabbit appeared from its burrow, he shot it quickly with a bolt.

Well-trained by the archers at Stafford Manor, this was not a problem. But he didn't get up to retrieve the animal. Not wanting to reveal his presence, he hoped his two visitors would leave. The longer he sat waiting, the colder he got. Why hadn't he brought his warm fur-lined cloak with him? Finally, he started shivering and then shaking from the cold.

Henry sat hunched over Roger, his cloak making a tent to keep them warm. The sun had peeked through the clouds only a moment, long enough to turn the snow's surface into a sheet of blinding white and reveal the English blue sky above, and then it hid again.

After waiting in the cold for a period of time, Henry suggested to Roger, "Son, I think we'd better check to see if we've trapped our rabbit and head home. We'll have to skin and dress our kill before your mother can start cooking it. She'll have just enough time if we're going to eat it tonight."

"What if we didn't trap one?" asked Roger.

"Ah well, my son, there's always another day."

With these final words, the two trudged across the snow to the traps, which proved to be empty.

"Can we leave them set until tomorrow?" pleaded Roger. "We can come check them then. We're sure to have caught something overnight."

Henry looked up at the sky. "The weather's not likely to change, so it will be cold enough. We'll leave them, but we'll have to come early, especially if the sun shines." Henry loved to eat wild rabbit, but leaving them in the traps for a long period was not a good idea, especially if they died.

Making sure the traps were still set and would work properly, Henry and Roger headed for the bridge. A movement from the *snow*-covered mound and muttered words stopped them.

"I'm sorry, b-b-ut I n-need your help," said young Ralph, the *not so smart* Knight, holding the rabbit out to them with the bolt still in it—almost as if giving an offering for their help.

Henry noticed the youngster was shaking visibly. "Here," he said, taking off his cloak and wrapping Ralph with it. "Who are you?"

"R-r-ralph."

"Where are you from?"

Ralph pointed a shaking hand up to Castle Hill.

"We'd better get you to some place warm."

"Roger, here, take the rabbit and shut the gate behind us." Henry picked Ralph up and carried him to the horse, placing the almost frozen lad in the saddle. He mounted up behind Ralph and pulled his cloak around them both. Then he grabbed Roger by the tunic, rabbit in hand, and pulled him up behind.

The boards were still across the brook. This time Henry did not dismount, but let the horse find its way on the wood. Soon they were home, Ralph's wet clothes had been removed, and he was warming on Roger's stool by the fire wrapped in a wool blanket.

Margery nursed baby Jane, and Anne sat sewing on some cloth near the fire.

Henry went to unsaddle the horse, putting the animal in the barn with Bossy and Sunshine. Roger came around with the rabbit which he was still holding.

"Are we going to cook it?" asked Roger, holding the furry gray animal toward his father with the bolt still stuck in its side.

"No. Let's dress it and let it hang to freeze. Your mother gave up on us and cooked another one I caught last week."

Back inside the house, Margery was taking Ralph's clothes and hanging them by the fire to dry. Running her fingertips over the material, she felt the richness of the wool compared to their own clothes, which were more homespun. Baby Jane lay in her crib nearby, waving her fists in the air.

When Ralph's teeth stopped chattering and he could talk, the Tiptons found out he was visiting Castle Hill with his mother. "Does your mother know where you are Master Ralph?" asked Henry.

Roger interrupted the answer and smiled as he offered Ralph a bowl of rabbit stew, a slice of bread, and a wooden spoon. "My mother makes the best rabbit stew. I think you'll like it." He nodded twice.

Ralph took the bowl and bread along with the spoon.

Henry asked the question again, "Does your mother know where you are?"

"No, she doesn't." Ralph ate a spoonful. He was beginning to warm up with hot food and fire helping.

Margery exclaimed, "She must be worried sick, Henry. He needs to go home as soon as he eats."

"There's time. Let the boy thaw out and give his clothes time to dry," said Henry.

Drying out his clothes gave Ralph a chance to talk to Roger. "Are you going back to check your traps tomorrow?"

"I think so. Do you want to come?"

"Mother may not let me out of the castle walls, but I'll ask when your Father takes me back. I left my crossbow and extra bolts at the warren."

"If you don't come, I'll find those and get them to you," promised Roger.

By this time, everyone had a bowl of soup to eat. The talk was friendly with Ralph joining the conversation. Soon the family knew that his mother's new husband, Thomas Pipe, was a friend of both Sir John de Somery and his sister, Lady Margaret. Lady Margaret was the wife of Sir John de Sutton, Lord of Dudley Castle, whom his mother was visiting.

Ralph, noticing the two swords hanging in their pride of place within the home, asked, "Is there a story behind the two swords?"

Henry stayed to hear the first of the story, and then winking at Margery, he drew on his cloak and left the room.

Roger pulled up Anne's stool and started telling his new friend the rest of the story. He was almost finished when his father interrupted the conversation. "Are you ready to go back to the castle, Master Ralph? The horse is saddled and outside the door."

"Yes, I'm ready." Ralph pulled on his dry clothes, and Margery gave him Roger's cloak to wear home.

She patted Ralph on the shoulder and said to her husband, "See you bring it back, Henry," motioning to the outer wear as the two went out the door.

"Good to meet you, Roger," called Ralph. "And thanks for the soup, Mistress Margery." He dipped his head toward Margery and waved at Anne.

Ralph's mother did not let him come to check the rabbit traps, but he did come back to Tipton — three days later.

In an unexpected twist of fate, his mother came down with a mysterious illness which quickly put her in bed with a high fever, leaving her very weak because she couldn't eat without losing her food. She did not want to nurse her baby for fear the youngster would be harmed by her milk. Not one person at the castle had a small child. Was there someone in Tipton who could nurse the baby until she felt better? Ralph slipped into her room.

"Mother, Roger of Tipton's mother has a baby. She might help."

Turning her head, his mother asked weakly from the bed, "Who's that?"

"The people who helped me when I went down to hunt rabbits. The mother has a small baby. She's nursing her."

A couple of quick trips later by one of Mistress Margaret's entourage, and all was arranged. The following day, Roger, his mother, and baby Jane arrived by horse at Castle Hill. After so many trips up and down the steep hill, the pathway was too slippery and dangerous to use a carriage.

The clatter of horse hooves, as they entered the courtyard sent an excited Ralph hurrying to meet his new friend.

Roger waved as Ralph exited the door to the Great Room beyond.

Ralph caught the animal's reins. "How was your trip?"

"Scary at times. I brought you something." Roger handed him the crossbow and bolts and jumped down from his pony.

"You didn't forget," exclaimed Ralph, upon receiving his precious hunting equipment.

The two stood aside, watching as the Constable of the castle brought a step, took Margery's baby in his arms, and helped Roger's mother alight from the horse.

"Leave the horses there," the Constable instructed, returning the bundled baby to Margery. He untied and pulled a pack from Roger's mother's horse and one from the young lads.

"No, I didn't forget." Roger whispered. "Father and I found them the next morning, and we had two rabbits in our traps. We've been eating rabbit stew for days. I think I may grow fur." Roger made a grimace as if tired of rabbit, and putting his hands beside his ears, he began to hop around the courtyard until he slipped on the icy cobbles.

"Roger, mind your manners," exclaimed his mother, turning to admonish her son for his actions. Then, being led by a chambermaid who carried the two bundles, she disappeared into the castle entrance hallway. She was taken immediately to Ralph's mother's room where she was introduced to mother and baby.

After they disappeared from the courtyard, Ralph laughed. "You are going to stay, aren't you?"

"Yes, until Mother goes home. The castle will provide meals each day to my Father and Anne, so we can ride back and forth on the ponies, if you wish."

"You'll get a variety of meals from here, including beef and lamb. We'll have fun," replied Ralph. "I've found lots of nooks and crannies to explore. And you must see the well. Although we are high on the hill, the water is only six feet below ground level, and it doesn't freeze. What fun in the summertime. Come let me show you. If we're careful, we can drop loose cobblestones in it. The water splashes almost to the top." If nothing else, Ralph was mischievous, teaching Roger to be slightly naughty.

~

Fourteen days later with his mother recovered, Ralph, his mother, and step father went home to Stafford.

Henry and Anne, who had gained a few pounds from the rich food they'd eaten from the castle, rejoiced to see the rest of their family.

Inside by the warm fire, Anne asked Roger, "What did you do *up there*?"

Roger's eyes lighted up, and he launched into a description of sieges and defending the castle from invaders.

"Yes," said Margery, looking at her husband. "And one time, the two got a good smacking because they were discovered trying to climb ropes which they'd attached to the top of the castle keep. Can you imagine? Even Sir John de Somery looked at them sternly and threatened to throw both of them in the dungeon."

"Oh no, Roger. You know the dungeon is haunted," said Anne, coming to give her brother a second hug—her eyes as big as a trencher. "I'm glad you didn't find out."

"After that, they were given tasks to keep them busy, like taking salted meat to the monks at the Priory of St. James and to the priests at the churches of St. Thomas and St. Edmund."

"Yes, and Anne, they call cow—beef, and sheep—lamb." Roger laughed at this revelation, so Anne did, too.

"Henry," said Margery, including her husband in the conversation, "Mistress Margaret explained these were Norman words used by the rich and powerful in the land."

Henry nodded. He was whittling again.

Roger continued, "And Anne, they eat fish caught from the moat or the ponds of the Priory and they have ducks which swim in the water, and…"

The conversation went on as the family gathered around the warm fire, happy to be together once again.

ঙ Chapter 18 ঙ

14th Century A.D

The Adventures of King Edward III, Roger of Tipton and Ralph de Stafford

Part I

The years between 1320-30 saw England recovering from the snow and ice filled years of the Little Ice Age. This was just in time for the start of the One Hundred Years War against the French and the turmoil taking place concerning the English throne.

During an intrigue between King Edward II, his wife Isabella, and her lover—Roger Mortimer, who was a long-time antagonist of the ruler—the King was forced to step down, having lost the support of the nobility. His son, young Edward III became King in 1327.

This was the year Ralph de Stafford, now aged twenty-six, became eligible to lead men into conflict. The year before he had married Katherine, daughter of Sir John de Hastang. She bore him two daughters before she died in 1332.

Ralph, now a widower, was given an appointment as a Knight Banneret. He was given the command of a company of soldiers, heading for war with Scotland as an accomplished archer.

~

Ralph de Stafford laughed at Roger. "You missed that one, my friend."

"If you'd shut up so I could concentrate, I wouldn't have." Roger shook his head and picked another arrow out of his quiver.

This time the arrow hit its mark which was a piece of wood nailed to a tree with a bullseye painted in the center.

"In the middle of the battle there is no silence, unless you are dead," Ralph said gently. He came and took the longbow in his hand.

In one movement, the arrow was from the quiver, placed on the longbow string, aimed, and fired, hitting a spot next to Roger's. "See what I mean? You need to practice that move—speed, that's what it takes to win battles. The more arrows flying through the air, the more dead enemy you will count." Ralph wasn't criticizing his friend. He was making a simple statement.

Roger made a move to try again, saying, "I remember when you scoffed at the use of the longbow, preferring the crossbow and quarrels (square-headed arrow)."

Ralph stopped him. "Let's not quarrel over quarrels, my friend and quit for today. You're tired and so am I. Your mother may have the afternoon meal ready. My mouth's watering for some of her rabbit stew. I'm beginning to favor it over our rich Norman fare."

For years, Ralph had returned to Tipton whenever he could to visit his friend but always in the summer— no more Tipton winters for him. This afforded the two growing lads a chance to get out and explore the King's game lands, which meant walking over numerous acres around Castle Hill and the Roughlea hills. Many times, he'd stayed a month and helped around the area with tenant's problems associated with flooding and winds, until the problem mostly abated, or the weather returned to normal.

This trip, he'd been in Tipton for a week. He and Roger had done the usual—hunted rabbits and deer, practiced archery, and helped Henry, whose health was failing.

"What will you two do tomorrow?" asked Henry on Tuesday at nightfall, as they sat around the fire after eating Margery's stew. They had eaten the last of the white bread, which Ralph had brought with him.

Ralph answered, "We need to replenish our arrows, and I thought we might go to Birmingham and look around the Thursday market. Is there anything we would need to buy for you?"

"A few more nails if you can find them," replied Henry. "I'd like to build a better door for the small barn we built out back and some iron hinges would be nice. I hear they have sturdy ones."

"We'll look for those. Mistress Margery do you need anything?" Ralph asked, turning in her direction. As usual, she was sewing on some cloth.

"Why don't you find something you especially like to eat and bring it back for me to cook—maybe something exotic. You'll know when you see it." She nodded at him.

"I've been meaning to ask you, Ralph, did you enjoy your trip to France?" Henry leaned forward in his chair, whittling away at a piece of wood.

"Very interesting. The big cities are much like London, but built of granite stone, not limestone, like our English ones. The villages are picturesque and crowded in-between hillsides. You'll be riding along, and you don't see a thing, then you get to a valley, and it's full of houses clustered in a tiny area. And of course, there's always a church steeple. Sometimes you see the spires first before you see the village."

"Like Tipton? We're in a valley, and we have a church." Henry stopped whittling and eyed his piece, turning it around to look at the opposite side.

"No, not like Tipton at all. The only word I can think of is tight—side to side homes crowded at the bottom of rolling hills."

"Who did you go with?" asked Margery.

"Hugh de Audley from Oxfordshire was in charge of the trip. I wasn't around him much, but I found out that King Edward relies greatly on him to conduct his business overseas. We went as a military force for his protection."

"Audley? Wasn't he the one who helped depose the King's father from the throne?" asked Henry, a perplexed look on his face.

"Yes. Along with Edward's wife, Isabella and her friend or lover, Roger Mortimer. Much has been said about the late King and his close friendship with Piers Gaveston, his involvement with the Despenser family, and the intrigues which led to his death five years ago at Berkeley Castle in Gloucester. I really can't say what happened. I wasn't there, but many rumours abound about that event."

"What do you think about our present Lord, the third King Edward?"

"He's definitely a warrior, but," was all Ralph said as he quickly changed the conversation. "What are you making, Henry?"

"It's a doll for Anne's little girl." He held up the chunk of wood for everyone to see.

"And I'm making it a tunic to wear," said Margery, offering a piece of sewn cloth for the two boys, as she still called them, to look at.

"I understand Sir William de Birmingham has increased the market town within his manor and secured his success as Lord with our young King, because of the tolls and rents he is charging and the taxes he adds to the King's coffers." Henry blew shavings toward the fireplace and looked knowingly toward his wife.

Margery smiled at him.

"Yes, my dear, I know where the broom stands."

She blew him a kiss.

Ralph chuckled at their antics. "Our King is always happy if his taxes appear on time."

Henry looked thoughtfully at Ralph, "If I remember correctly, Sir William was Knighted by our King's father."

"Yes, he was, and I believe there's some relationship between he and Hugh de Audley's wife, Margaret de Clare. I've heard them speak his name."

"It will take two days for you to travel to Birmingham and back. Will you leave early in the morning?" Margery asked, thinking of their trip.

"Yes. We'll stay the night at a local inn and return Thursday after shopping at the market."

"I'll see that you have food for the journey," she said.

"You three can talk all night. But I'm sleepy and heading for bed." Roger got up and walked to the ladder leading upward to the loft. With Anne, Jane, and two other boys gone and married, the huge upstairs was Roger's, which Ralph shared when he came to visit.

～

The trip to Birmingham by horse took most of Wednesday. The less expensive inns were crowded, so Ralph and Roger elected to stay at a private home which offered rooms for the night. Located on the outskirts of the village at Deritend, it was close to the ford over the River Rea into the town and the Lord's deer park.

"Are you going to the bullbaiting tomorrow afternoon?" asked Peter, who'd rented them a room.

"No. We will be going to the market, leaving as soon as we buy supplies," Ralph stated. "We need to return to Tipton before nightfall, if possible." He was dressed in a tunic with the Stafford Coat-of-Arms, as befitted his rank when attending tomorrow's festivities.

"What do you think of the sport of bullbaiting?" Peter inquired, as the three rested before a log fire. "I'm going tomorrow afternoon to watch."

"I've seen enough of blood in wars. Seeing an animal tortured or torn by dogs is not a sport I appreciate." Ralph stood and took off his cloak, handing it to Roger. Roger disappeared into their room for the night to hang it on a peg in the wall.

"You don't think making a bull angry tenderizes the meat before it's slaughtered?" Peter pressed his occupant. Some theorized the meat was more tender.

"The only meat I've eaten of an angry animal was a wild boar. The meat was so tough we used a mallet to beat the sinews apart. So, no, I don't think being angry has anything to do with eating meat—beef or pig."

"You are wearing the symbol of Staffordshire. Do you know Sir William de Birmingham? Isn't he the Steward of Dudley Castle close to Tipton in the shire?"

"Ah yes, he is at present. As far as knowing him, I've heard of him through Hugh de Audley. His wife, Margaret de Clare, is distantly related to him, I believe. Is the Lord in town?"

"Yes, his Lordship rode by here just this morning. He is enjoying what's left of the deer park, hunting with his greyhounds and friends. If the market keeps expanding around the green and the village maintains its growth, hunting deer will be obsolete in our area. But he has other places to hunt." Peter shrugged his shoulders.

Ralph inquired about the market's supply of items and where to find quarrels, nails, and hinges. After asking where to buy food, he and Roger bade goodbye to Peter and went to eat before turning in for the night.

∽

The trip to Birmingham produced more arrows for target practice and, with Peter's instruction and several inquiries, nails and hinges for Henry's door. Margery was harder to please. But they headed back with loaves of white bread, a jar of fig jam sweetened with honey, and a large, cloth bag of dried dates to use in cooking porridge or bread or nibbling straight out of the bag. As a special treat for Margery, a bolt of cloth with all the colors of spring was added to their pack horse.

Their return was leisurely, with talk of Ralph's travels and his marriage.

"Where are your two daughters?" asked Roger, knowing they were very young.

"I left them with my Mother. She loves them and will see that they are taken care of by the servants. Since I'm with the King's archers, I'm on call at all times. I think continuity is the best thing I can offer them. They don't need a father who's there a few days and then gone most of the time. I remember losing my father. I was not a happy child."

"I didn't know that," said Roger, amazed that he'd known Ralph for years, and he'd never mentioned this fact. At least, as far as he could remember.

"You do now." The two rode on for some minutes in silence — each thinking different thoughts. Finally, Ralph turned to look at his friend and said, "Roger, I'd like for you to return with me to Stafford Castle as my Constable. You'll make sure the castle is protected and keep my archers ready to fight. This will give you a steady amount of money each year and, as my assistant, you'll be able to join me on my trips abroad when I go with the King to do battle with England's enemies."

Roger did not answer immediately. "Father's not in good health, and I should be here for him."

Ralph didn't let him continue. "Yes, I know. Your mother may need help with him. I saw Richard yesterday while you'd gone to carry water from the spring. He's willing to come each day to check on him and to help your mother. I promised to see that he gets several sheep each year to increase his herd for his help. I didn't want to offer money. I don't think it's a good idea for people here to think your family's a place to go for coins."

Roger nodded. "Let's talk to Mother and see if she thinks that will work. As far as going to serve you, I have no problem with being your Constable, but I will have to find someone to look after the family's fields and beasts. Perhaps my youngest sister's man could do that. There's some talk of marriage between them."

⤳

After accepting Ralph's offer, Roger's first necessity at Stafford Castle was to take an inventory of men and supplies. He needed to find out the particulars of Ralph's possessions and meet the men whom he would direct according to Ralph's wishes — to become familiar with his new home. He did this as quickly as he could.

One of the first noblemen he met was Sir Hugh de Audley. He and Ralph arrived in Oxfordshire from Stafford to discuss Audley's approaching trip to France on the King's business. Ralph would accompany and command a group of military men who would protect the ambassador on the trip. This would be Ralph's second time in this capacity to Audley.

It was here that Ralph first noticed the young daughter of his soon-to-be superior. "She's a beautiful young girl," was the whispered comment he made to Roger. He didn't add that besides her dark hair, sparkling brown eyes, mouth with its perpetual hint of a smile, and an ever-graceful manner, that she was very rich. As the only child of a rich and doting father, she was a prize worth capturing, for she was ten times wealthier than he.

Hugh de Audley's post within the King's government was subject to change by the month. His expertise in English affairs and in Scotland where unrest ruled the northern kingdom and wars were being fought necessitated his frequent travel.

Audley and Ralph passed and sometimes accompanied each other on these journeys for four years, even visiting in each other's homes, until 1336. At that point, they both ended up at the manor of Thaxted in Essex, a county northeast of London, bordering the North Sea.

Ralph made up his mind. He asked Audley for his daughter, Margaret's, hand-in-marriage, and was refused very decisively. Sir Ralph took matters into his own hands.

"Can you believe he turned me down?" asked a greatly insulted Ralph of his friend Roger in the privacy of his quarters. He walked up and down, ramming his fist in his hand.

"No, I can't. I've always felt he didn't like you, but I couldn't guess why. You've protected him on his trips overseas and fought beside him in Scotland. Maybe it's because you've always backed the young King Edward, and he's not been sure at times which side he's on. I have heard others question whether he sided with Mortimer and our dowager Queen Isabella against the King."

Roger continued with his thoughts, saying, "The Nobles don't notice me. To them I am but a servant and they don't realize that I understand French, which they always speak at Court or in your august gatherings. So, my dear friend, I hear more intrigue than anyone can imagine. I am both your eyes and ears at these events, as you well know."

Ralph walked over and put his hand on his friend's shoulder. "I know my brother. Why do you think I encouraged you to take lessons in both French and Latin from the Augustinians at Greyfriars close to Stafford castle? My concern though is of the Lady Margaret. I know I'm older, but I'll be a good husband to her. I've noticed her watching me. I hope—" Ralph sighed and continued with another thought. "Maybe brother, my Lord Audley has someone else in mind, and I must be quick to get her."

A knock on the door interrupted their conversation. Roger went to the door and, shocked, walked outside to participate in a conversation with Richard from Tipton.

When he re-entered, Ralph took one look at him and asked, "Is it your father? Is it Henry?"

Roger nodded. "Richard says that my father has died. Do I have permission to head for Tipton?"

"Yes, of course. Stay as long as you like." Ralph put his arm around Roger and walked him to the door. "Give my regards to Mistress Margery and the rest of the family."

～

Without Roger to help, Ralph called in some friends— some who were truly loyal to King Edward and who he knew would willingly assist him.

Once before he'd participated in a raid which changed the English landscape. This was a tunnel plot at Nottingham Castle, and it was successful.

~

Ralph walked to a window, overlooking the manor's grounds, remembering the details of his former escapade. In the intrigue which followed King Edward II around, and after he was forced to step down as King and had died mysteriously at Berkley Castle, those considered to be his friends were being arrested.

One man remained a threat to the young son of the late King and those who supported him. He was capable of scheming and instigating a coup d'état against his lord—his name Roger Mortimer. Mortimer's inferiority complex caused him to surveil those he considered a threat to his power over the young King. Even Isabella, the King's mother was suspect because she'd learned to stand on her own two feet and loved nothing better than to control every situation. This included her young son, King Edward, causing at times, a literal tug-of-war in the monarchy.

A plot was hatched between Ralph de Stafford, Sir William Montagu, Robert Ufford and several others loyal to the young Edward. Montagu was heard to say, *"Bring the dog down, before it bites us all."* He was referring to Mortimer.

Young King Edward, now much older and a father himself, was chafing under his mother, Isabella, and her lover Mortimer's control. He was made privy to the plot.

The two lovers were at Nottingham, and everyone was ready to execute the plan.

The tunnel under Nottingham was well known but kept under lock and key. Finding someone with a key was done.

Dragged to the outside door, he was told, "You will unlock the doors." There was one on each end. "Or your life will be in peril." Wanting no part of the coming escapade, the key was handed to the men, and he ran with a few coins jingling in his pocket.

The men looked at each other. Failure was not an option. If they didn't get Mortimer, he would see them all hanged. "There's strength in numbers," said a determined Ralph, lighting torches with a candle and looking at his mates in the tunnel.

Using the candles to illuminate the dark, smelly passageway, the men along with their cohorts crept down the corridor, making no sound. At the last door, they bunched together and drew a sword or knife. Carefully, silently, they pushed open the tunnel door, and stormed into Mortimer's room. Mortimer's Steward flung himself in front of his master and immediately died. Taking Mortimer captive, they gagged him to Isabella's loud screams. Then the abductors dragged him down the tunnel, put him on a horse, and galloped away with the young King riding alongside.

Mortimer was later hanged. Isabella afterwards reconciled with her son, and the King never forgot the men who made his throne secure. This included Ralph de Stafford.

Ralph pondered this. If this kidnapping functioned one time, why wouldn't it work to release Margaret from her father's manor? He was sure some of those same men would help him now.

Yes, this was the way to go, and he was just foolhardy enough to do it.

～

The sun was down, and Margaret de Audley sat in her bed chamber at the manor of Thaxted. She had let her hair down and had combed it until it shone. Ready for bed, she got up to call her maid.

Suddenly, the maid burst into the room followed by several armed men. One she recognized — Ralph de Stafford.

"Why are you here? What do you want?"

"We're here to take you with us," said Ralph, holding her by the arm and steering her toward the open door, where two of his friends and fellow conspirators took charge of the Lady.

Margaret started to scream, but a hand over her mouth stopped any utterance. She reached out her hand to her maid, her eyes pleading. Three men carried her from the room, down the steps, and out of the castle.

Ralph dragged the maid with him. "You must come quietly," he told her.

She did, following her mistress into the cold, dark night.

~

Hugh de Audley and his wife, Margaret de Clare, came to Windsor Castle to complain to King Edward. Their beloved daughter, Margaret, had been abducted and what was he going to do about it?

Edward ordered two men to find out the facts.

~

Ralph's plan worked so well that it was days before anyone knew what had exactly happened to Margaret, where she was being held, or who had attacked the manor.

When the facts did come out, the King laughed, because he was a hopeless romantic and happily married to his wife, Philippa. He could well believe Ralph had done this deed, and he didn't plan on punishing him for it. He devised a plan.

When de Audley returned to see how the search was going, the King told him the results.

"Your Grace," said a horrified Hugh, "What are you going to do about my daughter's abduction? Ralph needs to be hanged for such a foul deed. He has taken and dishonored her."

"Hugh, I realize this is not the outcome you must have wanted for your daughter, but Ralph is one of my trusted confidants, and I feel sure he will be a good husband to Margaret."

The father opened his mouth to protest.

King Edward held up his hand, silencing him. "This is my offer. How would you like the Earldom of Gloucester? It has been retired to the crown since the death of Gilbert de Clare, the brother of your good Lady wife."

Gilbert had died during Edward I's campaign against the Welsh. Gilbert had commanded the southern campaign and lost. His holdings were extensive.

Hugh, raising his eyebrows, looked over at his wife. Their daughter, Margaret, was ruined in the eyes of any other man, so maybe Ralph wasn't a bad solution to the situation, especially with the riches of the earldom offered to them.

Noticing a change in their demeanor, the King, with a smile lurking on his face, went on to suggest. "Ralph and Margaret could be married here at the castle with all the trappings of a noble wedding befitting the daughter of an Earl, and I propose my Lady wife shall be a matron attending your daughter."

That cinched it. Hugh knelt before the King and, placing his hands between those of the King, he accepted the title and the lands, and the threat of troubles over the abduction of Margaret de Audley was over. She and Ralph were married at Windsor Castle with the King in attendance. Margaret bore Ralph six children — two boys and four girls.

Ralph continued to serve the King in many capacities. The year after he and Margaret were married, 1337, he was appointed Steward of the royal household. This is also the year that the battles with the French began in earnest.

When King Edward went to Flanders (at this time, an English territory in France), both Ralph and Roger went with him. They stayed until 1340 when the King returned to England. While there, he Knighted several men, who were privy to his confidence. Sir Ralph de Stafford was one of them.

What was the cause of the conflict with France? It started centuries before with Duke William of Normandy who crossed the southern English Channel and won the Battle of Hastings in 1066, to become crowned the King of England.

Ever since, the English had fought wars to keep claim to the lands he had left behind on the continent of Europe. The battles raged back and forth with the advantage sometimes with the French and another time with the English.

To complicate matters, King Edward's northern border with Scotland was not secure. He was distracted by numerous battles with the contenders for the throne of his neighbor, who had given their allegiance to support France in future struggles with England.

In the midst of this northern conflict, Philip VI of France confiscated the large Duchy of Aquitaine. This Duchy was part of the old English territory. Now, it was a large fief of the French crown. The start of this current conflict with France was over the seized Duchy. King Edward was determined to get the Duchy back under English rule.

Not only that, but because the English Kings were descendants of Philip IV, King of France, the English decided to claim the French Crown—another reason to risk lives and spend treasure.

Although France was rich and populous with military advantage, the English army was disciplined and, after learning accuracy and speed from their Welsh neighbors, had become experienced with the longbow. Their expertise with the longbow and arrow could stop mounted horsemen as they charged.

With their success at the naval Battle of Sluys, the English controlled the English Channel. Invading France was secured.

❧ Chapter 19 ❧

14th Century A.D

The Adventures of King Edward III, Roger of Tipton and Ralph de Stafford

Part II

In February 1345, at the age of forty-six, Ralph was appointed Seneschal or Steward of Aquitaine. King Edward sent orders for him to take command of a fleet of ships and sail from Bristol, England to Bordeaux. Once in France, he would join the Earl of Derby, Henry of Lancaster.

"You mean we're going to Bristol?" questioned Roger, when Ralph told him about his orders from the King. They'd managed to stay home for four months at Stafford Castle.

"Yes, and then to Bordeaux in the southern part of Aquitaine, close to the middle of the conflict."

Roger walked to a window and looked out. "Will we have time to take a detour to Shrewsbury? And a few extra days in Bristol to see my family would be nice. My father said the Tiptons have an export business located at Bristol and Portishead on the Avon River. My father tried to keep up with all of them."

"Has it been a long time since you were there?"

Roger returned to the middle of the room. "Oh, I've never been. My father went as a young man. Going there has always stayed in the back of my mind — one of those want-to-do things."

Ralph looked at Roger and smiled, "I have lands not too far from Shrewsbury which I too have never visited. So, we will go to Shrewsbury and take an extra day or two in Bristol. I'd like to go into the village and see what wares are bought and sold at the market. Perhaps, as we travel south, we can stay close to the River Severn and observe the sea bore that drives a mighty wave up-river. The war in France will still be around when we get there."

Roger was elated, because this meant he could make connections with distant branches of his family. He started packing for the trip.

Sending their armour and other supplies on ahead by cart to Portishead with a retinue of soldiers from Staffordshire, the two headed west to Shrewsbury. They rode out of Stafford armed only with swords and knives and such clothes as they would need. These loaded on their packhorse and accompanied by two men-at-arms.

Roger carried the most recent sword given to Sir Anthony by the King. The ancient one, given to Meta by the Lady of Mercia, Æthelflaed, was left in Tipton in the family home, hanging above the fireplace to keep it safe.

~

Roger and Ralph had planned on spending three days in Shrewsbury.

"How will we find out where the Tiptons live?" asked Roger.

Looking over the possibilities, the men had paused on the outskirts of Shrewsbury — gazing at the town on the hill, which was almost totally encircled by the great River Severn. They saw one of the largest towns in the Kingdom, the towers of a castle, steeples of churches, and dark smoke curling skyward from myriads of chimneys, amazed them. These added to the landscape of roofs seen in the distance, all trying to crowd into the loop of the River Severn.

Instead of fording the river like his ancestor Eggen and the Welshman Andras, they would ride across on a bridge into the town.

"I'm suggesting we go to the Abbey Church before we cross the river," returned Sir Ralph, pointing. "If anyone knows your family, the monks will."

"Yes, I agree."

⁓

The first long-robed monk, at the Abbey of St. Peter and St. Paul, didn't know Roger's family, but he directed them to someone who should. "Friar Joseph has roots here. He will know them," he responded.

Elderly Friar Joseph stood outside in the abbey garden with a hoe in his hand. Although he'd never laid eyes on the men before, he looked up, smiled, and said as they dismounted, "These are my babies." He indicated a patch of well-tended plants.

Taking a step forward, Roger gestured in an attempt to introduce Sir Ralph.

Not looking at the two men, the Friar shuffled around his plot and pointed at each as he continued, "I have garlic, rosemary, sage, dill, and other herbs growing in my small bed. I think food is much tastier with spices to give it flavor, don't you?"

Both men nodded, agreeing with him.

The Friar quickly added, "At my age, food doesn't taste as good." After giving the two a brief lesson in aging, he added, "Spices enhance the taste. For me, they make food edible."

"Friar Joseph," Roger interrupted him. "I'm Roger of Tipton, and this is my Liege Lord Sir Ralph of Stafford. We need to ask you a question."

The Friar was also hard of hearing. "And, there's mugwort," he said, stepping unsteadily into the small space. He bent over and pulled a leaf from a tall green plant, crushed it in his hand and, leaning on his hoe, he approached and handed it to Sir Ralph, who had on his Stafford Coat-of-Arms tunic, obviously the most important man of the two.

"Smell," he ordered, his head with its circle of gray hair bobbing as he continued.

Sir Ralph obeyed, and Roger looked amused.

"When made into an ointment, it's good for foot ailments. And if it doesn't help with that, it sure makes your feet smell better." He winked and chortled like the old man he had claimed to be. "We have one of our brothers at the Abbey, you can smell his feet..." Ralph held up his hand and the Friar, noting this movement, stopped midsentence, and then he asked, "Sorry, how may I help you, gentlemen?"

Roger loudly explained the reason for them being in Shrewsbury. He asked, "I was hoping you could tell me where the Tiptons live. I would like to visit them."

"It's a sad story," said Friar Joseph, shaking his head and taking a stab at an ill-fated weed with his hoe, "and it goes back some generations."

Roger and Sir Ralph exchanged a quick glance, wondering how long this would take. "How so?" asked Sir Ralph.

"When William the Conqueror started giving land to his friends from France, he settled Shrewsbury and the land surrounding to Sir Roger de Montgomery. Sir Roger needed a castle to live in because we are on the borderland with the Welsh and the area needed protection. Did you know, we still have problems with the Welsh. Would you believe they…"

At this point, Ralph threw up his hand, again, interrupting the Friar. "Please, the Tiptons," he reminded the man.

"Yes, yes, the Tiptons. Here's what I was getting at, when Sir Roger de Montgomery became the exalted Lord of Shrewsbury, he tore down fifty houses to build his castle, and the Tiptons stone home was one of them. Afterall, where the house was built dominated a choice spot."

"What happened to the Tiptons?" asked Roger.

"Oh, they went to Pontesbury."

"Where?" asked Roger, frowning.

"Pontesbury — not far from here." The Friar flung his hand in an undeterminable direction to the west, and then he gave them detailed instructions on how to reach the Tipton household, after which he added. "The family won't be there."

"What? Why?" asked Sir Ralph, getting slightly perturbed at the exchange, which had started with one simple question.

"They still own property, but most of them are at Bristol or Gloucester or Worcester."

Ralph looked discretely at Roger and rolled his eyes. There was no way of getting around this man's explanation. Better to let him get at it. "What happened, Friar Joseph?" Roger took the initiative.

"I think they all went south to help with the shipping business. I heard they may come back someday. But I don't really know for sure. The house is still there ... and the servants."

Ralph and Roger mounted up and prepared to leave. Friar Joseph took Roger's horse by the rein. "Go by the Market Hall in Gloucester. They may be there, or someone will know of them. They have interests in the town."

Both men nodded, agreeing with him.

"Thank you, Friar Joseph. We'll definitely look there." Leaning over, Sir Ralph put a silver penny in the old Friar's hand.

They rode off, while he stood watching them. "Should we go by Pontesbury, just in case?" asked Roger.

"Absolutely. Then we'll go on south to Ludlow and Hereford. This is a straighter track than following the meanders of the river. We will need to stay the night at each of these villages, and, finally, ride east to cross the Severn, heading on into Gloucester. I think that will cover all the possibilities."

"I believe you're right. Since it's so late, may I suggest we get a room and start early tomorrow?"

～

The old Friar was right. Pontesbury was a futile effort to find any Tiptons. They found the house, but were again told the family resided in Gloucester.

Three days later, the men crossed the bridge toward the east over the River Severn and rode to the Market Hall in Gloucester. They found the Tipton business on the square closest to the market.

Charles from Tipton, Pontesbury, and Gloucester explained, "We have a house in Pontesbury, but our activity is here in this city or Bristol, by way of Portishead. So, we split our time between the two."

The store was stocked with supplies to sell and a warehouse ready to receive wool, from the hot July sheep-shearing time. The wool would be sent down the River Severn to Bristol-on-Avon, for onward shipment to the dyers and merchants of Flanders in France. The large room was partially full of an assorted variety of water-tight barrels and chests.

"Are you the northern port of the Tipton export business?" asked Sir Ralph, trying to understand the family's ties to Bristol or Portishead. He found out that Portishead was a small community downriver from Bristol at the confluence of the River Avon and the Severn Estuary.

"I guess you could say that," stated Charles. "We sort, assemble, and ship the products from several small villages around Gloucester and even from Hereford and Worcester by barge to the estuary. Even so, our family works together. We are interconnected as a business."

Roger and Ralph stayed two days with Charles, learning more from him of the trade in which the

Tiptons were involved, and traveling to other suppliers within the town's guild.

Then Charles mentioned a daily occurrence on the River Severn he thought the two men would be interested in seeing. "Have you heard of the river's bore when the tide changes?" he asked.

"Yes, I have," Sir Ralph nodded. "On trips north to Scotland I've seen the one on the River Trent."

"Would you like to go tonight and witness the spectacle? On this particular day, with the moon out, the sight will be breathtaking."

Sir Ralph responded. "Yes, let's do. Roger's never seen a river boil upstream."

So, on the second night, with a full moon overhead, the three traveled to the bank of the River Severn. With other spectators, they lined up to watch as the neap tide was in full bore within the river's banks.

The increasing growl coming upriver was heard for several minutes. The sound made Roger wonder if one of the English dragons he heard about as a child was on the rampage. Finally appearing, the water churned and foamed, and the roar the water made running against the river's current—almost deafening.

Sir Ralph, thrilled at the sight, shouted to Charles and Roger, "I've seen the bore on the River Trent. This one is spectacular compared to it. What a sight." He waved his hand at the frothing waves, glistening in the moonlight as the bore or wall of water raced on past.

～

Saying goodbye the next morning, they headed further south towards the hills below Bristol and above

Portishead on the Severn Estuary. The plan was to visit Bristol, but not today.

Hours later they arrived at the Downs, a range of hills above the coast and below Bristol, separating this city — the second largest in the English Realm from the place called Portishead. Here, they stopped to enjoy the view as the sun dropped toward the earth in the west before them — the sun's blinding rays glistening on the vast expanse of open water — the Severn Estuary.

"There's nothing so beautiful as English ships resting at anchor, especially if you're going on a voyage or returning home," mused Ralph.

"They do make an impressive sight, especially flying the English flag of the Cross of St. George on the main-mast."

Side-by-side, fourteen sailing ships — with the flag of the red cross on a white background, fluttering with the wind — lay at anchor, waiting for troops to arrive from the Midlands and southern England.

"Wonder why they aren't moored in Bristol?"

Of course, Roger couldn't answer the question. He wondered at two more ships roped to pilings at a private, floating wharf.

"Who do they belong to?" Roger asked, taking their pause as an opportunity to eat an apple purchased from the Tiptons in Gloucester — grown in Hereford. He leaned over and shared the core with his horse.

From a bag tied to his saddle, he handed a Golden Beauty to Ralph.

"Could it be your family? The people up river at Pontesbury and Gloucester mentioned the Tiptons as being exporters and importers of goods, and you said your own father visited them in Bristol," said Sir Ralph, munching away and wiping the salty sweat off his forehead. Where they had paused, the western sun bore down on them. "Let's continue on. The breeze off the estuary should cool us down somewhat, and it's getting late. We must find lodging for the night."

"Sir Ralph, we could sleep on one of the ships," Roger suggested, since the area didn't look too promising.

They continued on the curved dirt path, leading down towards the small, coastal town. A couple of horse-drawn carts passed by, heading back toward Bristol. Once at the shore, they dismounted beside the floating wharf, built to solve the tidal changes of the estuary.

The English ships were anchored in deeper water offshore.

An assortment of carts pulled by horses off-loaded supplies to sailors, who carried them to men in small boats to be rowed to the sailing ships. The wharf, what there was of it, was alive with activity on its sturdy boards.

While Ralph, followed by the two men-at-arms, went to find out who was in charge of the English ships and to see if their own cart had arrived from Stafford, Roger poked around the area of the two-unknown craft.

Seeing one with *MaryRose* on the side and a man on the deck, Roger decided to climb the gangplank and talk to him. The man on the ship, lifted his hand, acknowledging him. Roger introduced himself.

"I'm Roger of Tipton from Staffordshire here with my Lord Sir Ralph de Stafford of Stafford Castle. He's to take command of the English ships in the harbour, heading to Bordeaux."

With a frown on his face as if digesting the words just spoken, the man looked at Roger. Suddenly, his face lit up, and he closed the distance between them, embracing Roger and exclaiming, "Then we're cousins. At least, somewhere down the years. My ancestors came from Tybbington in Staffordshire."

"One and the same place, for its name changes with each generation" returned Roger, smiling from ear-to-ear, and clapping his newfound relative on the back.

"My name is William. This is my ship and that is my import/export business." He pointed to a large building built next to the wharf with the sign, *Two Brothers, Shipping*, on the front. "That wasn't always the name. One of my *greatest* grandfathers," he grinned at the word greatest, "was named Eggen. I eventually inherited the business from his heirs. He was married to a woman named Alina—from Bamburgh in Northumbria. But you'll read the whole story when you come home with me, for it is all written down. We'll catch up on our family, and I'll show you the book of our family history. We've been calling it the Ancestry Book, because of all the information within its pages. Have you heard the stories of Tybba or Dever?"

"I've heard about a book of our family. I'd like to see it. Isn't there a ship impressed on the front?" he asked.

"Yes, there is. You must come. My wife, MaryRose, will be so happy to meet you. She loves company, especially since the children have flown the nest. She keeps telling me it's too quiet here. I don't know what she wants me to do about that." He winked at Roger. "I keep telling her our grandchildren will take care of it."

Obviously, William wasn't going to take no for an answer. Roger found Ralph, and instructions were given as to where the house was located.

"It's only a short walk," he pointed. "Lord Ralph, you and Roger are welcome to stay with me until you set sail." William said. "My wife and I have plenty of room, and she's a good cook."

When William said plenty of room, he meant it. The stone house was sprawling with several upstairs bed chambers, supported by large wooden beams. The men climbed stone steps, and Roger was shown the rooms he and Ralph would occupy. Roger walked to the glassed window in his room. The opening overlooked the Avon, and upstream he could see the great gorge carved by the river through the range of hills. In another direction, the Severn Estuary was visible until the sea mists obscured it. "What a view!"

"Yes, exactly. The one reason we wanted this place."

"How many children do you have?"

"Six, and they have young children. Are you married, Roger?"

"No. I've been busy following Sir Ralph around. I'm not griping, but there's been no time to even get interested in a young woman. And, being in my forties, it's a little late to start."

"I'm not much older than you."

A call from downstairs put an end to the conversation. William turned and went to the head of the stairs. Roger trailed him. At the end of the steps, a woman with gray streaking her hair smiled at both men.

"I thought I heard voices. I see you've brought us a guest, William."

"Yes, this is Roger of Tipton from Staffordshire. Roger, this is my wife, MaryRose."

"Ah, Tybba's old home," she said. "We're honoured to have you."

Roger bowed and nodded at her. "Yes, I guess you could call it the birthplace of the Tybbingtons or Tiptons, as it's now called, at least in England."

"William, are you going to show Roger your ancestral book? I'm sure the pages will interest him. While you do that, I'll go ahead and start the afternoon meal."

"There'll be one more, dear. Robert's friend and Liege Lord, Sir Ralph de Stafford, will take his meals and stay here with us."

"A Lord! My, my, then he is truly welcome. I'll see that the rooms are ready for visitors." MaryRose disappeared from sight.

～

The ancestral book was fairly large, since it had been around for eight hundred years. Roger could still make out the image of the ship, although the stamping wasn't as crisp as it surely was when given to Tybba by Cassius at Snotta's village. He kept reading until he came to, "Didn't you say Eggen was your ancestor?"

"Yes, come and look." They walked to a room where house materials were stored, and there leaning up next to the back wall was a sign which read, *Eggen-Merchant and Trader*. The coloring was faded and gone in places, but it could still be read.

"The old sign," Roger said, nodding his head.

"Yes, the very one. History is important to me. I've tried to make it vital to my children."

The clattering of a cart made noises outside the house. When Roger and William went out, Roger recognized the men. They had the traveling supplies he and Ralph had packed in Stafford. Ralph had sent the cart with two men to unload it.

"William, we'll need some of the supplies here, but most need to go back to our ships."

"Why don't we take them to my warehouse? We can put the whole cart inside, and you can sort through and pick out your necessities."

"You don't mind?" asked Roger.

"No. I have plenty of room. My ship is fully laden with empty casks for Bordeaux, some wool, and other supplies for parts of France, so the warehouse is fairly empty. After we have unloaded in France, we'll pick up wine for delivery to London on its return voyage."

"William, have you thought about accompanying us to France?"

"I was hoping to travel with your fleet for protection. You never know when pirates are around, especially at Devonshire or when we round Cornwall. There's security in numbers."

The rest of the day was spent in taking the cart to William's warehouse, finding Ralph to see if he'd found the captain of the main ship, and then returning to place their traveling supplies in the sleeping room. Roger went through the rest of the ancestral book and asked, "William, you say you have six children. Do any of them live close to you?"

"My oldest two, Hugh and Jonathan, live at Worcester. Did you pass through there coming here?"

"No, we came west of the River Severn on our way south and missed Worcester."

"My sons maintain our workplace at Worcester and package the supplies we ship from that area, mostly bales of wool from three of the closest shires. This goes to our warehouse at Gloucester. At present, I have them and their workers making barrels and chests for our shipping operation. They'll have enough by the time sheep shearing starts in July, and both will go to France as well. Our reputation for making quality barrels is becoming known throughout the shipping area here in England and in the other ports we service."

"You have four more children?"

"Yes, two more live at Gloucester with their wives and children. And the last two, Henry and Samuel, live in Bristol, where they supervise the loading of the ships and make lists for the shipments, going to London or other ports. Henry is one of my ship captains.

"The Bristol harbour is sheltered, not unprotected like here on the coast. We use this wharf to free up space in Bristol, to finalize shipments if a product is late arriving for shipment, and sometimes to wait for better weather, as the seas on this western coast can be extremely rough. Since the loading is done, they're probably fishing on the estuary, or they've gone hunting in the hills. I give them a loose rein."

"We met Charles at Gloucester. You have a nice shop loaded with supplies for the residents, and the warehouse was full of goods to ship."

"William's family maintains our shop in Bristol."

"Sir Ralph wants to visit Bristol before we leave."

A horse's hooves sounded on the outside cobblestones.

Ralph had arrived, along with the smell of food wafting from what appeared to be the kitchen area.

After more greetings, Sir Ralph said, "I've been so busy, I didn't realize I was getting hungry."

Soon, MaryRose appeared, and Sir Ralph bowed and kissed her offered hand, causing her some embarrassment and blushes because she wasn't used to hand kissing. The men laughed at and with her as they went in to eat.

The room was more or less bare. Two tapestries hung on opposite walls. One was of black horses grazing in a meadow with rolling hills in the background. The other showed the River Severn after a rainfall with dark clouds resting above the angry bore of water as it rose on the river's banks.

A tall, heavy chest was pushed against the wall coming from the kitchen. An array of food sat on it with spoons for dipping. Boiled chicken in a thick cream sauce with mushrooms was the main course. There were carrots, peas, fresh leeks, and slices of white bread to sop the sauces left on the wooden trenchers. Salt and even pepper in bowls to season the repast sat in the middle of the cloth-covered table. William's wife had outdone herself.

MaryRose handed trenchers to the men. She walked to the table and placed a knife and spoon at each setting. She would not eat with the men but eat later in the kitchen. Her focus for the next few minutes was making sure the men at her table had everything they needed. She was an excellent hostess.

"How long until your ships are ready to sail?" William asked Sir Ralph.

"We're ready. All we need is our troops to appear. I received a message from a courier saying that they are about two days away. We'll sail as soon as they get here, and we can load them and their supplies."

"William wants to sail with us for protection," Roger said, digging a piece of chicken off his trencher with his finger and knife.

"Of course. Just be ready to go. You are welcome to accompany us."

More noises from outside the house, and a young man came into the dining room with two bouncing children who headed straight for their grandfather. "This is our youngest, Samuel, and his two rowdy lads," explained William, pushing back from the table and grabbing one arm of each. "This one is William, and this one who wants on my lap is James."

After explaining the reason for their being on the River Severn, Roger asked, "Samuel, I understand you live close by."

"I do, in Bristol. Father and mother can stay down here on the river. My wife prefers the society of the city, its churches, and markets. Did you know, Bristol claims to be second only to London in size and noise?" He smiled and asked, "Will you be staying long?"

William, noticing his wife's wave from the kitchen said, "Gentlemen, let's move to the Great Room. We can talk there, and MaryRose can clean up and feed the children."

"Samuel, Sir Ralph would like to visit Bristol while in the area."

"Of course, Sir Ralph. Come any day."

~

After the men and supplies were loaded onto the cog sailing ships and everything secured for departure on the morrow, Sir Ralph, Roger, and William took the afternoon to travel into Bristol. Samuel waited for them at the Tipton market and headquarters on the stone Bristol Bridge.

"I can certainly see why His Majesty's ships are anchored in the estuary," exclaimed Sir Ralph, leaning out the window at the back of the store. Not one slip remained empty on the quay.

William chuckled, "Yes, Bristol is a busy place—much like London."

"Did you know the Britons or Welsh called Bristol, *Caer Odor*—the fortress or town of the gap or chasm?" asked Samuel.

"I certainly understand why, after riding here from Portishead. The depth is staggering from the ragged cliffs above to the River Avon's water below. Is this the only crossing of the river?"

"Yes, for miles in any direction. Sir Ralph, what do you especially want to do while in Bristol?"

"I have heard of a church built into the city walls."

"Yes. We have several of them. I'll take you to the one on Broad Street called The Church of St. John-on-the-Wall. Are you intending to pray for a safe journey tomorrow?"

Ralph nodded. "Yes, when you go in the service of the King, you never know what will happen. Roger and I will be in the hotbed or thick of the fight, and England and our fighters need God's presence. Prayer is essential for our country's victory or even as comfort in defeat."

～

At dawn's break the following morning in May, Sir Ralph stood beside Roger as the lead vessel left Portishead. The two men waved at William and Samuel, who stood on the wharf.

"God speed," yelled William. Of course, the two could not hear his comment, but knew his call must include best wishes for their journey.

Sir Ralph and Roger waved again.

The men working for William cast off lines so *MaryRose*, with Henry in command, could join the King's fleet.

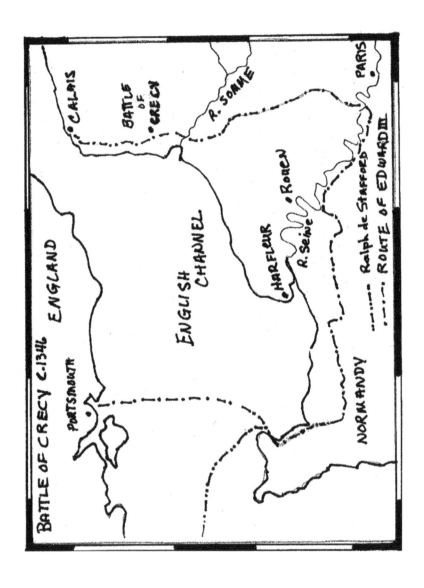

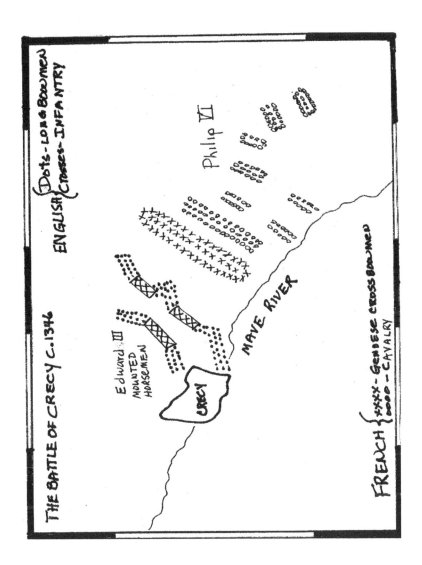

THE BATTLE OF CRECY C.1346

ENGLISH { Dots - LONG BOWMEN / Crosses - INFANTRY

Philip VI

Edward III MOUNTED HORSEMEN

CRECY

MAVE RIVER

FRENCH { xxxx - GENOESE CROSS BOWMEN / oooo - CAVALRY

❦ Chapter 20 ❦

14th Century A.D

The Adventures of King Edward III, Roger of Tipton and Ralph de Stafford

Part III

The Battle of Crecy

The English navy, founded in the reign of King Alfred the Great, had become a force to be reckoned with and more so after they mastered the longbow. Leaving Portishead and the Severn Estuary, Sir Ralph de Stafford had several hundred archers on board his ships. Enough to give the English an advantage. Nothing the French had for arms could come close to the distance of the longbow arrows.

~

This was evidenced more than once in the battles they were soon to fight with the French.

The first naval battle, the Battle of Sluys, 1340, destroyed the French fleet in the English Channel, proving they had mastery of the seas. Because of the accuracy of arrows shot from the English ship decks, the bowmen eliminated any possibility of the French navy's inclusion during the battles to come. Especially the first serious land battle at Crecy.

This battle was between the longbow, the crossbow, and the horse.

In July, King Edward had landed a force of 14,000 men at Normandy. Sir Ralph, coming from Bristol, and the Earl of Derby were ordered to join him there. They marched almost to Paris, plundering the countryside, before encountering a massive French army. The English turned north, toward the port of Calais, where they could possibly get help from Flanders—an English territory.

On August 26, 1346, they arrived at Crecy within a few miles of Calais, and turned to confront the French army following them. The French had 25,000 heavily armed men on horses and 6,000 Genoese crossbowmen. The Genoese were mercenaries hired because of their prowess in battle and their success with the crossbow. The English forces were greatly outnumbered.

Preparing the battlefield, the English dug deep holes in the wet, soft earth and drove sharpened, pointed stakes to impale horses, intending to wreak havoc on the cavalry, which made up most of the French army. These were positioned in front of their battle lines and would slow down and thwart the onslaught of the French horsemen when they came across the battlefield.

The English battle lines consisted of longbow archers and men-at-arms. The longbowmen were positioned at each end and in the middle. The men-at-arms were between each section of archers. King Edward and his mounted horsemen dismounted at the rear and came forward to fight in hand-to-hand combat. One side of the line of armed men was under the command of the 16-year-old son and heir of King

Edward, Edward of Woodstock, soon to be known as The Black Prince.

∼

Sir Ralph of Stafford, in his mail and helmet, stood in the middle section of his longbowmen. "How are you feeling, Roger?"

Roger did not answer his question. He was staring in disbelief at the opposing foe on the other side of the field. They were in line to attack. "Do they really think the crossbow can compete with our longbows?" He adjusted his sword, the same one which had hung over the fireplace at Tipton.

"I don't think they realize what kind of fire power we have here." Ralph pulled the taunt string of his longbow, making it sound—a vibrating twang. Made from the yew tree imported from Germany or Austria, it was one-piece, strong, and if kept waxed, long-lasting.

"There's something strange about their archers." Roger furrowed his brow, checking out the opposing side.

"You're right. They don't have shields." Normally those who shot crossbows had shields they stuck in the ground to keep them from getting shot while they restrung a bolt and set the trigger to release.

Ralph made a strange sound in his throat. "They're not making this hard, are they?"

"No. Definitely not, and that's to our advantage."

At 5:00 p.m., the French made the first charge by the sounding of trumpets, the pounding of drums, and the loud shouts of 6,000 men—the Genoese crossbowmen. They came forward to shoot their bolts. The flood of bolts flew across the battlefield sky and fell short, not having enough distance to reach the English. As the crossbowmen advanced, closing the distance to the French lines, the longbowmen had no trouble shooting their arrows rapid fire into the Genoese. Without their shields, dying and wounded men were scattered all over the ground.

After several attempts and with men dropping all around them, it became apparent their crossbow quarrels would not reach the other army. The Genoese broke and ran.

This prompted the French King Philip to order his cavalry to, *"Kill me those scoundrels, for they stop up our road without any reason."* This the mounted Knights did, running over those leaving the battlefield, as they rode hastily toward the English lines.

The French cavalry soon got a taste of what the bowmen were running from, because the English arrows cut down men and horses. The French fell back, regrouped, and charged again—fifteen times they came at the English. Those who managed to get close to the English lines were killed by swords and battle axes—King Edward's men who were waiting on them. The French retreated when it became dark—not to return. They had had enough.

When the sun came up the next morning, the English counted 10,000 dead of the opposing side. This did not count the 1,542 Lords and Knights left on the field. The English lost 2 Knights and 80 men.

King Edward was ecstatic. This battle was the greatest of his reign, and all because of the superb skill of his archers. He continued to Calais, on the English Channel, and after a brief siege, took the town. It would remain an English possession for two hundred years.

Still elated at this great victory, he returned home and ordered the construction of St. George's Chapel at Windsor Castle. He wanted to honor his warriors. What better way to set them apart than to establish a new Order of Knighthood — The Order of the Garter — and induct an exclusive band of his men. Number five on the list was Sir Ralph de Stafford.

Sir Ralph and Roger continued in the country, returning to England at news of Margaret's declining health. She died in 1347 and was buried next to her father and mother at Tunbridge Priory in Kent, England. Sir Ralph was now a very rich man. Although many thought he abducted Margaret de Audley for money, he grieved Margaret's death and, though King Edward let him stay home for a few months, he was soon at battle for the King again.

～

In 1348, on one of his brief trips to Windsor to see the King, Sir Ralph and Roger walked down the hill from the castle to see St. George's Chapel, which looked complete although scaffolding was still in place.

"What do you think, Roger? Will this be a fitting place for the King to hold his ceremony?" The two men stood outside the building. "This part is an addition to the other chapel constructed nearly 200 years ago."

Roger looked up at the tall columns which made the building look like it touched the clouds floating in the sky above.

Sir Ralph noticed Roger's head movement and said, "It's perpendicular architecture. It does stretch to the sky."

"Very impressive." He'd seen just about everything, following Sir Ralph around England, Scotland, and France, but this building was an imposing edifice.

"Sir Ralph, I see you're looking at my addition to our chapel," King Edward saluted his new Knight.

"Your Grace," Ralph turned and bowed, greeting the King.

Roger bowed his way out of the conversation but remained close at hand.

"I wanted to see for myself how the construction was progressing. And yes, my Lord, because I've heard so many comments, I was interested in the design and architecture."

"Come inside. I'll show you around."

The King proceeded into the entrance hall with Ralph just behind him and Roger following at a close distance. "Only a few more finishing touches and the building is done. The scaffolding hasn't been removed," he waved his hand, indicating the cross bars and boards, reaching to the ceiling, "because I wanted to wait until the last minute, in case I change my mind or add something else to the interior or exterior of the structure. For a King," he continued, now smiling, "that's a good idea."

The King was a good guide, demonstrating the different parts of the chapel. "These are the seats for the choir," he said, indicating three tiers of wooden seats on either side of the central aisleway. The seats stretched toward the front of the chapel where the altar was prominent. Then he pointed to twenty-four upper stalls. These were located above the choir seats, paralleling them to the front. "The Knights will have their own padded seats. Your heraldic banner, My Lord of Stafford, will fly above your stall. Come."

The King walked toward the front of the building where the altar was located and pointed, "See there, My Lord of Stafford, your name enshrined within this building."

Looking up, Ralph could barely read his name on a shiny plate beside one of the upper stalls.

"This is your seat, my friend, in a place of honor to the front of the chapel."

"I don't know what to say, Your Grace." Ralph stopped talking. He was speechless.

"There's nothing to say, Sir Ralph. Your actions have proved to be everything I need, to demonstrate your allegiance to me, and my Kingdom. And, you know I value a man's loyalty above all."

"You have my respect and fidelity, Your Grace."

"Here at Windsor Castle, St. George's Chapel will be a testament to England's superior military strength and to its elite Knights—only twenty-four men honoured here, the home of the Order of the Garter."

"When will you have the ceremony?" asked Ralph, following his King from the chapel.

"I haven't picked a firm date. But I'm thinking in October at the Feast of St. Edward the Confessor, who as you know founded Westminster Abbey and was also my namesake."

"I like that idea," Ralph nodded.

"Why don't you and Roger walk with me back to the castle. Remember, we're having a small party tonight, and you are both welcome to attend."

"We definitely won't forget your party, Your Grace."

On the walk up to Windsor Castle, Sir Ralph asked about an obvious construction taking place next to the castle. "Your Grace, is this a new addition to the castle mount?"

"I've kept my intentions regarding the structure to myself. But what more fitting place to call meetings of my chosen twenty-four, here in a place much like the Arthurian tale of yore. Twenty-four of the greatest military minds and King's men in a place where discussion of strategy and chivalry can take place. Come and see."

The King, Sir Ralph, and Roger walked over to look at the round footing and the start of the stone foundation. "A real roundtable," murmured Ralph.

"Yes, exactly," replied the Lord King. "Here the legend of King Arthur's round table shall come to life."

The three men turned and continued their trip toward the castle gate. The rest of the walk was given over to a discussion of the war in France, which was never far from King Edward's mind.

This is not the end.
To continue this story, please go to Book Two.

Books of the Tipton Chronicles

In England and the West Indies

The Tipton's of Tybbington, Before and Beyond,
Part One – 500 to 1300 A.D.
The Tipton's of Tybbington, Before and Beyond,
Part Two – 1300 to 1700 A.D.

In America

Butterfield Station – 1858 to 1859
Chilhowee Legacy – 1911 to 1930's
My Cherokee Rose – 1930's and Present
Tipton's Sugar Cove — Matthew – 1917 to 1921
The Six at Chestnut Hill – 2008

There will be sequels to some of my books. I can't write but so fast. Be patient. R.R.

The books are available at Amazon.com or may be ordered through your local bookstore. If you like what you're reading, go to Amazon.com/Reba Rhyne, and leave a review for any book you've read.

Ms. Rhyne may be reached at rebarhyne@gmail.com.